W9-CEI-469

The Caine Prize for African Writing 2011

To See the
Mountain
and other stories

The Caine Prize for African Writing 2011

To See the Mountain
and other stories

cassava republic
feeding the African imagination

JACANA

KWANI?

New Internationalist

The Caine Prize for African Writing 2011

First published in 2011 in Europe, North America and Australasia by
New Internationalist™ Publications Ltd
Oxford OX4 1BW
www.newint.org
New Internationalist is a registered trademark.

First published in 2011
in Southern Africa by
Jacana Media (Pty) Ltd
10 Orange Street
Sunnyside
Auckland Park 2092
South Africa
www.jacana.co.za

First published in 2011
in West Africa by
Cassava Republic Press
Edo House
Plot 75, Ralph Sodeinde Street
Central Business District
Garki, Abuja
Nigeria
www.cassavarepublic.biz

Cover photograph: Dag Sundberg/Getty

Design by New Internationalist.

Printed by Bell and Bain Ltd
who hold environmental accreditation ISO 14001.

Mixed Sources
Product group from well-managed
forests and other controlled sources
FSC   www.fsc.org Cert no. TT-COC-002769
© 1996 Forest Stewardship Council

British Library Cataloguing-in-Publication Data.
A catalogue record for this book is available from the British Library.

Library of Congress Cataloguing-in-Publication Data.
A catalogue record for this book is available from the Library of Congress.

National Library of Nigeria Cataloguing-in-Publication Data.
A catalogue record for this book is available from the National Library
of Nigeria.

New Internationalist ISBN 978-1-906523-86-2
Jacana ISBN 978-1-4314-0204-5
Cassava Republic ISBN 978-978-50238-8-6

Contents

Introduction

In an interview on the BBC with Aminatta Forna shortly after the Prize was awarded last year, Nigerian writer Helon Habila, our winner in 2001, said: "The phenomenon of the Caine Prize is really helping raise awareness... I see a connection between the Caine Prize and this boom we are having – an almost direct link. People are more aware of African writing... It is being published more than it has ever been published before." Helon's remarks were echoed in a review in the *Financial Times* by Bernadine Evaristo in January: "The Caine Prize has been instrumental in rejuvenating African literature... There is now a growing roll-call of African writers, several of whom are Caine Prize winners, or alumni of its annual fiction-writing workshops, who have successfully published novels worldwide."

Well, here are the stories from the 12th annual Caine Prize shortlist, along with those from our ninth workshop for African writers. The shortlist includes for the first time a story by a writer from Botswana; and the collection includes a story by the first writer from Zambia to participate in one of our workshops. By a happy coincidence, another story by one of the participants in this year's workshop has now been shortlisted for this year's Prize.

The 2011 shortlist comprises:
- NoViolet Bulawayo (Zimbabwe), 'Hitting Budapest', from *The Boston Review* vol 35, no 6, Nov/Dec 2010.
- Tim Keegan (South Africa), 'What Molly Knew', from *Bad Company* (Pan Macmillan SA, 2008).
- Lauri Kubuitsile (Botswana), 'In the Spirit of McPhineas Lata', from *The Bed Book of Short Stories* (Modjaji Books, SA, 2010).
- Beatrice Lamwaka (Uganda), 'Butterfly Dreams', from *Butterfly Dreams and Other New Short Stories from Uganda* (Critical, Cultural and Communications Press, 2010).

- David Medalie (South Africa), 'The Mistress's Dog', from *The Mistress's Dog: Short Stories 1996-2010* (Picador Africa, 2010). The winner will be decided by a panel of judges chaired by Booker Prize-shortlisted novelist Hisham Matar and including Ellah Allfrey, Deputy Editor of *Granta*, award-winning novelist Aminatta Forna, Vicky Unwin, publisher, film and travel writer, and David Gewanter, poet and professor from Georgetown University. As has been the case in recent years, the winner will be invited to undertake a residency at Georgetown University.

This year's workshop took place in Buea, under Mount Cameroon, in the new Centre of our partners, the Langaa Research and Publishing Common Initiative Group. We are greatly indebted to the Managing Editor of the RPCIG, Dr Roselyne Jua, and the Centre's staff, especially Walter Nkwi. The 12 workshop participants, from seven different African countries, were guided by the celebrated writers Véronique Tadjo (Ivory Coast) and Jamal Mahjoub (Sudan).

Once again, the principal sponsor of the Prize was the Oppenheimer Memorial Trust, and very generous help was received from Miles Morland – without whose timely intervention, indeed, the workshop could not have taken place. The Booker Prize Foundation, Actis and the British Council also gave valuable support, and Kenya Airways and the Beit Trust both provided travel grants for workshop participants. There were other generous private donations, and vital help in kind was once again given by the Royal Over-Seas League, Bodley's Librarian, the Rector of Exeter College, Oxford, the Royal African Society and the Institute of English Studies, London University. We are immensely grateful for all this help, most of which has been given regularly over past years and without which we simply could not have achieved the results credited to us above.

Nick Elam
Administrator of the Caine Prize for African Writing

Caine Prize 2011
Shortlisted Stories

Hitting Budapest

NoViolet Bulawayo

WE ARE ON OUR WAY to Budapest: Bastard and Chipo and Godknows and Sbho and Stina and me. We are going even though we are not allowed to cross Mzilikazi Road, even though Bastard is supposed to be watching his little sister Fraction, even though Mother would kill me dead if she found out; we are going. There are guavas to steal in Budapest, and right now I'd die for guavas, or anything for that matter. My stomach feels like somebody just took a shovel and dug everything out.

Getting out of Paradise is not so hard since the mothers are busy with hair and talk. They just glance at us when we file past and then look away. We don't have to worry about the men under the jacaranda either since their eyes never lift from the draughts. Only the little kids see us and want to follow, but Bastard just wallops the naked one at the front with a fist on his big head and they all turn back.

We are running when we hit the bush; Bastard at the front because he won country-game today and he thinks he rules, and then me and Godknows, Stina, and finally Chipo, who used to outrun everybody in Paradise but not any more because her grandfather made her pregnant. After crossing Mzilikazi we slither through another bush, gallop along Hope Street past the big stadium with the glimmering benches we'll never sit on. Finally we hit Budapest. We have to stop once for Chipo to rest.

"When are you going to have the baby, anyway?" Bastard says. Bastard doesn't like it when we have to stop for her. He even tried to get us not to play with her altogether.

"I'll have it one day."

"What's one day? Tomorrow? Thursday? Next week?"

"Can't you see her stomach is still small? The baby has to grow."

"A baby grows outside. That's the reason they are born. So they grow."

"Well, it's not time yet. That's why it's still a stomach."

"Is it a boy or girl?"

"It's a boy. The first baby is supposed to be a boy."

"But you're a girl and you're a first-born."

"I said supposed."

"You. Shut your mouth, it's not even your stomach."

"I think it's a girl. I don't feel it kicking."

"Boys kick and punch and butt their heads."

"Do you want a boy?"

"No. Yes. Maybe. I don't know."

"Where exactly does a baby come out of?"

"From the same way it gets into the stomach."

"How exactly does it get into the stomach?"

"First, God has to put it in there."

"No, not God. A man has to put it in there, my cousin Musa told me. Didn't your grandfather put it in there, Chipo?"

She nods.

"Then if a man put it in there, why doesn't he take it out?"

"Because it's women who give birth, big-head. That's why they have breasts to suckle the baby."

"But Chipo's breasts are small. Like stones."

"They will grow when the baby comes. Isn't it, Chipo?"

"I don't want my breasts to grow. I don't want a baby. I don't want anything, just guavas," Chipo says, and takes off. We run after her, and when we get right in the middle of Budapest, we stop. Budapest is like a different country. A country where people who are not like us live.

But not an ordinary country – it looks like everybody woke up one day and closed their gates, doors and windows, picked up their passports, and left for better countries. Even the air is empty; no burning things, no smell of cooking food or something rotting; just plain air with nothing in its hands.

Budapest is big, big houses with the gravelled yards and tall fences and durawalls and flowers and green trees, heavy with fruit that's waiting for us since nobody around here seems to know what fruit is for. It's the fruit that gives us courage, otherwise we wouldn't dare be here. I keep expecting the streets to spit and tell us to go back to the shanty.

We used to steal from Chipo's uncle's tree, but that was not *stealing* stealing. Now we have finished all the guavas in his tree so we have moved to strangers' houses. We have stolen from so many, I cannot even count. It's Godknows who decided that we pick a street and stay on it until we have gone through all the houses. Then we go to the next street. This is so we do not confuse where we have been with where we are going. It's like a pattern, and Godknows says this way we can be better thieves.

Today we start a new street and so we carefully scout around. We pass SADC Street, where we already harvested every guava tree two weeks ago. We see white curtains part and a face peer from a window of the cream home with the statue of a urinating boy with wings. We stand and stare, looking to see what the face will do, when the window opens and a small voice shouts for us to stop. We remain standing, not because the voice told us to stop, but because none of us has started to run, and because the voice does not sound dangerous. Music pours out of the window onto the street; it's not *kwaito*, it's not dance hall, it's not anything we know.

A tall, thin woman opens the door and comes out of the house. She is eating something, and she waves as she walks toward us. Already we can tell from the woman's thinness that we are not even going to run. We wait for her, so we can see what she is smiling for, or at; nobody really ever smiles at us in Paradise. Except Mother of Bones, who smiles at anything. The woman stops at the gate; it's locked, and she didn't bring the keys to open it.

"Jeez, I can't stand the heat, and the hard earth, how do you guys ever do it?" the woman asks in her not-dangerous voice. She takes a bite of the thing in her hand, and smiles. A nice, pink camera dangles from her neck. We all look at the woman's feet peeking out from underneath her long skirt. They are clean and pretty feet, like a baby's. She is wiggling her toes. I don't remember my own feet ever looking like that, maybe when I was born.

Then I look up at the woman's red, chewing mouth. I can tell from the vein at the side of her neck, and the way she smacks her big lips, that what she is eating tastes good. I look closely at her long hand, at the thing she is eating. It is fat, and the outer part is crusty. The top looks creamy and soft, and there are coin-like things on it, a deep pink, the colour of burn wounds. I also see sprinkles of red and green and yellow, and finally the brown bumps, like pimples.

"What's that?" Chipo asks, pointing at the thing with one hand and rubbing her stomach with the other. Now that she is pregnant, Chipo likes to play with her stomach every time she talks. The stomach is the size of a soccer ball, not too big. We all look at the woman's mouth and wait to hear what she will say.

"Oh, this? It's a camera," the woman says, which we know. She wipes her hand on her skirt and pats the camera. She then aims what is left of the thing at the bin by the door, misses, and laughs, but I don't see anything funny. The woman looks at us, like maybe she wants us to laugh since she is laughing, but we are busy looking at the thing, flying in the air like a dead bird before hitting the ground. We have never seen anyone throw food away. I look sideways at Chipo.

"How old are you?" the woman says to Chipo, looking at her stomach like she has never seen anybody pregnant.

But Chipo is not even listening, she is busy looking at the thing lying there on the ground.

"She is ten," Godknows replies for Chipo. "We are nine, me and her, like twinses," Godknows says, meaning him and me. "And Bastard is eleven and Sbho is eight, and Stina we don't know."

"Wow," the woman says, playing with her camera.

"And how old are you?" Godknows asks her. "And where are you from?" I'm thinking about how Godknows talks too much.

"Me? Well, I'm 33, and I'm from London. This is my first time visiting my dad's country."

"I ate some sweets from London once. Uncle Polite sent them when he first got there but that was a long time ago. Now he doesn't even write," Godknows says. The woman's twisted mouth finishes chewing. I swallow with her.

"You look fifteen, like a child," Godknows says. I am expecting the woman to slap Godknows's big mouth for saying that, but then she only laughs like she has been told something to be proud of.

"Thank you," she says. I look at her like what is there to thank? and then at the others, and I know they think the woman is strange too. She runs a hand in her hair, which looks matted and dirty; if I lived in Budapest I would wash my whole body every day and comb my hair nicely to show I was a real person living in a real place.

"Do you guys mind if I take a picture?"

We do not answer because we are not used to adults asking us anything; we just look at the woman take a few steps back, at her fierce hair, at her skirt that sweeps the ground when she walks, at her pretty peeking feet, at her big jewellery, at her large eyes, at her smooth brown skin that doesn't even have a scar to show she is a living person, at the earring on her nose, at her T-shirt that says 'Save Darfur'.

"Come on, say cheese, say cheese, cheese, cheeeeeeeese," the woman enthuses, and everyone says "cheese". Myself I don't really say, because I am busy trying to remember what cheese means exactly, and I cannot remember. Yesterday

Mother of Bones told us the story of Dudu the bird, who learned and sang a new song whose words she did not really know the meaning of, and was caught, killed, and cooked for dinner because in the song she was actually begging people to kill and cook her.

The woman points at me, nods, and tells me to say "cheeeeeese" and I say it because she is smiling like she knows me really well. I say it slowly at first, and then I say, "cheese" and "cheese", and I'm saying "cheese cheeeeese" and everyone is saying "cheese cheese cheese" and we are all singing the word and the camera is clicking and clicking and clicking. Then Stina, who never really speaks, just starts and walks away.

The woman stops taking pictures and says, "Are you ok?" but Stina does not stop. Then Chipo walks away after Stina, rubbing her stomach, then the rest of us all walk away after them.

We leave the woman standing there, taking pictures. Bastard stops at the corner of SADC and starts shouting insults at her, and I remember the thing, and that she threw it away without even asking us if we wanted it, and I begin shouting too, and everyone else joins in. We shout and we shout and we shout; we want to eat the thing she was eating, we want to make noise in Budapest, we want our hunger to go away. The woman just looks at us, puzzled, and hurries back into the house and we shout after her still. We get hoarse shouting. Our throats itch. When the woman closes her door and disappears, we stop and slowly walk away to find guavas.

Bastard says when we grow up we will stop stealing guavas and move to bigger things inside the houses. When that time comes, I'll not even be here; I'll be living in America with Aunt Fostalina, doing better things. But for now, the guavas. We decide on IMF Street, on a white house so big it looms like a mountain. In front is a large swimming pool, empty chairs all around it.

The good thing with this pretty house is that the mountain is set far back in the yard, and our guavas are right within reach, as if they heard we were coming and ran out to meet us. It doesn't take long to climb over the durawall, onto the tree, and fill our plastic bags with bull guavas. These ones are big, like a man's fist, and do not ripen to yellow like the regular guavas; they stay green on the outside, pink and fluffy on the inside. They taste so good I cannot even explain it.

* * *

Going back to Paradise, we do not run. We walk nicely like Budapest is now our country, eating guavas along the way and spitting the peels all over to make the place dirty. We stop at the corner of AU Street for Chipo to vomit. Today her vomit looks like urine, but thicker. We leave it there, uncovered.

"One day I will live here, in a house just like that," Sbho says, biting a thick guava. She looks to the left and points to a big blue house with the long row of steps, flowers all around it. Her voice sounds like she knows what she is talking about.

"How are you going to do that?" I ask.

Sbho spits peels on the street and says, with her big eyes, "I just know it."

"She is going to do it in her dreams," Bastard says to the sun, and throws a guava at the durawall of Sbho's house. The guava explodes and stains the wall pink. I bite into a sweet guava. I don't like grinding the bull guava seeds especially because they are tough and it takes a long time to do, so I just grind them gently, sometimes swallow them whole even though I know what will happen.

"Why did you do that?" Sbho looks at the now-dirty durawall of her house, and then at Bastard. Bastard giggles, throws another guava. It misses the wall but hits the gate. The gate does not make noise like a real gate is supposed to.

"Because I can. Because I can do what I want. Besides, what does it matter?"

"Because you just heard me say I like the house, so you are not supposed to do anything to it. Why don't you pick another house that I don't care about?"

"Well, that doesn't make it your house, does it?" Bastard wears a black tracksuit bottom that he never takes off, and a faded orange T-shirt that says 'Cornell'. He takes off the Cornell T-shirt, ties it over his head, and I don't know if it makes him look ugly or pretty, if he really looks like a man or woman. He turns and starts walking backwards so he can walk facing Sbho. He always likes that whomever he is quarrelling with look right at him. He has beaten us all, except Stina.

"And besides, Budapest is not a toilet where anyone can just walk in. You can never live here."

"I'm going to marry a man from Budapest. He'll take me away from Paradise, away from the shacks and Heavenway and Fambeki and everything else," Sbho says.

"Ha ha. You think a man will marry you with your missing teeth? I wouldn't even marry you myself," says Godknows, shouting over his shoulder.

He and Chipo and Stina walk ahead of us. I look at Godknows's shorts, torn at the back, at his pitch-black buttocks peeping like strange eyes through the dirty white fabric.

"I'm not talking to you, big-head!" Sbho shouts at Godknows. "Besides, my teeth will grow back. Mother says I will even be more beautiful, too!"

Godknows flings his hand and makes a "whatever" sign because he has nothing to say to that. Everybody knows that Sbho is pretty, prettier than all of us here, prettier than all the children in Paradise. Sometimes we refuse to play with her if she won't stop talking like we don't already know it.

"Well, I don't care, I'm going out of the country myself. I will make a lot of money and come back and buy a house in this very Budapest or Los Angeles, even Paris," Bastard says.

"When we were going to school, my teacher Mr Gono said you need an education to make money, that's what he said, my own teacher." Chipo rubs her stomach, and says Mr Gono's name so proudly like he is her own father, like he is something special, like maybe it's him inside her stomach.

"And how will you do that when we are not going to school?" Chipo adds.

"I don't need school to make money. What Bible did you read that from, huh?"

Bastard screams at Chipo, bringing his face close to hers like he will bite her nose off. Chipo caresses her stomach and eats the rest of her guava quietly. She walks faster, away from us.

"I'm going to America to live with my Aunt Fostalina; it won't be long, you'll see," I say, raising my voice so they can all hear. I start on a brand new guava; it is so sweet I finish it in just three bites. I don't even bother chewing the seeds.

"America is too far," Bastard says, bored. "I don't want to go anywhere where I have to go by air. What if you get stuck there and you can't come back? Me, I'm going to South Africa or Botswana. That way, when things get bad, I can just get on the road without talking to anybody; you have to be able to easily return from wherever you go."

I look at Bastard and think what to say to him. A guava seed is stuck between my gum and my last side teeth and I try to reach for it with my tongue. I finally use my finger. It tastes like earwax.

"America is far," Chipo says, agreeing with Bastard. She stops briefly, her hand under her stomach, so we can catch up with her. "What if something happens to your plane when you are in it? What about the terrorists?"

I think fat-face, soccer-ball-stomach Chipo is only saying it to please ugly-face Bastard since he just screamed at her. I give her a talking eye, but my mouth just keeps chewing.

"I don't care, I'm going," I say, and walk fast to catch up with Godknows and Stina because I know where the talk will end if Chipo and Bastard gang up on me.

"Well, go, go to that America and work in nursing homes and clean poop. You think we have never heard the stories!" Bastard screams to my back but I just keep walking.

I think about turning right around and beating Bastard up for saying that about my America. I would slap him, butt him on his big forehead, and then slam my fist into his mouth and make him spit his teeth. I would pound his stomach until he vomited all the guavas he has eaten, pin him to the ground. I would jab my knee into his back, fold his hands behind him and then pull his head back till he begged for his life. But I shut up and walk away. I know he is just jealous. Because he has nobody in America. Because Aunt Fostalina is not his aunt. Because he is Bastard and I am Darling.

***

By the time we get back to Paradise the guavas are finished and our stomachs are so full we are almost crawling. We will just drink water for the night, listen to Mother of Bones tell us a story, and go to sleep. We stop to defecate in the bush. It is best to do so before it gets too dark otherwise no one will accompany you; you have to pass the cemetery to get to the bush and you might meet a ghost.

We all find places, and me, I squat behind a rock. This is the worst part about guavas; all those seeds get you constipated when you eat too much. When it comes to defecating, we get in so much pain, like trying to give birth to a country. Minutes and minutes and minutes pass and nobody shouts, "I'm done, hurry up."

We are all squatting like that, in our different places, and I'm beating my thighs with fists to make a cramp go away when somebody screams. Not the kind of scream that comes from when you push too hard and a guava seed cuts your anus; it says "come and see", so I stop pushing, pull up my underwear and abandon my rock. And there, squatting and screaming, is Godknows. He is also pointing ahead in the thick trees, and we see it, a tall thing dangling in a tree.

"What's that?" somebody, I don't know who, whispers. Nobody answers because now we can all see what it is. A woman dangles from a green rope. The sun squeezes through the leaves, and gives everything a strange colour that makes the woman's light skin glow like there are red-hot coals inside her.

The woman's thin arms hang limp at the sides, and her hands and feet point to the ground, like somebody drew her there, a straight line hanging in the air. Her eyes are the scariest part, they look too white, and her mouth is open wide. The woman is wearing a yellow dress, and the grass licks the tip of her shoes.

"Let's run," Stina says. They are the first words Stina has spoken since country-game. When Stina speaks you know it's something important, and I get ready to run.

"Coward, can't you see she's hanged herself and now she's dead?" Bastard picks a stone and throws; it hits the woman on the thigh. I expect something will happen but then nothing does, the woman just does not move.

"See, I told you she is dead." Bastard says, in that voice he uses when he is reminding us who is the boss.

"God will punish you for that," Godknows says.

Bastard throws another stone. It hits the woman on the leg with a *khu* sound. The woman still does not move.

I am terrified; it is like she is looking at me from the corner of her white, popped eye. Looking and waiting for me to do something, I don't know what.

"God does not live here, idiot," Bastard says. He throws another stone that only grazes the woman's yellow dress, and I am glad he missed.

"I will go and tell my mother," Sbho says, sounding like she wants to cry. Stina starts to leave, and Sbho and Godknows and I follow him. Bastard stays behind for a little while, but when I look over my shoulder, I see him right there behind us. I know he can't stay in the bush by himself, with a dead woman, even though he wants to make like he is the president of Paradise. We start walking together again, but then Bastard jumps in front of us.

"Wait, who wants bread?" he says, tightening the Cornell T-shirt on his head. I look at the wound on Bastard's chest, just below his left breast. It's almost pink like the inside of a guava.

"Where is it?" I say.

"Listen, did you notice how that woman's shoes look almost new? If we can get them then we can sell them and buy a loaf, or maybe even one-and-a-half. What do you say?"

We all turn around and follow Bastard back into the bush, and we are rushing, then we are running, then we are running and laughing and laughing and laughing.

NoViolet Bulawayo was born and raised in Zimbabwe. She recently completed her MFA at Cornell University in the US, where she is now a Truman Capote Fellow and Lecturer of English. Another of her stories, 'Snapshots', was shortlisted for the 2009 SA PEN/Studzinski Literary Award. NoViolet has recently completed a novel manuscript tentatively titled 'We Need New Names', and has begun work on a memoir project. 'Hitting Budapest' was first published in *The Boston Review*, vol 35, no 6, Nov/Dec 2010.

What Molly Knew

Tim Keegan

AT FIRST MOLLY RETIEF didn't know who it was on the other end of the phone. Tommie had never phoned her before, as far as she could remember. He sounded agitated, his voice shaking. Sarah's dead, he said. What do you mean, Sarah's dead? It can't be. But it was. Molly had never hidden the fact that she didn't like her son-in-law. She blamed him for everything that had gone wrong in her family. She liked to think they'd all been happy before he came along.

"Somebody shot her," he was saying. "In the back of the head. She's just lying there in her dressing gown on the kitchen floor. The police are here now."

That's all there was. What more was there to say? Molly wasn't sure what she should do now. What do you do when your only child is dead? She sat for a moment by the phone, running her fingers over the eczema on her arms. Sarah was all she had left after her first husband had been killed in a car crash near Laingsburg twenty or so years ago. She felt like the world had ended, much the same as she'd felt when Neville died. All the anger and pain that existed between mother and daughter, the gulf of misunderstanding and mistrust, charge and recrimination, was like a balm, a reassurance, compared to this. They had been held together by their differences. They'd lived out their unhappiness and their guilt and their shame in mutual embrace, scratching each other's scabs, never allowing wounds to heal. But they always had each other. And now – what now?

Molly did what she always did. She turned on the kettle, got down the tin of Five Roses tea bags, got the milk out of the fridge. The cat purred from her spot on the kitchen table, as if this were a day like any other, waiting for the saucer of milk that was her due. Why should you change the habits of a lifetime just because your reason for being had come to an end?

While she waited for the slow kettle to boil, Molly took the carpet sweeper out of the broom cupboard and began doing the rugs in the hallway. Housekeeping would keep her busy until eleven, when she allowed herself a break in front of the telly. That's how every day went.

As she was pouring the water into the chipped teapot, she felt a sharp pain in her ribs. She clutched her arms together under her breasts as she sat down at the table. She knew it was Tommie. Who else would kill her? Sarah had no enemies. She had nothing anyone would want to steal. And who could get into a third-floor flat in a secure block in Goodwood? She thought of phoning her husband Rollo at the Autoglass place in Milnerton where he was workshop manager. He should know. But she didn't phone him. She didn't want to interrupt him, especially now that they were short-staffed. What could he do anyway? He never got on with Sarah. As a girl she'd resented his presence, the speed with which her mother remarried after her father's death. She'd got it into her head that Rollo was a rival, someone who was out to ruin her and her mother's lives. She never understood how little choice Molly had. Molly was always caught in the middle, trying to keep the peace, accepting the battering she took as the price she had to pay.

And then along came Tommie Nobrega, the psychologist, with his theories and suspicions. Sarah was a nurse aide in the clinic where she met Tommie. Of all the men her daughter could have fallen for... The horrid little man was determined from the beginning to poison her mind. She got it into her head that she'd been victimized, abused, interfered with, and it was all her mother's fault for allowing it. Recovered memory, he called it, as if you can make things up and suddenly it becomes real. All because of her resentments against the man who had always stood between them and destitution. Alright, Rollo wasn't perfect: he drank too much; he stayed out at night playing darts at Wally's Bar in Koeberg Road; he'd visited prostitutes in his time, had girlfriends. And he had a temper, used his fists when he was boozed up, used foul language. The neighbours had sometimes called the police in. But what was she supposed to do? Move out and starve? Go and live in a shelter? At her age?

"It's always the husband," agreed Inspector Duvenage. "Mr Nobrega is definitely top of the list, just between you and me. We reckon he had the opportunity. It happened between seven when she was seen picking up the paper downstairs, and nine when her neighbour came in to see why her door was wide open and found her lying there. The husband says he left at 7.30 to go to work. The neighbours say they heard nothing, though we're still busy going from door to door. No forced entry. That's the thing. The security gate is always closed. So whoever did it must have been known to her."

"I'm sure it's him," said Molly. "I never liked him. He filled her head with hate. She only married him to punish me. I never understood what I did to deserve it."

Molly stroked the cat sleeping on her lap. She looked drawn, worn out. Her brown, thinning hair showed streaks of grey. She was wearing a pinafore over her shapeless lavender jersey. She always wore the pinafore when she was doing housework.

Inspector Duvenage took a sip of tea, holding the cup with his fingers gripping the rim. He checked the ring-bound notebook he held in his left hand. "Mrs Retief," he said, clearing his throat. "I need to clear up a few things with your husband. I presume Mr Retief is at work?"

"Yes. Why?" The colour rose to her cheeks. "There's nothing my husband can tell you. I know Tommie will tell you lies, Inspector. He's trying to shift the blame. He's been telling lies about us from the beginning. That's why my daughter didn't speak to me. He turned her against me."

"I suspected he might be making things up. They do, you know, when they think they're cornered. But still, I think I should talk to him. Your husband, I mean."

He scratched his head, looking at the notebook with a frown. "You say your daughter didn't talk to you, ma'am? Was there any particular reason for that?"

"No, not really. I mean, she was never easy. But it was Tommie who came between us. He seemed hell-bent on destroying us all. Now he's got his way. It's wicked, that's what it is. Wicked!"

She offered Inspector Duvenage another Marie biscuit from the glass plate she'd arranged them on. He declined. He was looking around the room, almost unnaturally clean and tidy, nothing out of place. Modest, but comfortable; old furnishings, pictures on the walls, a few ornaments carefully placed on the mantel. A room used only for entertaining, perhaps. Not that much entertaining went on here, by the looks of her. One of those stay-at-home women, in her fifties, with not much of a life outside these walls. Seemed like a family in which you didn't expect things to go wrong.

In Inspector Duvenage's experience, there are two kinds of investigations. Those, the everyday ones, where it's difficult to sympathize with the victims, people for whom life is cheap and death routine. And then there are those where violent death is as far from the victims' expectations as it can be, normal, good people living normal lives in homes like this one, whose existence is overturned in an instant for reasons that no one can fathom. It's at times like this that he finds the job a strain, when he feels he has to nail the culprit just to calm the jangling in his nerves that doesn't go away when he gets home at night. He knows that all citizens are equal in the new South Africa, but he can't help but feel some people's pain more than others'.

That's just the way he is, and the newspapers and television people seem to think the same way, to judge by the posse of reporters and cameras outside Sarah Nobrega's flat in Goodwood when he left.

"Mrs Retief, why don't you tell me all about your son-in-law? Where did they meet?"

"I hate it when you call him my son-in-law. I never thought of him as part of my family."

Rollo Retief was a big, balding man with grey sideburns and rolls of fat under his puffy eyes. He breathed heavily and smelled of cigarettes and he needed a close shave. His round face was lined and his skin was yellowish, parchmenty, with little veins near the surface of his large nose. Yellow teeth, yellow fingers too. He didn't look healthy. Nearing retirement age, assumed Inspector Duvenage, and not a moment too soon. Nor was he pleased to see the cop, the way he stared at Duvenage as if he was to blame for wasting his time with enquiries when all these people with their broken car windows wanted same-day service. High crime rates made for good business in Rollo Retief's line of work, but clearly didn't do much for his temper. It was obvious his staff were wary of him, glancing at him with surreptitious looks through the glass partition of his small office to make sure he wasn't watching what they were doing.

"I'm sorry to hear that, but I don't know what I can do to help you," Rollo said when Inspector Duvenage told him of Sarah's death. The inspector was surprised to discover that Rollo Retief knew nothing about it, that his wife hadn't got in touch with him.

"I suppose you'll want to go home, to be with your wife, Mr Retief," he said.

Rollo shook his head. "I would, except we're run off our feet here. It's a terrible thing to happen but life must go on.

We're short-staffed, you know. The buggers come and go. The turnover's terrible."

He sat behind a desk piled with folders and files. It was an untidy place, with dirty cups and glasses and dust on the shelves. Not the sort of office to give clients confidence in the way the business was run.

"When last did you see Sarah, Mr Retief?" asked Inspector Duvenage, pulling the notebook and the blue Bic out of his inside pocket.

"I never saw her. Not since before she was married. She wouldn't have anything to do with me. Or her mother, either. You know she didn't even invite her mother to her wedding? She brought that man over to the house when they first got engaged, just to shock us, then there was a big fight and that was that. They sometimes spoke on the phone, she and Molly, but it always ended with a screaming match and Molly in tears for the rest of the day. Sarah was sent to torment her mother. Ever since she was little. The trouble I had from her! Her mother thinks it's because her father died, but that doesn't explain anything. Some of these kids these days are just naturally bad. Her mother won't tell you anything about it, but the boyfriends and the drugs! Molly always had her head in the sand over that girl. She doesn't know but I paid for more than one abortion. And then she goes and marries that man! I suppose you've seen him. Figures, doesn't it? She was bound to come to a sticky end after that. Thank God they didn't produce any children, that's all I can say!"

"She was a nurse, wasn't she?" asked Inspector Duvenage. "I mean, she couldn't have been such a bad case."

"Ja, well…" he shrugged, as if that meant nothing to him.

Not the friendliest, thought Duvenage. A man of fixed opinions, not to be swayed from his antagonisms by the girl's death. He felt sorry for the wife, putting up with this sad sack of a man, who presumably took his sourness home with him at night.

When Rollo came home, he wanted his supper ready, whatever time it was. It was after ten when Molly heard the Mazda turn into the drive. She hadn't spoken to anyone all day, not since Inspector Duvenage had been there before lunch. Except for Mrs Henning from next door, who came over to say it was on the radio, and was there anything she could do? Molly said no, it was very kind but she was coping, and didn't let her in. Trust Mrs Henning to know Sarah's married name. She seemed to know everything. Rollo didn't like Mrs Henning, who'd phoned the police before and was always snooping.

Otherwise, it was a day like any other for Molly, except there was a big hole inside her that ached and ached. She'd thought of phoning her sister in Saldanha, but what could Lettie do? Lettie was married to a warrant officer in the navy and lived in a navy house, and thought herself superior. She'd say how sorry she was, but wouldn't really mean it, and that would be that. Her own sons were both qualified and gainfully employed and successfully married, one an electrician, the other an accountant, and that's all that mattered to her. Molly could do without Lettie's smugness right now.

She'd made chops and mash and gravy, the way he liked it, put it in the warmer, and waited in front of the telly. She always laid the table meticulously, just for one, with the linen tablecloth always clean and the pepper and salt shakers and the paper napkins in their container within reach. He came in, smelling of whatever it was he drank and wheezing heavily. He sat down at the table and looked closely at the food in front of him, as he did every night, with a frown, looking for faults.

"You heard anything more about Sarah?" Rollo asked after a while.

"No. The policeman said he'd phone or come by if he found out anything more."

Molly sat opposite him and watched him as he ate, ready to fetch whatever he wanted from the kitchen. Sometimes he wanted water, sometimes a beer or the bottle of brandy and a glass, sometimes tomato sauce or chutney. She sat stiffly on the edge of the chair, gauging whether he was in one of his moods or not, relaxing after a while when she was satisfied he wasn't about to explode.

Rollo ate without speaking, smacking his lips and clearing his throat as he always did, shaking his head now and again. Then he said, the fork hanging in the air in front of his mouth, "Jeez, that bastard!" He chewed and swallowed. "I'm sorry to say it, but I knew there was going to be a bad end to all this from the moment she brought him here to show him off to us. You don't marry someone like that if you come from a normal home. I know you cared for that girl, but she didn't deserve you, and if you knew what's good for you you'd be relieved she's gone to her maker. She wouldn't have stopped until she'd destroyed the both of us." He shovelled another forkful into his mouth and chewed away noisily, shaking his head again. "With all her lies. She wanted us both in prison, and you know it. Now at least you can get on with your life without that girl spreading shit about us."

Molly knew better than to say anything. Not that there was anything she wanted to say. She weighed up what Rollo had told her and thought, maybe he's right. He usually was, and even if he wasn't, there was no point disagreeing with him. It wasn't her place to argue with him. After all, he had her interests at heart. He always did have, and even if he didn't express himself with any kindness, he meant well deep down.

"That's what it's all about, Molly," he said as she put the tinned pears and custard in front of him. "What goes around comes around. She only got what she asked for. At least now you can sleep at night without worrying about her, without putting up with her lies and deceit. You're free of all that now. There's that to think about, once you get over the shock and all."

He was in a strange mood, oddly placatory but belligerent at the same time. Disturbed by what had happened today, but unwilling to yield an inch in his self-righteousness about it all. I told you so, so don't blame me for any of this, seemed to be his attitude.

"That husband of hers can rot in prison for all I care," he added, as if to himself, stirring the custard in with the syrup from the tin, as he always did.

Molly felt tears rise to her eyes. She held a tissue to her face, not wanting him to see her in this state. She hadn't felt like crying all day, but now, at such a time, there they were, hot tears welling up and spilling out. She stood quickly and went into the kitchen, busying herself with coffee cups. Rollo didn't like to see her crying. It upset the natural order of things. He didn't like to think there was unhappiness in the house. He had enough on his shoulders without having to put up with his wife getting in the way, demanding attention, implying there was something wrong with the way they led their lives. There were things he expected from a wife, and crying and complaining and carrying on weren't amongst them. When he came in late from the bar was the worst time, the time when things were most likely to go wrong, when she had to be on her best behaviour. Not a good time for tears.

"It hasn't been on the telly, has it?" Rollo called from the sitting room. "The cop said there was a camera crew there, outside the flat."

"I don't think so," Molly called back, trying to sound normal. She wouldn't know. She never watched the news.

Molly was always relieved when Rollo got home and there wasn't a fight. It made everything alright again, whatever the rest of the day had been like. Only today hadn't been an ordinary day. It was the day her only child had been killed, shot in the back of her head in her kitchen, by her own husband. Molly had been holding it in all day but couldn't hold it in any more. She sat at the kitchen table and let the tears flow silently down her cheeks. When she took the coffee in, hoping he wouldn't notice her raw face and swollen eyes, Rollo was asleep.

Inspector Duvenage phoned the next day to report progress, or the lack of it. They had collected lots of evidence at the scene, but were still looking for the murder weapon. They'd taken Tommie in for questioning, but so far he was sticking to his story.

"The man is clever," he said, "and he knows how to sound convincing. After all, he has a psychology degree from UWC and knows all the tricks." The inspector counselled patience. He was sure they'd nail him sooner or later.

Then a man called Comrade Titus phoned to say there was to be a memorial event at the Congregational Church hall in Goodwood on Saturday afternoon at three o'clock, and the family would be welcome. Molly wrote it down and sat and looked at the piece of paper. She didn't know what to make of it. She wondered what Rollo would have to say. If he decided he wasn't going, she could hardly go by herself. Molly and Rollo hardly ever went out together, only to the movies sometimes or to the Wimpy or the fish and chip shop for supper over weekends. Not that often, really.

Molly didn't know what she'd wear. She had an old felt hat with a veil she hadn't worn in years, and a pair of good shoes she never wore either. Her floral dress wouldn't do – something more sombre was required. Perhaps the navy woollen two-piece suit, if it wasn't too warm.

"Titus?" Rollo was sceptical, as she knew he would be, when she told him that evening. He sat at the dining table, an angry scowl on his face, looking at the piece of paper he'd taken from Molly.

"Who's he? You didn't ask him who he was? Why didn't you ask him? I suppose he didn't leave a number."

"He was in a hurry. I didn't have time to ask."

"I can just imagine. And what's a 'memorial event'? Is that what he called it? And why's it in the church hall? Funerals are normally in churches."

"It isn't a funeral. They haven't released the body. I think they'll cremate her. The inspector said it's up to the husband. He's next-of-kin."

"Well, I'm not going – that's for sure."

"You don't think we shouldn't just show up, just for a short while? It might be my only chance to say goodbye to her."

Rollo snorted, stuffing pork sausage into his mouth, washing it down with a Castle straight from the bottle, but didn't say anything more.

On Friday morning, Molly did what she always did on Friday mornings. She went to have her hair done at Mary-Jane's on Voortrekker Road, followed by a cake and coffee at Nino's. She saved all the spare cash she had left over after the grocery shopping and spent it on herself. It was her favourite morning of the week. She always felt pampered and special having her hair washed and set, listening to the hairdresser, fat, unnaturally blonde Marcelle, carry on about her mother and her child and her boyfriend and all the small dramas of her life, feeling reassured that other people's lives were also far from perfect, but that they, too, somehow managed to struggle through.

Marcelle knew not to pry into Molly's life. She knew her life at home was difficult. The telltale signs were there often enough. It sufficed to ask every week how Rollo was, getting the same answer. "He's fine. Nothing ever changes with Rollo." "And Sarah?" "She's fine too."

"Did you see that terrible story about that woman in Goodwood who was murdered by her husband?" asked Marcelle, who always read *Die Son*, because it provided her with talking points that kept her going through the day. "Shot in her head, she was, in her kitchen. My cousin lives in the same block of flats, and she says she's not surprised. She says the husband is one of these illegals from Mozambique.

"They say he's half-Portuguese, but he's more black than white, to judge by his appearance. Can you imagine it, he's living there in a respectable block of flats in a white area, dressed up in ANC gear all the time, with all these blacks coming and going, having meetings and things? And with a white wife who always looked like there's something wrong with her, with these dark rings around her eyes. She's married to one of them, that's what's wrong with her! What do you expect? My cousin says people heard him threatening to do things to her, and now it's happened. So why am I not surprised, hey?"

Molly said nothing. She felt her fists balled tight under the sheet, her nails digging into the soft flesh of her palms. A moment later Marcelle said, "You alright, Mrs Retief? You don't look so good."

Molly was feeling faint and wanted to go home. Come over all funny, she said, looking anxiously at her white face in the mirror. They called a taxi and Marcelle helped her in, saying she should see a doctor just in case.

When Molly got home, the phone was ringing in the hallway. She sat down heavily and picked it up. It was Inspector Duvenage, just checking in, he said, reassuring her they weren't going to let up until they'd nailed the culprit.

"We're getting some useful information from neighbours," he told her. "You know how it is. Leave them for a day or two to jog their memories and they come up with all sorts of stories. Shake the tree a bit and who knows what falls out. They know nothing when you first ask them, nothing out of the ordinary, just ordinary neighbours, but two days later – then they remember all kinds of things. Did you ever hear they fought a lot, Mrs Retief? Did you ever see her with bumps or bruises?"

"No, I didn't."

Molly didn't want to hear anything more about the subject. She felt a headache coming on. She just wanted to take a couple of aspirins and lie down.

On Saturday morning, Rollo went down to the bar at 10.30, as he always did. "You better get my suit ready if we going to this thing," he said as he went out the door. Molly was full of nervous energy after he said that. She got out the suit, a pin-striped, double-breasted thing that probably wasn't in fashion any more, and a good shirt and the ironing board. She took out his good shoes and polished them, and found a decently sombre tie and sponged it. She then took out her navy outfit and made sure it was clean and free of musty smells and moth holes. It was once in a blue moon they ever got dressed up like this. She rushed through her housework, fixed lunch and then sat and waited with the cat on her lap for company. He'd be smelling of drink when he got in. Pray God he wouldn't fall asleep and forget all about it. Or that there wouldn't be a rugby match on that he'd decide was more important.

But there were no hitches and they arrived at the hall on time. Molly was nervous. She felt Rollo's hackles rising, his breathing getting louder as they parked the Mazda. The first thing they saw on entering the hall was the large ANC banner hanging from the table in front. A steady, echoing buzz of voices arose from the twenty or thirty people there, almost all coloureds and Africans, several in ANC Youth League T-shirts. At the front, surrounded by his friends, sat Tommie, his back to them. Molly feared Rollo might create a scene or decide to turn around and head home. He stood and stared with that look on his face that warned there was trouble brewing. Then they saw Inspector Duvenage sitting at the back against the wall, well out of the way. He nodded to them.

They sat down, on plastic chairs spread around from the piles stacked against the walls, feeling self-conscious and out of place. Rollo was not one to put up with situations that made him feel uncomfortable. Molly knew she'd take the brunt of his anger once they were home, he'd let rip later, but that was a small price to pay. For her, being here was important. It wasn't her life, but it was Sarah's, and she couldn't turn her back on her now that she was gone.

A young man came up to them, introduced himself as Comrade Titus, and said there were chairs for them in front. Rollo said they were staying put, at the back, out of the way. He was restrained, but Molly could tell that there was real anger in him, violent anger.

The proceedings began. Comrade Titus welcomed them. Heads turned to look at them, two old white people staring back. She looking embarrassed and anxious, he scowling and displeased. Two men and one woman at the head table stood up and spoke in turn, about Sarah, what a committed partner she was for Comrade Tommie and a committed member of the branch too, about the good work she'd done amongst the victims of violence and the homeless. They talked about Tommie as if he was a victim too, about his family that had fought the Portuguese, although his father was Portuguese himself, and about how he'd joined up to the struggle against apartheid oppression in South Africa. Then people were invited to make contributions from the floor. Molly didn't follow much of what was said after a while, keeping a nervous eye on Rollo, who looked red and puffy in the face as if his blood pressure was going through the roof again.

When it was finished, Rollo was out of the hall while everybody else was still slowly getting to their feet. Molly followed him. They drove home without saying anything. Rollo gripped the steering wheel tightly and chewed his teeth. He went through at least two red traffic lights as if his life depended on it. People hooted at him, but he wasn't in a mood to take heed. As she let herself in the house, Rollo sped away, back to the bar, she knew, to calm his nerves and let off steam. He wouldn't be back till late, she was certain of that, and then very likely his temper would come out and she'd have to put away the breakables. But she was quietly pleased she'd been there, reclaiming part of her daughter for herself, making it known she had a mother.

Molly didn't know why she went out into the unkempt back garden. She might have been looking for dill or parsley left from the lot she'd planted in what had once passed as a vegetable patch. What she found was something else, which explains why she could not recall later what she was doing there. It was a scrunched-up envelope pushed into the compost heap behind the shed. Only a bit of white was visible under the pile of brown lawn clippings that Rollo dumped there when he mowed the lawn. She didn't know why she pulled it out, what on earth she thought she was looking for. Perhaps it was just the incongruity of it, a fresh-looking bit of white paper underneath grass that had been there for weeks, moist and mouldering, disturbed by the cat that had climbed up and rummaged in the warm mulch. Almost as if someone had deliberately pushed it down out of sight, only to be revealed because of a cat's curiosity. She picked it up, shook off the dirt, straightened it out. It was Sarah's handwriting. No question about it. Addressed to Rollo Retief, just the two words on the front of the envelope, the Rs sloping forward and the ls backward. The envelope had already been torn open and there was a letter inside on crinkly airmail paper, a single sheet that had been crumpled into a ball in someone's fist before being reinserted in the envelope and disposed of.

Molly looked around, frightened someone might be watching her. She put the letter in her pinafore pocket and rushed back inside. She sat down at the kitchen table, trembling, and held the thin paper open flat on the tabletop as she read it.

Rollo (it said) –
You know what you did to me as a child and yet you keep on denying it. This can't go on any more. My own life is at a standstill until I get closure on this issue, which still haunts me and makes my life a living hell. My husband knows all about it. We have decided that you should be confronted and made to own up to everything or else we are going to the police. I have already written a thirty-page statement. So, we are coming, Tommie and me, on Saturday morning to your house at ten for an intervention, where you will have an opportunity to admit the wrong you did me and ask for my forgiveness, failing which I will have no choice but to go to the police and lay a charge. Please make sure my mother is present, because she has to know the truth as well.
Sarah Nobrega

Molly sat and stared at the piece of paper for a while, not knowing what to make of it, thinking maybe it isn't what it seems to be, maybe there's an explanation. Then she noticed the date written in the top right-hand corner – two days before Sarah was killed. She got up, took out the frying pan, found the matches she kept for blackouts, put the letter in the pan and lit it. She watched it take fire, those poisonous words decomposing into blackened fragments, curling up, breaking off, dissolving into ash. She lit another match until there was nothing left of it. She shook the pan out in the garden and washed it in the sink.

Molly set about making supper, cutting up potatoes and tomatoes and carrots for the lamb shank stew. When she'd laid the table and cleaned up the kitchen, she sat down in front of the telly and waited for her husband's return, much like any other Saturday night. Of all the nights of the week, Saturday was the most fraught, the night there was most likely to be a scene. She knew she might end up locking herself in Sarah's old room, as she had often in the past. But whatever happened, she knew that tomorrow he'd apologize, say he'd had too much to drink, and then they'd get on with their lives.

Tim Keegan, a Capetonian by birth, started his working life as an academic historian, with spells in Britain and the US before returning to South Africa. He left academic life in his forties in order to write full-time. In addition to several books of history, he has published three novels, one of which, *Tromp's Last Stand*, is a detective story set in Cape Town. His last novel, *My Life with the Duvals,* was shortlisted for the Commonwealth Writers Prize, Africa section. 'What Molly Knew' first appeared in *Bad Company*, published by Pan Macmillan SA, 2008.

In the Spirit of McPhineas Lata

Lauri Kubuitsile

THIS TALE BEGINS AT THE END; McPhineas Lata, the perennial bachelor who made a vocation of troubling married women, is dead. The air above Nokanyana village quivers with grief and rage, and not a small amount of joy, because the troubling of married women, by its very definition, involved a lot of trouble. But, maybe because of his slippery personality, or an inordinate amount of blind luck, McPhineas Lata seemed to dodge the bulk of the trouble created by his behaviour, and left it for others to carry on his behalf. He had, after all, admitted to Bongo and Cliff, his left and right sidekicks, that troubling married women was a perfect pastime because it was "all sweet and no sweat".

Women in the village of Nokanyana, named after a small river that no one had yet been able to discover, were notoriously greedy, and, without exception, surly. Husbands in the village were all small and thin with tight muscles worked into knots because they spent all of their lives either working to please their wives or withstanding barrages of insults and criticisms for failing to do it up to the very high expectation of Nokanyana women. For Nokanyana men, it was a lose-lose situation and, as a result, each and every one of them despised McPhineas Lata merely for remaining single – he had made the right decision and they had not.

McPhineas Lata, though thus despised by most husbands, was adored by most wives. His funeral was full of dramatic fainting and howls of grief echoing as far as the Ditlhako Hills. Tears fell by the bucketful and nearly succeeded in creating the village's missing namesake. The husbands stood at the back of the gathering wearing variations on the theme 'stern face' while the minister said his last words. When it was time to pour dirt on the coffin of McPhineas Lata, the husbands rushed past their crying wives and grabbed up the shovels. Some even came prepared with their own to make the work faster. Indeed, no one could remember a burial that had lasted for so short a time. No sooner had the wives heard that first shovelful of soil hit against the wooden coffin, as they were still organizing themselves for their final grand crescendo of wailing, than the soil was seen to be heaped into a great mound over the grave. The men then piled stones on top, of a great number sure to keep McPhineas Lata firmly in his eternal bed. The men stacked the shovels by the grave, slapped the soil off their hands, and led the way back to the village leaving all their McPhineas Lata problems in the cemetery for good. Or so they thought.

As the husbands made their happy ways to Ema Rengwe Bar, MmaTebogo, one of McPhineas's greatest fans, lingered behind looking longingly at McPhineas Lata's grave. She wondered how the women of Nokanyana would manage without such a talented man. She also wondered what the women would do with all of their spare time. There was only so much husband haranguing a woman could stand. She thought about how much she personally would miss McPhineas Lata and without so much as a warning her mind floated away into McPhineas Lata Land.

Naledi Huelela stopped on the thin lane leading from the cemetery to the village and looked back at McPhineas Lata's grave and spotted MmaTebogo. "What does she think she's doing?" she asked with indignation. The wives stopped and turned to see MmaTebogo lying on top of McPhineas

Lata's grave. "She can't do that!" Naledi said. She felt quite proprietorial over McPhineas Lata since he had died in her bed in the middle of one of his more gymnastically performed sessions. It really had been quite extraordinary what he could get up to. People said he read books.

*** ***

"Read books?" Bongo responded with a sceptical air when asked by the husbands who had gathered at Ema Rengwe Bar after the funeral.

Though they had left the cemetery in a jovial and confident mood, a comment by Zero Maranyane put paid to that. He had looked up from his first beer and said, "I doubt our wives will forget him as quickly as we will."

It was a bitter taste of what their McPhineas Lata-less future was going to hold. No, Nokanyana wives would not forget McPhineas Lata. It would have been better if he had lived to a ripe old age where his muscles and frail, old man body would have let the wives down and would have had them drifting back to their hard-done-by husbands.

Instead, he died as virile as ever, for god's sake, he died in the act of one of his more acrobatic performances, or so the husbands had heard.

The husbands were in a predicament. They knew enough to realize that a dead and buried McPhineas Lata didn't mean dead and buried McPhineas Lata memories. Memories that would likely swirl and twirl in their wives' minds, adding salt and strength until McPhineas Lata became an untouchable super-sex hero with whom they could never compare. They realized then that they had quite a problem with McPhineas Lata dead and buried. Their wives had been almost manageable when he was around, but now the husbands expected the worst.

So they grilled McPhineas Lata's left sidekick, Bongo. "McPhineas Lata reading books? No, he was far too lazy for that. Mostly, I always put it down to a good imagination," Bongo offered. "Imagination?" the husbands asked. If that was the case, they were most certainly doomed.

RraTebogo stood up to address the husbands. He was in the same rudderless boat as they were, but he knew they needed a plan if there was to be any hope at all. "Men! Men! If McPhineas Lata had imagination, why can't we get some of it? Why not? Just because we never had imagination before, doesn't mean we can't change. To be honest, I don't think we have a chance if we don't." Then he turned to McPhineas Lata's right-hand sidekick, Cliff. "So did he ever give you any pointers? Any advice?"

Cliff, not the brightest bulb in the box, looked to Bongo for help. "He did say once that it was good to regulate speed," Cliff offered up as assistance. The crowd nodded in approval.

Some took out pocket-sized notebooks and wrote down the advice, but before they put a full stop on the sentence, Bongo added, "But he said speed was also dependent on the woman's likes and dislikes." The crowd's elation at their perceived progress fell like a lead balloon when they found they were back to the start line.

A particularly gnarled and knotty fellow named Tobias Oitlhobogile stood up. Hunched over, he said in a battered voice, "Maybe we should work together to come up with McPhineas Lata's method. I don't see any of us finding it out on our own." The husbands nodded. It was better that way – at least if they failed, which in all likelihood would be the inevitable outcome, together it wouldn't feel so personal. And they could always meet at Ema Rengwe to commiserate; at least that would be something to look forward to.

So while the wives were fighting it out, trying to climb on top of McPhineas Lata's rocky grave to give him a few last humps, the husbands made a plan of how together they would, by the process of elimination, come up with McPhineas Lata's secret for satisfying their wives.

RraTebogo, the headmaster at the local primary school, rushed to collect a blackboard which he and Ntatemogolo Moeng carried back to the bar. They would use it to map out their plan. They knew that there were only so many things that one could do when it came to making love so they divided the work into a few main categories. The husbands had decided to work in a logical, deductive manner. They would start broadly and work down to the intricate details. All evidence collected would be brought back to Ema Rengwe, discussed, and compiled into notes by the elected secretary, Mr Mokwadi Okwadile, the local accountant. They were going to be systematic and with a good effort by everyone, they were almost assured of success.

The women trickled home from the cemetery over the next week, tired and hungry and more surly than usual. A thunderstorm on the weekend meant no woman could buck and ride on the grave as she mourned McPhineas Lata, and the men knew the time had come to begin collecting the information they needed.

RraTebogo was given the broad topic of foreplay. Once Tebogo, their son, was born almost 36 years previously, RraTebogo had thought, as the natural course of things, foreplay should be abandoned in lieu of sleep. Reintroducing such a long-forgotten activity after such a substantial period of time proved to be a bit touch and go. On his first attempt, which even he recognized later as slightly overambitious, MmaTebogo stuck her head under the covers and responded "What the hell do you think you're doing, Old Man?" Lost for words, RraTebogo rolled over and went to sleep.

The next day he decided he'd have to take things a little slower. Before getting down to business, he rubbed her right shoulder for three minutes. The time-span he knew for certain as he made sure the digital alarm clock Tebogo had bought them for Christmas was positioned at the correct angle as to be seen from the bed. Then he stroked her left side four times in sequence and promptly proceeded with the business. Since MmaTebogo neither shouted nor hit him, he marked it up as a success and passed his news on to the others that night at Ema Rengwe.

Mokwadi looked up from his notebook, his eyes swimming behind his thick, Coke-bottle glasses. "Was that four minutes on the shoulder and three strokes on the side?"

"No," RraTebogo corrected. "Three minutes on the right shoulder and four strokes of the left side. Don't forget that left. I might be a bit subjective, but it seemed that the left side is the right side for the stroking. Anyway, we'll know soon enough."

And indeed they would, for once something was seen to work all of the husbands took the bit of information home and put it into practice in their beds. So for a week of nightly sessions in each and every home in Nokanyana, husbands were giving their wives three-minute rubs of the right shoulder and four strokes of the left side before getting down to the business. The wives were curiously quiet throughout the week. A few hardcores still climbed up the hill to the cemetery to cavort with the memory of McPhineas Lata, but the rest stayed at home, more confused than anything. Something strange was happening in Nokanyana and they didn't want to be up on top of McPhineas Lata's grave and miss the uncovering of all this mysterious activity.

✳✳✳

Back at Ema Rengwe the husbands were in a jubilant mood. Things were going well with the foreplay. "It is time to move on!" RraTebogo said, bringing out the heavy blackboard from the bar storeroom. "Okay, Ntatemogolo Moeng. You've been assigned breasts, any progress there?"

The husbands' eyes moved to the old man sitting on a stool in the corner. He stood up straight and repositioned his jacket, circa 1972, evidenced by the massive lapels and

4 cm by 4 cm checked pattern, red on tan. "Thank you, Modulasetilo. I am happy to report that I have nothing at all to report." The old man bowed slightly and repositioned himself, with no small amount of effort, on the tall stool.

"Well, have you tried anything?" RraTebogo asked in desperation. "Even a negative result is helpful." The husbands nodded their heads. They all knew that a hard smack from a big, disagreeable wife would teach them a lesson they wouldn't soon forget.

Ntatemogolo Moeng stood up again. "Thank you, Modulasetilo. Yes, I have tried a few things but they seem to have just made MmaMoeng very annoyed. She has taken to bringing a softball bat to bed, so considering my age and the fragility of my bones, I thought it best to stop along the way. It was a matter of health." He climbed back up on the stool.

RraTebogo was annoyed. "Bloody hell, man, just tell us what you did so we all avoid it. I don't think any of us cherish the idea of getting hit in the head with a bat!"

"Thank you, Modulasetilo. I can say that it appears squeezing of breasts is a bit tricky – considering all of the patterns and rhythms and varying levels of pressure – I really didn't know where to start. And then, I know some of you more ambitious young men might even add in some mouth activity. I just didn't know where to start, honestly, so I thought since the two milk cows in my kraal seemed to accept the pattern I used on them, I started there. Sort of a milking action. But as I said, MmaMoeng didn't take kindly to that." As he climbed back up on the high stool, the husbands let out a collective groan and shook their heads.

RraTebogo tried to be respectful of the old man's age. "Are you saying you were milking your wife?"

Ntatemogolo stood up. "Yes, Modulasetilo, that is exactly what I am saying, but be warned, I wouldn't advise it." He sat back down.

RraTebogo looked at Mokwaledi. "Did you write that down? We certainly don't want to go that route again." He turned to the husbands. "Does anybody have anything to report? Anything at all?" He couldn't help but sound discouraged. He knew a few shoulder squeezes and side strokes were not going to push the legend of McPhineas Lata out of the wives' minds. "I have noticed a few of our wives have taken to drifting back to the grave in the late afternoon. We husbands are losing ground!"

RraTebogo looked around and saw nothing but a crowd of disappointed faces. "Come on, men, we need to put in more effort." Then, hesitantly, the secretary raised his hand. "Yes, Mokwadi, do you have something for us?"

"I'm not quite sure. As you know, I was given speed as my area, but I discovered something that has nothing to do with that. I don't know if it is in order to mention it or not."

"Give it over, man! Can't you see we're desperate here?"

"Well, I was experimenting with quite a fast speed and MmaMokwadi shifted to get a better view of the TV and I slipped off her and fell to the side. I happened to settle right next to her and since I was slightly out of breath, being not used to such high-energy activity, I was breathing hard right in her ear. Suddenly she picked up the remote and shut off the TV. As the week progressed, I added a few licks of my tongue and kisses on her neck and I believe I'm on to something."

The Nokanyana husbands burst into cheers. Some rushed forward and slapped the shy accountant on the back.

RraTebogo stood up to get some order. "Okay, okay. This is only going to work if we can reproduce the moves in our own homes. Mokwadi, show us on the blackboard." The slight man stood up and took the chalk. He quickly drew a diagram complete with arrows and times as to how the husbands should approach this new move. The house agreed it should be inserted in the routine after the shoulder rubbing and the side-stroking, and before the business. That night the Nokanyana husbands went home a happy lot. They began to believe that they actually could replicate McPhineas Lata's moves and that their wives would forget all about that dead wife-troubler.

***

MmaTebogo was at the communal tap filling her water tank when Sylvia Okwadile pushed up with her wheelbarrow loaded with two large buckets. They greeted each other and sat quietly together; Sylvia on the edge of the wheelbarrow, MmaTebogo on a turned-up cement block, both nibbling at the words they wanted to say while watching the thin stream of water fall from tap to tank. "Too bad about McPhineas Lata," MmaTebogo started, hoping that Sylvia would pick it up and lead them to the topic filling both of their minds.

Sylvia adjusted the purple and red *doek* on her head, and then glanced at MmaTebogo from the corner of her eye. "Everything fine there at home?" she asked.

"Yes," MmaTebogo answered. "Why do you ask?"

"Nothing unusual?" Sylvia wanted a bit more before she let her tongue wag freely.

"Well, now that you mention it." And MmaTebogo began explaining the changes taking place in her matrimonial bed.

Sylvia listened but, like most people, she listened through ears that filtered things to be skewed in a general direction already decided by her. When MmaTebogo finished, she asked, "So is it three minutes on the right shoulder and four strokes on the left side?"

MmaTebogo's eyes widened. "Yes! Yes! That is exactly it! Every night like clockwork. Then there are a few minutes of blowing in my ear, five to seven kisses on the neck, and then the business."

"Aha! I knew it!" Sylvia said, jumping to her feet. She now had enough evidence to confirm what she already believed. She told MmaTebogo her theory. "He's here... with us. I knew he couldn't just leave like that. McPhineas Lata has taken up the bodies of our husbands. He has taken spiritual possession of the husbands of Nokanyana."

MmaTebogo, a practical woman, said, "Do you think so? Can that even happen?"

"Sure, why not? What else could it be?"

MmaTebogo had to agree she had no answer to that question. Maybe Sylvia was right. The two decided to call the wives to see if in their bedrooms they were experiencing the same transformation.

"It starts with three minutes on the left shoulder," Karabo John said the next morning, at the meeting at the church at the end of the village.

"Left? Now that's an interesting twist," MmaTebogo commented.

"Why would McPhineas Lata change things for only one of the wives?" The wives nodded their heads in agreement. It was indeed unusual. Maybe the theory was not correct after all.

But then Karabo John remembered, "Okay, no... you know Dimpho has a problem, he never could keep left and right straight."

The wives giggled. That was the answer then. It was true, they decided – McPhineas Lata had not left them when he died, he had only taken up residence in each of their husbands' bodies. They were so relieved. Many had wondered how they would go on without their weekly visits with McPhineas Lata and the grave humping was just not cutting it.

"Now it's even better," Naledi Huelela added. "Now we all get McPhineas Lata – every night. No more sharing!"

"He really is a wise man," MmaTebogo said, nodding thoughtfully.

***

As the sun set in Nokanyana, husbands and wives had big, wide smiles planted firmly on their faces and deep in their hearts. Once darkness descended, they hurried off to their bedrooms, leaving children to fend for themselves; favourite television dramas were abandoned in the rush, as husbands and wives could hardly wait to discover what new between-the-sheets tricks and treats McPhineas Lata had in store for them.

Lauri Kubuitsile is a full-time writer living in Botswana. She is the author of 14 works of fiction (for adults and children) and numerous textbooks. Her short stories have twice been highly commended in the Commonwealth Short Story Contest (CBA) and in both 2009 and 2010 she won the Golden Baobab Literary Prize. This year will see the publication of her young adult book, *Signed, Hopelessly in Love* (Tafelberg) and a third romance novella, *Mr Not Quite Good Enough* (Sapphire). 'In the Spirit of McPhineas Lata' first appeared in *The Bed Book of Short Stories*, published by Modjaji Books, SA, 2010.

Butterfly Dreams

Beatrice Lamwaka

LABALPINY READ OUT YOUR name on Mega FM. This was an answer to our daily prayer. We have listened to the programme every day for five years. You and ten other children had been rescued by the soldiers from the rebels in Sudan. For a minute we thought we heard it wrong. We waited as Labalpiny re-read the names. He mentioned Ma's name. Our village, Alokolum. There could not be any other Lamunu but you.

During the last five years, we had become part of the string of parents who listened to Mega FM. Listening and waiting for the names of their loved ones. We sat close to the radio every day. Our hearts thumped every time we heard Lamunu or Alokolum.

Without saying words for one hour and each day we sighed after the programme. When the days turned into years, we prayed more often. Your name seemed to have disappeared and our chance of seeing you faded. We waited. We bought Eveready batteries to keep the radio going.

Lamunu, we may never tell you this: we buried your *tipu*, spirit, when word went around that you would not come back to us. The neighbours had begun to tell us that you would never return. Bongomin, who returned after four years of abduction, said he saw your dead body bursting in the burning sun. We never believed you were dead. We also didn't want your *tipu* to roam northern Uganda. We didn't want you to come back and haunt us. Ma never believed for one moment that you were gone.

It was her strength that kept us hoping that one day you would return. She said she dreamt that butterflies were telling her to keep strong. The night after the dream there were so many butterflies in the house. We thought she was running mad. We thought you had taken her mind with you.

Ma wore *opobo* leaves for three days to let your *tipu* rest. We knew that she did it to make us happy. We advised her to let you rest so that she could move on with her life. She never did. She walked around as if her *tipu* had been buried along with yours. Your *tipu* was buried next to Pa. We didn't want you to loiter in the wilderness in the cold. Ma said you deserved to rest. To rest peacefully in the other world. Then, we heard your name on the radio. And we didn't know what to do. Run away? Unveil your *tipu*? Let you go on without knowing what we had done? We may never find the courage to let you know this. Maybe one day you will see the grave with your name on it and then the butterflies will give us the right words and strength to tell you.

You were at World Vision, a rehabilitation centre for formerly abducted children. You were being counselled there. You were being taught how to live with us again. Ma cried and laughed at the same time. Yes, you were alive. We couldn't believe at long last our anxiety would come to rest. That night, Ma prayed. We prayed till cockcrow. We were happy. We were happy you were alive. Pa might have turned in his grave. We were happy to know you were alive.

***

You returned home. You were skinny as a cassava stem. Bullet scars on your left arm and right leg. Your feet were cracked and swollen as if you had walked the entire planet. Long scars mapped your once beautiful face. Your eyes had turned the colour of *pilipili* pepper. You caressed your scars as if to tell us what you went through. We did not ask questions. We have heard the stories before from Anena, Aya, Bongomin, Nyeko, Ayat, Lalam, Auma, Ocheng, Otim, Olam, Uma, Ateng, Akwero, Laker, Odong, Lanyero, Ladu, Timi, Kati. We are sure your story is not any different.

When you returned home, Lamunu, we were afraid. We were afraid of you. Afraid of what you had become. Ma borrowed a neighbour's *layibi*. Uncle Ocen bought an egg from the market. You needed to be cleansed. The egg would wash away whatever you did in the bush. Whatever the rebels made you do. We know that you were abducted. You didn't join them and you would never be part of them. You quickly jumped the *layibi*. You stepped on the egg, splashing its egg yolk. You were clean. You didn't ask questions. You did what was asked of you. It's like you knew that you had to do this. Like you knew you would never be clean until you were cleansed. Ma ululated. You were welcomed home. Back home where you belonged.

We watched you silently. In return, you watched us in silence. We gave you food when we thought you were hungry. You gulped down the sweet potatoes and *malakwang* without saying a word. We didn't want to treat you as if you were a stranger but in our hearts, we knew that you were new. We knew that you would never be the same again. We didn't know what to expect of you. We waited to hear you say a word. We wanted to hear your husky voice. Hear you do the loud laugh you did before the rebels snatched you from us. We wanted to tickle you and watch your body move with laughing. But you were silent. You watched us with awe. You had grown now. Your breasts were showing through the blue flowered dress that you wore.

We greeted you. We thanked God when we saw you. You didn't answer our greetings. You looked at us. We saw your eyes glistening. We knew you were happy to be back. We knew you were happy to see us alive.

That night Ma cried in her bed. She whispered your name time and again as if wishing you would at least say Ma. Although she was happy you were back, she never said it. She expected you to say something. Something that would make her believe your spirit was in that body you carried around. We wanted to know whether your *tipu* had been buried with your voice. We had never been taught how to unbury a *tipu*. We only hoped that your real *tipu* was not six feet under.

We wanted to see you alive again. Although you were fifteen then, we wanted to know if you were still interested in becoming a doctor. We wanted to see you smile again. We wanted to see your eyes brighten as your mother gave you water and did the dance that you liked when you were a child. We wanted something that would make us know that you recognized us. We wanted to do our best to make you happy.

Ma never spoke of the butterflies again. We never heard of the butterfly dreams any more. We wanted the butterflies to come and say something to Ma.

*** * ***

We watched you as you studied our new home. Our new home had become something new. We watched the neighbours watch you with disgust. They were not happy you were back. Some of them still clutched the radio waiting for Labalpiny to read their son's name. They waited to hear him call out their names like *lupok cam* call out our names to give us yellow *posho* and beans.

Lamunu, we no longer till our land. Our children no longer know how to hold a hoe. They have forgotten how the groundnut plant looks. Now, our land buries our children. Our gardens grow huts. We now live in a camp. *Lupok cam* call it internally displaced people's camps. From the sky our camp looks like a farm of mushrooms. We have empty huts with empty people whose *tipu* have been buried or have taken a walk.

Look at the huts, Lamunu. This is something that we don't expect you to understand. Something you couldn't recognize. This is something that we don't understand. This is our home, something that we don't know how to explain to you. Something we took refuge in. This is our home that keeps us alive. Keeps us sane. Just huts. Grass and bricks. Just huts to hide our nakedness. When Latim and his neighbours built their huts here, they said Alokolum was safe. Their children will not be abducted. Their wives will not be raped. They will have something to eat. Then so-and-so built in our gardens all with the same hopes and dreams. Then everybody wanted to build their huts on our land. We couldn't dig any more. We had no more food. We later learnt our home had been marked in the map of Uganda as a camp.

Don't look at us like that, Lamunu. Yes, we now eat yellow *posho*. Yes, yellow *posho* that Ma used to feed Biko, Pa's hunting dog, before the war. We wait for *lupok cam* to provide us with cooking oil and beans, and of course, yellow *posho*. That's all we eat now. Sometimes we don't have enough. Sometimes *lupok cam* don't even come at all. We scramble to get out of the camp to look for something to stop the gnawing feelings in our stomachs. Just a little something. Some wild plants. Some *malakwang kulu*.

Some things that our ancestors never ate. Then we found out there were soldiers guarding us. They don't want us to get out of the camp. Why? we asked. They said they don't want rebels to abduct more of us. These days, my dear, they abduct anybody. Anybody who they can force to stand and be shot in the battlefield.

We asked the soldiers, where were you when Lamunu was abducted? Where were you when the rebels came and took our young ones? Where did you go to when the rebels came and raped our women as we watched? They told us they had not been paid. Sod off! we told them. Let us go to look for food. Then they came with their sticks to beat us as if we were schoolchildren.

***

You spoke in your dreams. You turned and tossed in your mud bed. We held your hands. You were like a woman in labour. You spoke of ghosts. You spoke of rebels chasing you in Adilang because you tried to escape. You spoke of Akello, your friend, who they made you and your team beat to death because she tried to escape. You said you didn't want to kill her. You said you remembered the commandment 'thou shall not kill'. You said you didn't want to participate. You didn't want to hurt anybody. You said you saw Akello covered with sticks. You saw the blood in her mouth. You watched as the older rebels checked to confirm that she was dead. You were nauseated. You tried to vomit but there was nothing to let out. The last meal, raw cassava and boiled chicken, which you had looted from a camp, had already been digested.

We listened to you. We wanted to feel your pain. We wanted to know what you knew. We squeezed your hand. We wanted you to let out what you had been holding onto. You let us squeeze your hand. You didn't wince when blood flowed. We never could drain all your pain away.

***

Today, we watched you get drenched in the rain. You stood there still as the rainfall poured on you. You were not disturbed by the loud thunderstorm. We made space for you in the hut. Waited for you with warm clothes. We thought you were letting out something. We didn't interrupt you.

As the rain became a drizzle, you entered the hut. You bypassed Ma with the warm clothes in her hands. You sat with your wet clothes on. We noticed that it was the time of the month for you. You let the rain wash the blood away. You let us watch the blood streak down your leg. You didn't see the tears rolling down your mother's face.

Later that day, we listened to you curse under your breath. We watched you tremble when you heard the government fighting planes flying over Katikati. We knew that you were worried about the people you left behind. We knew that you knew what would go on when the planes went after the rebels. We didn't ask you for stories. We have heard the stories from Anena, Aya, Bongomin, Nyeko, Ayat, Lalam, Auma, Ocheng, Otim, Olam, Uma, Ateng, Akwero, Laker, Odong, Lanyero, Ladu, Timi, Kati.

✳ ✳ ✳

Lamunu, we remember as if it were yesterday when the rebels came to our home. That night was the night we knew that there would be many more nights like that one. We heard the butts of the guns hitting people's heads. We heard the screams. We heard the rebels demanding our children from our own homes. We were helpless.

You were still dazed with sleep. One rebel not much older than you grabbed you by the hands. You were only wearing a t-shirt. Ma grabbed a skirt for you to wear. You went out of the house with it still in your hand.

Ma's pleas and cries were only answered with the butts of guns on her head. She asked them to take her instead. But the rebels demanded medicine. They wanted the medicine she brought from the government hospital in town. Lamunu, Ma would never have let you go. You were only eleven. Reading for your Primary Leaving Exams. You always wanted to be a doctor. You said you wanted to do what Ma was doing, not as a nurse, but as a doctor.

We later learnt that they went house to house in Katikati as well, taking all boys and girls around your age with them. They said that the rebels would train the children to fight.

Train them to lure other children. Join the big war to save the Acholi. Oust the government. Overthrow Museveni's government. We didn't know what that meant. We didn't want to ask anyone. What we knew was that we didn't want our children to get involved in that war.

***

We watched as you always prepared to go to school like it was a special ritual. Brushing your teeth and then taking a bath. You carefully splashed the water from the *galaya* onto your slender body. You didn't eat the breakfast that Ma made for you. You packed it in your school bag so that you wouldn't be late for school. We admired you for that. Even when the war started and many children were waylaid, you managed to get there. You cursed the teachers and called them cowards when you didn't find any children or teachers. Days after a heavy fight between the rebels and soldiers you continued to go to school. You never gave up, even when you didn't find anybody there.

You said that the war only affected the education of the children in the north. The rest of the children in Uganda studied. And the exams were all the same. You went to school when everyone was hiding in the bush. Ma begged you not to go. Children were waylaid by rebels on their way to school, she pleaded. You always managed to get to school. Found an empty class. Disappointed, you would come home. Ma later became your teacher. Ma taught you about reproduction even if she knew she shouldn't say such words to her daughter. You were eager to learn. Pa wanted to teach you too, even though he didn't know how to read and write.

***

Lamunu, we don't know how to tell you that Pa is no longer with us. You may have noticed that he is not around. We don't know with which mouth to tell you that he was cut to pieces by those who you were fighting for. He was found in a garden he rented in Lalogi. He said he could not depend on *lupok cam* to provide him and his family with food. You know your father. He was a proud man. He believed that a strong man should show his strength by the amount of food he had in his granary. Before the war, there was a lot of food in the granary. The neighbours were jealous of that. He dug like a tractor. His cows were the best in Alokolum. Everybody wanted to buy milk from him. Even the lazy Lutukamoi, he tried to dig night and day but couldn't get done half of what your father could achieve.

The rebels found him digging and asked him what he was doing since everybody was supposed to be in a camp. He said a man has to provide for his family. They mocked him and told him to join them to fight if he was a strong man. He said he would not join them because he did not start the war they were fighting. Ten young men beat him up with whatever they could find. They later cut his body into pieces. Lamunu, we did not eat meat after we buried your father and we have not eaten meat since then… We could never understand why another human being could humiliate another, even in their death.

Each day we pray that we get the strength to tell you. And one day when the war ends, you will tell us your story. And we will tell you our stories.

***

We learnt from the neighbours that you went to school. You asked the headmaster to register you as a primary six pupil. We didn't know that you could talk. We were happy that you said something, even though it wasn't to us. The headmaster looked at your skinny body. You told him you wanted to become a doctor. He asked you whether you could pay. You didn't answer that. You knew that we didn't even have a coin to put food on the table. You said you didn't care and that all you wanted to do was to study. You said you could pay when you were finished with your education.

You entered a primary four class. The pupils watched you silently. They thought you were a mad girl. They muffled their screams, worried that you would hit them or something. They knew that the war had brought something that they didn't understand. They wanted to survive, so whatever didn't kill them they would watch to try to find a way.

Ma ran to school when she heard that you were there and argued with the headmaster. She wondered why you didn't tell her anything. She wanted to help you. She wanted you to talk to her but she didn't want to push you as well. She loved you though she could not say it.

* * *

Ma spoke to the headmaster of Lacor Primary School. The headmaster agreed to let Ma pay your school fees in instalments. She said that she is happy that you still want to go to school.

You said *apwoyo*. You said thank you to Ma. That's the first word we have heard you say. We're happy to hear you say something. We hope that you will be able to say a lot more. Tell us more than Anena, Aya, Bongomin, Nyeko, Ayat, Lalam, Auma, Ocheng, Otim, Olam, Uma, Ateng, Akwero, Laker, Odong, Lanyero, Ladu, Timi... Most of all, we want to hear your voice.

* * *

You look very beautiful in your new uniform. The headmaster of Lacor Primary School for formerly abducted children has donated the uniform to you. Ma says that you will get special treatment. Most of the children are like you. They too have killed, tortured other children. They too fought in a war that they didn't understand. The teachers will treat you well, Ma says. They have had special training.

You are very happy. We can see you have woken up early. You have packed your bag with your new books. You have written your name neatly on the books.

We know that your dreams will come true. You will be a doctor some day. Do the work that Ma does but wearing a white coat.

There are tears in Ma's eyes. You look the other way. We know that you know they are tears of happiness.

Beatrice Lamwaka is the General Secretary of the Uganda Women Writers Association (FEMRITE). She was a finalist for the 2009 SA PEN/Studzinski Literary Award and was a fellow of the Harry Frank Guggenheim Foundation/African Institute of South Africa Young Scholars programme that year. Her stories have been published in national and international journals and anthologies. She is currently working on her first novel and a compilation of her short stories and is studying for an MA in Human Rights at Makerere University. 'Butterfly Dreams' first appeared in *Butterfly Dreams and Other New Short Stories from Uganda*, published by Critical, Cultural and Communications Press, Nottingham, 2010.

The Mistress's Dog

David Medalie

THE NIGHT WIND TUGGED at the house and slammed against the windows. Nola drank a glass of dry sherry, ate honey nougat and slices of camembert on poppy-seed crackers, and watched TV. The mistress's dog lay on her lap, snoring and twitching. Once he looked up, gazing at her with milky eyes. Then he lowered his head again.

At half past ten she prodded him. "It's time for final ablutions," she said. "I want to go to bed." She picked him up and put him on the floor. Then she unlocked the patio door. The mistress's dog padded behind her, his nails making clicking sounds on the tiles in the passage. The wind had died down a little, but still pushed against them as they made their way down the steps and into the garden. The smell of the sea was strong. Above them loomed the dark mass of the mountain. The mistress's dog sniffed the damp paving-stones and stumbled against a pot-plant. "Hurry up," she said to him. "It's cold." After a while he lifted his leg against a fuchsia. "Thank you," she said. A dog barked in the distance. The mistress's dog barked in response, a shrill, reedy sound. He made scratching movements in the grass with his back legs. Nola carried him indoors.

She fed him again. He spent a long time hunched over his plastic bowl, but ate little. Most of his teeth were gone. His diet, for the last five years, had consisted exclusively of soft food. He suffered from chronic halitosis – or, to be more accurate, others suffered from halitosis in him. There was nothing that could be done about it.

He slept in a basket – which had accompanied him when he flew from Johannesburg, seven years ago – at the foot of Nola's bed. He followed her to the bedroom and hopped into it. She read for twenty minutes and then switched off the light. The dog's sandpaper breath rose and fell in the darkness. Occasionally he whimpered – but whether in the gratification of a dream or the rasp of its disappointment, she could not tell.

Nola had always preferred cats to dogs.

The mistress was considered attractive according to the fashion of that time. But for Nola there was always too much of her – too much laughing, too much heartiness, too much peroxide, too many teeth. Nola's word for her was 'blowsy'. Sometimes she described her as 'blond and blowsy' because she liked the demeaning effect of the alliteration. At other times she just said 'blowsy', confident that the two syllables would hold sufficient scorn.

The mistress thought of herself as bold, daring, unconventional. And in the context of the poor, religious, rural family she came from, she was. She remained single, devoted herself to what she called her 'career' (she was a powerful man's secretary), and had an affair that endured for over a decade with a married man (that same powerful man). She bought a flat, bought a vermilion car, bought the advice of an interior decorator, bought elocution lessons, bought cookery lessons, bought Italian olive oil, bought crushed garlic, bought tickets to the ballet, bought the records of Callas and Caruso, bought sunglasses that resembled the ones Callas used to wear.

She severed all contact with her family. She never went to church. But in the unfettered darkness of night (the mistress was a chronic insomniac), she would sometimes weaken and, ashamed of her weakness, beg God to look indulgently upon her and at least understand her rebellions, even if He could not condone their sinfulness. She wanted God to know that she longed only to be free. She asked God to consider what it meant for a woman like her to have to live in the crimping South Africa of the 1960s.

The powerful man who was her boss and her lover saw her as spirited and strong. She excited him for seven years. She interested him for another five. Then she neither excited nor interested him. But Nola (who was married for over forty years to that same powerful man) sensed that the mistress, for all her bravado, was a fearful person. She understood that, although she presented herself as independent, flagrantly independent, she was in fact frightened of being alone, terrified – to the point of obsession – of abandonment.

Sometimes the mistress invited Nola and her husband to her flat for dinner and Nola would feel obliged to admire the food, the wine, the work of the interior decorator. She would pat the mistress's little dog. (There was a succession of small, yappy dogs over the years; the mistress was never without one.) But she preferred cats to dogs. And the food was always a little too oily, a little too salty, the wine too sweet, the flat too cluttered. Nola saw in the mistress the hesitation that the hearty laugh could not hide, the timorousness that was silent but present all the time, like a heart murmur. It was evident to her that the mistress had become a snob largely because she dreaded the judgement of snobs.

In everything she did and said, the mistress declared her determination to be free. She was, she believed, making and remaking herself. It was very hard work. It was expensive too. But it would be worth it if, by chipping away at herself, she could set herself free forever: a complete metamorphosis.

Nola knew, however, that the mistress had not even begun to emancipate herself. And she suspected that she never would. For she, Nola, was not free either, except from anxieties about money. She knew what the mistress had not yet discovered, which was that nothing grew in the shadow cast by the powerful man.

But it didn't make her sympathetic to the mistress's predicament. 'Blowsy,' she would say. 'Blond and blowsy.'

The next morning the sun shone, but the wind was cold. The mistress's dog, after performing successfully the first ablutions of the day, slept on a rug in the lounge, in a patch of sun. He was less wheezy than he had been during the night, but his breathing was shallow. He lay so still that whenever Nola walked past him, she bent over to see whether or not he was dead. But each time, she heard the tenacious little breaths, saw the rise and fall of the scrawny belly.

She would have liked him to die like that, during his sleep – not because she wished him gone, but because she lived in dread of having to have him euthanased. The vet was prepared to do it at any time: the mistress's dog, he said, was at least eighteen years old, almost toothless, almost blind, more than a little deaf, suffering from heart failure. She need have no qualms, the vet told her. It would be perfectly appropriate; even humane. But Nola couldn't bear the responsibility. She didn't want the needle to do its work at her prompting. She clung still to the hope that the life of the mistress's dog would end of its own accord. She didn't want to have to choose the moment of extinction, to say "today is the day; now is the time".

Was she keeping him alive, she wondered, simply because she was too cowardly to make that choice? Wasn't avoiding that choice a choice in itself? All her life, whenever she had had to make momentous choices, she had felt the pressure to choose as a weight that lay upon her, squeezing and stifling her. Sometimes she had chosen wisely, sometimes foolishly; but, whatever the outcome, the act of choosing had been in itself an agony.

The mistress's dog was old when he came to them; he would not live long, the powerful man had assured her. But he was wrong. The dog lived on in increasing decrepitude.

And now it was not only his life for which she was solely responsible, it was his death too. Near the end of her life, when the anguish of having to make choices ought to be fading at last, the mistress's dog threatened her with the choices associated with his death.

It would be much, much better, Nola thought, if death would come to him there and then; if – with all the euphemistic kindness death is reputed to be capable of – it would gather him in as he slept in a patch of sun on a cold day.

Isn't that what we all want?

But it did not happen.

No one ever told Nola that her husband was having an affair. No one needed to. The powerful man's studied indifference towards a woman whom he so evidently admired, the excessive friendliness of that woman towards her, the gushing pretence that she desired a friendship to develop between them (it never did) – all these things told her unequivocally that the secretary had turned into the mistress.

Nola chose to say nothing. She allowed herself to be invited to the mistress's flat; occasionally, when she felt she had to, she invited the mistress to her home. But whereas the mistress would invite just the two of them, Nola and the powerful man, Nola always ensured that the mistress was invited to her home as part of a large dinner party. She selected the other guests carefully. They were always people the mistress had never met. They had old money. They had read old books. They had seen old paintings. They had visited old cities. They were soft-spoken.

The mistress, in their company, became heartier than ever, as abrasive as a typewriter in a room in which people were writing on soft vellum with quills and ink. In the garrulous terror of the mistress, the resulting discomfort of the powerful man and the condescension of the soft-spoken people, Nola found a small but piquant revenge.

The mistress's dog woke up in the afternoon and went from room to room, looking for Nola. He found her in the entrance-hall, about to leave for the supermarket. "I'll see you later," she said, closing the door. He whined. Nola opened the door again and carried him to the car. "Oh, all right," she said.

In the car she rolled down the window a few inches. The mistress's dog pushed his face into the wind, his ears back and his tongue hanging out. He sneezed several times.

It was a day of clear light and cold blue skies. The supermarket was not far away; still, Nola found the trip arduous. Even when she kept to the speed limit, other motorists seemed to be annoyed with her for travelling too slowly. And when she backed into a parking-space, someone hooted at her – she was doing that too slowly too. A young man knocked against her as she walked into the shopping centre and didn't even apologize. He was talking on a cellphone.

Nola pushed the trolley with one hand and held the mistress's dog in the other. He quivered against her arm. The honey nougat was on the top shelf. Nola put the dog down so that she could reach it more easily. She heard him make a little sound, almost as if he were sneezing again; but when she looked down, she saw that he had vomited on the shiny supermarket floor. The vomit was runny and yellow. "Oh, no!" she said. "Oh, no!" He looked up at her.

There was no one about – Nola could have crept away and slipped out of the supermarket, leaving the misdemeanour to be discovered later. But she did the right thing: she reported it and returned to the aisle, standing guard over the vomit, warning people not to tread in it. Eventually a young woman arrived to clean it up. She was sullen, resentful. "I'm really sorry," Nola said. "I truly am."

"You mustn't bring your dog in here," the young woman said. She was big and her uniform was too tight for her. It strained against her as she bent down to clean up the mess. Her face, when she looked up, had a greasy sheen.

"You're right," said Nola. "You're absolutely right. I won't bring him here again. I promise." She was as contrite as the circumstances demanded. But something also made her want to put in a plea, to soften this thick resentment. "You know," she said, as the young woman heaved herself to her feet, "he's a very old dog. These things happen when you're old." This produced no response. "We all get old," Nola said pointedly.

The face of the supermarket employee came perilously close to Nola's as she brushed past her. "They must shoot me first," she said.

Nola knew when the affair was over, just as she knew when it had begun. The mistress continued to work for the powerful man, but now she was just a secretary, no longer a mistress. When the powerful man retired, so did she, declaring she could not work for anyone else. She was loyal to the end, even though the clandestine days were long gone. And no doubt she envisaged a continued relationship of sorts with the powerful man: the succour of reminiscences, of anecdotes of the years spent together.

But the powerful man retired with Nola to the coast, to Cape Town (his idea, not Nola's); and the mistress remained in Johannesburg. She wrote, she phoned every week (expensive as it was); she did whatever she could to wring a last drop of solicitude from him. But all he gave was money. "She's hard up," he said to Nola. "I must do what I can to help her. After all, she worked for me for over thirty years." When she moved from her flat to a retirement village, he financed the move, for the cottage in the retirement village cost far more than she received from the sale of her flat.

Nola said nothing about the money, but she protested when the powerful man spoke to her (with unwonted awkwardness) of the mistress's dog – the current one, the last of the many small, yappy dogs.

"She can't take it with her to the retirement village," he said. "No pets allowed. Ridiculous, isn't it? You'd think they would realize that elderly people need the company of pets."

"There must be someone else who can take it," said Nola.

"There isn't."

"Then she must ask the SPCA to find a home for it. Or have it put down."

"It's an old dog. If she takes it to the SPCA, they will put it down. That will break her heart."

"It's not my problem."

"Please, Nola. It won't be for long. As I said, he's an old dog. He's on the way out."

It was one of the few occasions in their marriage in which Nola had had the power, the absolute power, of decision. The choice was truly hers. If she had persisted in saying no, the mistress's dog would have remained in Johannesburg and, no doubt, would have been euthanased. It was an opportunity for revenge such as she had never had before.

But it had come too late. The powerful man had gout, an enlarged heart and a flickering memory. The mistress was no longer robust. They would never see each other again. It was too late, far too late, to triumph over them.

The mistress's dog was flown to Cape Town in a crate.

"I prefer cats," Nola said when he arrived.

That night they sat once more in front of the TV. Nola drank dry sherry, ate honey nougat and slices of camembert on poppy-seed crackers. The mistress's dog lay on her lap.

"That was your last trip to the supermarket," she said to him. "Never again. No matter how much you cry."

He bent his head towards her hand and licked it.

We are the survivors, she thought, the two of us. The powerful man had died in a Cape Town hospital after weeks on a ventilator. The mistress died in the frail-care section of the retirement village in Johannesburg. The mistress's dog had outlived them both. And so had she.

Who would have thought that she would spend her last days with this ancient animal – with a dog that used to belong to her husband's mistress? Had she chosen him? Or had she ended up with him by default because she had not, during her life, made the wise, the adroit choices? If we are our choices, then what did it say about her that the mistress's dog was her last companion?

She sighed. He looked up at her with milky eyes. "It's time," she said, "for final ablutions."

David Medalie is a Professor in the Department of English at the University of Pretoria. He published his first collection of short stories in 1990. He won a Sanlam Literary Award for one of his short stories in 1996; and 'The Mistress's Dog' won the Thomas Pringle Award in 2008. His debut novel, *The Shadow Follows*, published in 2006, was shortlisted for a Commonwealth Literary Award and the M-Net Literary Award. 'The Mistress's Dog' appeared in his second collection of stories, *The Mistress's Dog: Short Stories 1996-2010*, published by Picador Africa, 2010.

The Caine Prize
African Writers' Workshop Stories 2011

Bridge

Jide Adebayo-Begun

LAGOS APPEARED TO JIMI as a city that swallowed its millions nightly and spat them out daily to be at the mercy of rain, sun and fumes, to scrape a living and die. For years, he had spurned invitations to visit the city, and had even refused to attend the final stage of a job interview with Shell, simply because it was to take place in Lagos. He excused his fear by calling the city a whore greater than Babylon, the bloated scrotum of Nigeria, and in contrast, extolling the virtues of a quiet existence as a teacher of English in Ijebu-Ode.

But there was no escaping Lagos. Everybody was in Lagos, including his aunt, Mrs Oyekan, who had been working as a nurse in Victoria Island for the past twenty years and was his only link to his mom. Jimi's mother had left him when he was two, and her departure had provided, over the years, both an inexhaustible sap from which his poems sprang and a niggling irritation at his loss of moorings, made worse because he had not received one reply to the 87 letters he had sent her in the past twelve years. So when he got a text message announcing his aunt's desire to see him, he decided to go.

At about 4pm, he arrived outside the hospital where Mrs Oyekan worked. She pulled off her glasses when she finally met him, looked at him from head to toe and burst into tears. Jimi did not know what to do.

"I am pleased to meet you, ma'am," he said, with a tentative smile playing on his lips.

"Pleased to meet me? I was by your mother's side when she brought you to this world. I gave you your first bath. Get into the car."

Before starting the ignition, she said a silent prayer and took off her shoes in readiness for the homeward drive. The sun was of a ferocity one got by burning refuse with petrol and standing close to it. They began to move along with a sea of cars, slowly, noisily; it was the rush hour. The veins of her neck stood out as she steered the vehicle, a second-hand Toyota Carina. Then the traffic stopped moving and she ransacked her collection of tapes before settling for a gospel track in a plethora of Nigerian languages.

"I can't believe my Jimi is now a man. You don't even recognize me."

"It's not my fault. I never heard from anybody on this side of the family."

"I am sorry, I am so sorry," she said.

"Everything is all right, you don't have to be sorry, ma."

"If not for your father, I would have kept in touch. The last time I came, I was with my late husband. Your father threatened to behead us if we didn't leave his house."

"My father left Nigeria seven years ago."

"Oh, that is surprising. I mean, we did not hear!" She paused to think about the implications. "Seven years? Who took care of you? How old were you then, fourteen? How could he have deserted you at that tender age?"

"It wasn't that bad. I was seventeen," he said, "already at the University of Ibadan then."

"*O ma se o.* You know your father is cruel, *sha*. He should have buried his pride and brought you to me. He knew I would not have turned him down." Her mind was set on his father's cruelty. He changed the subject.

"So have you heard from my mother recently?"

"Your mum? You will see your mother, don't worry. Everything in its own time."

They began to move again, towards the Third Mainland Bridge, passing a trailer that had broken down right in the middle of the road. But this was not the major cause of the go-slow. The real culprits were the long queues in almost all the filling stations. While most of them claimed they had no fuel, hundreds of cars still formed an iron trellis in front of their gates. He marvelled at the thousands of vehicles trickling from many roads into the bridge. It was like the broad road that leadeth unto destruction.

"Do you know you have three uncles in this Lagos?" his aunt asked. "Brother Dele is a surgeon at Idi-Araba. Brother Kunle is a big *oga* now at NNPC. Siju is a lawyer... but since Mama passed on, I have not smelled any one of them. What is happening to us in this country? No one knows anyone again; a time is coming when people will just be free to choose any name they like! I hope I will be gone by then."

She called a boy selling Gala sausage rolls.

"Your gala soft?"

"Yes, madam, touch am."

She picked three pieces. The traffic eased a little and she gunned ahead without paying. Jimi looked back, the boy selling Gala didn't show any alarm. He simply adjusted his bathroom slippers and started running towards them as the woman drove on.

"I know your mother has hurt you," she said.

"Not at all, ma. I just want to see her."

"She has hurt you. Don't run away from the truth." She tossed a gala in his direction.

"I just ate, thank you, ma."

In Jimi's experience, most people had expectations of how a child abandoned by his mother was supposed to feel. And he never rose to their expectation. Deep down, he knew who he was: however much he wrote poetry or spoke with feeling, he lacked the sensitivity (or the energy) needed to appreciate this theme of desertion; to give it weight, treat it seriously, start unravelling the tracery of a suppressed childhood. Was he supposed to be mad at her? Or should he embrace her with mercy? What words of wisdom or indignation must he compose to garnish these emotions?

But the truth was that, more often than not, he felt nothing but gratitude towards his mother. She brought him to the world; that could not be discounted. And who was he to demand anything from anyone? She owed him nothing, except that, in moments of fancy, he had imagined his father wasn't really his, since a drunken classroom teacher told him at age twelve that the Bible in the Book of Ezekiel used the adjective 'foolish' to describe any man who felt certain about his paternity.

Perhaps he would ask his mother for his true surname. Just that – afterwards, she owed him nothing. The little he had from life was enough. Jimi liked keeping to the fundamentals: good food, interesting books, cold beer, nice Juju music and women; no, just one in fact. A woman: pleasant, empathetic, thoughtful yet a trifle insouciant, beautiful but not to an alarming degree, restrained in temperament but wild in bed; a woman who could tame him for the workaday pleasures of living. From that abundant domesticity he would study literature and craft great poems – this woman was the most difficult for him to get. But it was all right, by and by everything good will come – childhood had nothing to do with it.

"Look at him. Always brooding. Just like Tunji," she showed him the wallpaper on her cellphone, with the photo of a young man in an academic gown. "That's Tunji, my first-born. He is now a neurosurgeon in Toronto. He likes to brood. Just like you. My boy always has an axe to grind. Never giving his own mother a moment of the day." The more she spoke, the more her eyes gleamed. "Your generation is an axe-grinding one. Don't worry, you will meet your cousins. Sayo and Kemi are at home."

The traffic slowed. She called a hawker over, offering him a 500-naira note for a bottle of water.

"Madam, I no get change."

"Take your water then."

"No, hold am, I go find change." Then the Gala boy, who Jimi had thought was forgotten, materialized with a fistful of notes and Jimi called back the water boy. They settled their account and she wound up. They had spent two hours in the traffic. Thunder rumbled overhead like an empty stomach; a drizzle started. But it didn't bring coolness, just a liquid accompaniment to the sun, the kind of rain that folks on his street in Ijebu-Ode would describe as "the lion is giving birth".

They heard a blast of siren. Three bullion vans approached, with police brandishing guns and cowhides. The road briefly cleared. It always amazed him, the power of noise to make things happen. A *danfo* bus lurched after the vans and stopped in front of his aunt's car, drowning the gospel lilt from the car stereo with Fuji music.

"What kind of a useless song is that?" his aunt asked.

Before Jimi could answer, a man appeared in the traffic with chunks of meat on a wooden slab complete with a set of knives.

"Thank God," she said. They stopped to buy meat.

"Is there any way I can see my mum?"

"That I won't tell you. Relax! For now, just know that wherever she is, she's doing the work of the Lord. You'll see for yourself. God has touched her life. God can use anyone, I kept telling this to my husband. Thank God he answered the altar call before he passed on."

"May God rest his soul."

"I'm telling you this so that you'll know that God never forsakes his own. He can also heal your family."

"Thank you."

The danfo bus kept managing to overtake them, and each time they were hit anew by the groan of its exhaust pipe and the Fuji music. It was overloaded with passengers. The vehicle has seen better days, Jimi thought. What hasn't in this country? Even the bridge quivered. Constructed less than sixteen years ago, it had grown tired. Too many people, too much life ferried up and down its span, too much spit of frustration sliding on it; the sad fate of a yeoman bridge.

"What do you do at the moment?" she asked.

"I am a teacher."

"Teacher *ké*? Are you comfortable with that?"

"We are managing, thank God."

Hawkers on the road sold all kind of wares: shoes, bags, cooking utensils, chess boards, motivational books, mineral water, rat-poison, windscreen wipers, cellphones, carpets, toilet seats and many more. And his aunt kept buying. Adding to the sausage and water and meat, she bought plantain chips, 'non-alcoholic' wine, credit for her phone and a pirated copy of a book titled *Forty-Eight Laws of Power*. This was the only thing she did not offer him.

There were also beggars with great deformities: bulbous eyes and goitres, cancers of the mouth, foot and groin. They sat on wheelchairs right in the middle of the road; looking deathly as men and women in uniforms solicited alms on their behalf. They amplified the shock value of their ailment by singing Christian tribulation hymns on a megaphone. Jimi heard 'By the waters of Babylon' and 'Don't forsake me O my saviour'. His aunt dropped a hundred naira note and lifted her hands in gratitude to God. A Hummer Jeep swept past them and Mrs Oyekan let out an involuntary sigh.

"You won't get to buy that as a teacher. What did you read at the university?"

"English and Philosophy."

"Philo- what!"

"Philosophy."

She looked at him and asked in a very solemn voice: "Are you a Christian?"

"No."

"Are you a Muslim?"

"No."

"What are you, then?"

"I am Jimi Aditu."

"You don't believe in God?"

"Not in that way."

"Your mum shouldn't have left you. Why would a God-fearing person read philosophy in school? You must move closer to God. It's not good to forsake the path of one's ancestors."

"Then I should take the worship of Eshu more seriously…"

"God forbid that in my car, in Jesus' name. Is it so bad you want to go to hell?"

"I'm sorry, I was thinking aloud."

"You will see my pastor," she erupted, "he will help you, he will pray for you, he will cleanse your mind, it is not too late, God has a plan for you, he will make a way for you, he never forsakes his own, your life will not remain the same, you will see the light, you can even go back to school…"

That got him: "To do what again?"

"Study. There is no end to learning."

"No… I don't want to do a masters, I'm comfortable with my first degree."

"Not masters, you will study Law. You read English, so law shouldn't be that difficult for you. Don't worry about the fees, God willing, I shall take care of it. We may have wronged you in the past, but we are not such beasts that I will sit here and allow you to destroy yourself."

But Jimi did not really think his lack of the Christian faith would destroy him. In fact, he thought otherwise, remembering his childhood as a kid in the Christ Apostolic Church. There were fiery pastors then. They foamed at the mouth. They monitored the latest methods of torture in hell and reported these at the Sunday school, especially whenever one failed to close one's eyes in prayer or the mind wandered off to more earthly things during the praise and worship session. They would say in Yoruba that Satan is rank, on the loose, prowling, sour: he suffers the pangs and poisons of the end of days like a snake cut by the tail. And Jimi started associating dead snakes with Satan. It was also about this time he encountered the dolorous English song, *My Darling Clementine*. This tune, whose existence he discovered in Orwell's *Animal Farm*, even to date never failed to evoke sorrow on the account of Boxer's death. The tune had fared well on Nigerian soil. The next time he heard a friend sing it, it was to pay homage to a slain Nigerian leader:

"In Nigeria, West Africa,
There was once a bloody coup
On the 13th of February
When they killed our head of state
Muritala, Muritala
Muritala Mohammed
You are gone and lost forever
We shall never forget you."

Then the tune changed again to accommodate an ace journalist bombed to pieces in his own home:

"In Nigeria, West Africa,
There was once a letter bomb
On the 19th of October
When they killed the journalist
Dele Giwa, Dele Giwa..."

His mind refused to forget the tune or the doleful instances attached to it. And as a kid, whenever he was sent by his dad to get a packet of candles or a quarter of oil at night, probably after watching some scary Yoruba movie, the song would come back to him. Not the melodious whole, but in fleeting snatches, or just a phrase of the song repeating itself over and over, like a scratched compact disc. He would picture Boxer as a huge black dead horse: half-buried, half-rotten, with a million flies circling it. Then he would begin to see forms in darkness; frenzied movements in open spaces. He would see spirits with claws and fangs; laughing at him, ready to tear him to pieces, running after him and screaming in a clear voice: "We will get you! We will get yyyyyooooooooouuuuu!"

In these visions there was also a motif of Christian torment. He feared hell and beautiful Lucifer. The morning star who was beloved of God; who could sing better than any angel, yet rebelled against God. Then he entered university and under the seduction of Socrates, Kant and deductive reasoning, he lost it. He turned agnostic. Hell was an example of the violence of the Judeo-Christian world order. It was inane, destructive. He scorned the cross, he became a poet. He lost his fear of dead snakes in obscure streets where electricity had been cut. But these hapless demons, decentred by logic, still flexed weak muscles now and then in his sleep, or in an image or two in his poems: formerly kings, now abject squatters in the tenement of his unconscious.

The traffic eased up again. They were behind the Hummer Jeep, which was painted yellow, with a customized plate that read: Zizzy 3. The number 3 meant the car was the third in the collection of expensive cars the owner had. Some had up to fifteen digits. Some people even bought four units of the same car and numbered them accordingly. Then, when going to parties, they would bring out a convoy of the same cars, in different colours, with sirens blasting... and even a god come to life couldn't be more glamorous.

Ahead, the danfo bus jostled for space with the Hummer Jeep. Jimi had to give it to the danfo driver. The Jeep might be worth thirty buses, but that did not deter the danfo guy. He moved from a tight lane to a freer one, keeping abreast of the Jeep. But just then, the traffic in their lane eased up and, spying the gap, the danfo driver accelerated. But the Hummer driver was expecting this; he made a hard lunge and the danfo driver was forced to swerve. Collusion of iron, dust and water defeated human control, and Jimi saw the danfo bus rub its metallic body hard against the bridge culvert and, finding a chink in the bridge railing, it lifted clear into the empty space. The lagoon reverberated with a thud.

Mrs Oyekan screamed through a mouthful of plantain chips; spattering both the dashboard and her dress with a yellow paste. His aunt kept muttering to herself, her hand clutching the steering wheel. He managed to piece together what she was saying; a biblical quotation: "I shall not die but live to proclaim the glory of God! I shall not die but live to proclaim the glory of God!" He spoke to her, but there was no answer. She kept chanting this over and over.

The traffic began to move again with the tireless efforts of the wardens.

"Aunty, it's okay," Jimi said. "May we never experience such mishap again. May the gods continue to watch our ways. May we not fall into the jaws of death and the belly of the lagoon."

She tried the ignition but the engine sputtered and died. She tried again and again. But it wouldn't start. The engine had overheated. She threw her hands up in despair. The time was 7pm. They got out of the vehicle. She opened up the bonnet and stared at the car's innards. Having no skill whatsoever in things mechanical, Jimi merely watched as she touched a knob here and twisted a fuse there. She went round and tried again. This time, there was not even a sputter.

They pushed the car to a reserve lane; noticing that more than six vehicles in their lane had developed similar problems. Somebody in a Mercedes Benz 'V boot' spotted his aunt. A colleague, he volunteered to take her to the mainland where a tow vehicle or mechanic might be found and suggested Jimi wait in the car. Or else there might be no car for them to tow or for the mechanic to repair when they came back. Her aunt picked up her bag. Their eyes met.

"Forget the car," she said, "let's go home." But Jimi declined and decided to brave the wait.

On the bridge, a man with dreadlocks came out of his car and slammed the door. His car, which was in the middle lane, would not start and he walked towards Jimi. A thickset man in a French suit, whose car had also broken down, joined them. The man in dreadlocks kept shaking his head and muttering the word modernity. Jimi asked him what he meant and the man declared to him:

"Today, I saw Ogun on the road."

Jimi wasn't sure which *Ogun* he was talking about – the god or the metal, and he said:

"Ogun is everywhere, were you not riding one?"

"I don't mean that crap," the man said, pointing to his vehicle. "I mean the great god. Ogun's face was huge and angry. Just right before the car skidded into the lagoon."

"Rasta man, you lie there."

"Who are you that I'd lie to you? I saw Ogun on this bridge today and he claimed his own, period. Modernity! Modernity! This madness of modernity is the cause of our troubles. When last did they sacrifice to Ogun on this road?"

"Well, Ogun or no, if the bridge had the proper bridge railing, the bus wouldn't skid off it," Jimi said, but without much conviction. The dreadlocked man gazed at the sky and replied: "May Ogun not bathe in our blood."

"Amen." Jimi said.

The man in a French suit shook his head, wiping his brow; his sweat mingled with the thinning gloss on Mrs Oyekan's Toyota Carina.

Jimi peered at the lagoon fishermen who had brought their greying canoes to the spot of the accident. About four of the passengers had been rescued from the bus. They were lying in the canoes and Jimi could not tell if they were dead or alive. The hold-up had become totally intractable, and hundreds of people were watching the unfortunate bus in the water. The LASTMA traffic wardens talked into their radios. When they saw they couldn't do much in the way of rescue, they harangued careless watchers.

A woman clutched the bridge railing with one arm and flailed the other unto God, with her wrapper falling off, screaming: "Ah, see people, see death! *Ikunle Abiyamo o!*"

A man was being led away by the traffic wardens but he resisted stoutly, shouting: "Why you dey hold me, my brother dey inside there, my brother dey there!" Without loosening their grip, they comforted him: "What has happened has happened. You have to be a man."

Jimi did not feel sorrow or pity for the victims. The only thing he felt, staring at the water and with a breeze hitting him, was exhilaration. His belief in the hereafter, though far from thorough, sustained him in moments like this. He believed that after the body dies, the soul treks on a lonely road filled with dishes of maggots and earthworms. And the soul, so revulsed, would ditch the flesh and cease its existence. Not as air or trees or grass or thought or shit, but lulled by the music of nothing. Afterwards the soul would reunite with the cycles of life and have its pick of many worlds, many universes. Only the most faithful or the most short-sighted chose to come back to earth. Then they were taken to *agbala*, the compound of the gods, to await their return. In this belief, he saw humility. There were no Elysian Fields or Heaven. But at least one went somewhere, one could start afresh. Eternal learning. Jimi felt free and different, and the wails and sighs no longer appeared to him as signs of sorrow but a call to adventure; an adventure where it didn't matter whether he had a mother or not.

The man in a French suit was still shaking his head and when he saw Jimi was paying attention to him, he said: "My friend, it is not Ogun."

"What do you know?" the dreadlocked man replied.

"It is not Ogun," the man repeated fiercely, "it is the lagoon, can't you see? Ogun has no hand in this. That same spot. An accident happened on that same spot five months ago; exactly where the vehicle went into the lagoon."

"Then isn't it quite obvious it's the damned bridge railing?" Jimi asked.

The man in a French suit shook his head again.

"There is a powerful queen inside, with a host of marine spirits," the man said, "and when they need blood they simply stretch their hands and pull. Tell me, what protection can you build against the queen of the coast?" And as if to answer his own question, the man clapped his hands on Jimi's back and laughed.

That was it then, Jimi thought. Felicity was all Lagos was about: an inexhaustible felicity pulsing at the dregs of every authentic Nigerian tragedy.

Jimi looked at him and said: "No, you tell me. How can I protect myself against your queen of the coast?"

But the man, just like the lagoon, was silent.

Jide Adebayo-Begun is a Nigerian who writes prose, poetry and drama. Born in 1983, he attended Obafemi Awolowo University, Ile-Ife, and has worked as a farmer's apprentice, a teacher and a copywriter. His short stories have appeared in *Internazionale*, *Kwani* and a few anthologies. He is currently working on a novel.

To See the Mountain

Ken Barris

THE LEADER OF OUR WRITING workshop is an affable, exacting man. His name is Antrobus. We have no hot water here, but he shaves every morning with what used to be called a safety razor. He sometimes appears for breakfast with cuts on his chin or throat, dangling scraps of tissue paper.

As I write this, he walks past my open door and peers in briefly, as if to check that I'm at work. I'm not certain if this is his motive – perhaps it is idle curiosity – but I follow his footsteps down the corridor as he seems to check on the other writers. He moves on, describing a circuit from his own bedroom up to the second floor where he marshals the kitchen staff and pores over accounts. About fifteen minutes later he comes down the stairs and the cycle begins again.

The rhythm of his movement is distracting. I lose interest in my work and listen to his pacing. I begin dreaming of boarding school, dribbling cold showers, echoing halls, the dank scraping of chairs, woodwork gleaming under dust, stentorian commands, brick-hard pillows, gold-lettered boards of honour, masters' robes cut from black umbrella, and the chill wind penetrating window frames that are too swollen to close properly. I am rescued by a rustling of banana leaves outside my room that sounds so much like rain.

My need to work is pressing but, to be honest, it is easier to lose myself in everything else. Someone outside our building is using a battery-powered screwdriver. It utters little moans of pleasure. Perhaps it is only a toucan, a hornbill. Someone turns a brass key in his bedroom lock, the heavy door thuds open.

There is a flourish of trumpets from the building site down the road. A bird chuckles, splattering palm wine from its voice.

At lunch Antrobus warns us: "Don't let me catch any one of you taking an afternoon nap." A few residents take him seriously enough to be disconcerted. They don't realize that he has a dry sense of humour, drier than old varnish.

* * *

Patience Dolo is badly named. She is the last to come, and walks into lunch with anger boiling off her almost visibly. She missed her flight at Nairobi and arrived a day late. I have no idea whose fault it is, but her rage is directed silently at Antrobus. She responds indifferently to his introductions, to the point of rudeness. She toys with her plate of coco yam and stewed goat, though the yam is excellent to my taste. She is a large woman, built on a trapezoidal frame. She sits down next to me and keeps bumping my elbow, even though she eats without vigour. I shift my chair an inch to the right – it is a heavy chair which scrapes loudly – and she turns and glares. For an appalling instant, I believe she might hit me.

I find it impossible to talk with her. She stares sulkily over the heads of the people opposite, and goes after lunch to the balcony, where she smokes two Camels in a row. Restraint settles on her then, if not exactly calmness. I cannot read her expression because she wears sunglasses that glint. Their shape appears to magnify the curve of her cheekbones, which is generous in any case, and a sullen cast settles over her mouth. I feel a bit safer when she takes on the rigour of a mask, but even her static presence is massive.

"That mountain," she says to me, stabbing at it with her Camel. "Do you ever see it properly?"

"I haven't been here much longer than you, but so far it's been misted up like this every day. I'm sure it will clear up sooner or later."

"I need to see it."

I imagine that her expression softens a little as she speaks, though I am unsure. Does she gaze at the mountain with longing, or is it in fact a darker shade of anger?

She is in a better mood at dinner. She arrives with a moth on her shoulder. It is large, over two inches at its widest, and keeps perfectly still.

"What on earth is that?" cries an American writer. Her alarm attracts attention. People cluster around Patience and the moth, creating a bedlam of delight about the tame beast.

"It is my daemon!" she roars, her rich voice cutting through all others. "It appears on my shoulder only when I am satisfied with life!"

For the record – as I speak to her, I furtively study the insect – it is a deathly cream, offset by striations of lime. The moth is so big that I can make out the fur on its head, its burred eyes. Patience wears it as a jewel. It is lit by her mantilla, her umber skin. As I study the creature, I catch the joke. Her moth is dead.

"Where did you find it?" I ask.

"I picked it up on the stairs, in that corner under the broken light."

"What possessed you to pick it up?"

A peal of laughter falls out of her: "It was very dusty, I had to hold its little body and blow it off! Then I put it on my shoulder to be my scarab, my own scarab moth."

"Your bon moth?" I suggest.

Another gust of laughter, and a clap on my shoulder that literally rocks me sideways. Our friendship is sealed.

* * *

I take a walk in late afternoon heat, trying to find my bearings, trying to find an engine for this project. There are plenty of examples of industry on the road that runs through Molyko. People sell things from under awnings, from tables, from the ground, from containers on their heads, from chairs under umbrellas. Yet they do not sell actively, they wait. Hoops of prestressed steel, charcoal, grilled pig's trotters, skin-lightening cream, airtime, ornamental masonry, used tyres, pedicures and manicures, foreign exchange, beer, palm oil, cellphones, Johnny Walker Black Label. I walk past a white plastic table crowded with white plastic feet cut off at the ankles. The shoes on them are for sale. A boy walks by, balancing a transparent container on his head. It holds roasted Congo meat, blackened salamanders twisted on skewers. Another boy passes the other way, balancing a tray of bananas on his head. It remains horizontal, though the bananas lie to the side of his tray. There is no lack of balance to be seen anywhere. An invisible gyroscope steers this market and all the people in it, allowing slack here, tightening things there, calibrating all action. Can I achieve such careless balance?

Not far from the building site adjacent to our dormitory, a gravel seller sits under his own awning. I know that he is a gravel seller because a cardboard placard on the ground advertises him as one. The awning is a makeshift roof of animal skins, strips of scrap metal and plastic sheeting stretched over four poles. It is weighted down by yams, cassava roots and gourds I cannot name. The gravel seller is a muscular young man with bare arms. He seems perfectly at rest in the heat, free of discomfort or anxiety.

There are four piles of rocks arranged before him. Two consist of volcanic rocks roughly the size of cricket balls, the other two are presumably the same material smashed into gravel. His heavy hammer rests where he dropped it. Now he sprawls on his chair, taking his ease. He grins at me. I struggle to believe the euphoria he projects, but he has produced his gravel. What have I done?

***

Breakfast this morning is punctuated by friction between Antrobus and Patience. He listens in bemused courtesy while she berates him, eyes and arms driving her agitation outward.

"The showers are slower than the internet!" she complains. "How can I shower in cold water? It hardly comes out, it is an unreasonable expectation! Do I have to suffer like this to be a writer? We suffer enough already, from the publishers, from each other. It is too much."

"I'm afraid there's not much I can do to improve the water supply, Patience. It's entirely out of my hands."

"This is a travesty," she mutters, spearing her avocado so hard that her fork squeals against the plate.

He raises an eyebrow, shrugs, and makes no comment.

Patience and I take our coffee to the upper balcony, and gaze at the mountain. Today the mist is thin enough to see it, but not clearly. It remains vague, bleached of colour and texture.

"I would like to walk up there," she remarks.

"I think you should ask Antrobus to organize an excursion."

"He will not listen to me. He will never listen to me. That man is obstructive, he doesn't like me. He doesn't like me at all."

"Then I suggest that you and I take a walk this afternoon, and see how far we get. I'm sure we won't reach it, but we might get a clearer view."

We set out later in the day, when it is slightly cooler. I have an ulterior motive, to escape my work. I'm finding it more and more oppressive. Call it *folie à deux*, but perhaps I will find the clarity I need if I can see the mountain. Our expectation is to clear the town and go as far into the country as we can, in search of a better vantage point.

Although it is after four, it is still terribly humid and hot, and it is difficult to build up momentum. There are long stretches of road bordered by an open concrete drain a metre deep and half as wide. There is no barrier to separate it from the road, no signage, no painted line to indicate its presence. In places the pavement is obstructed by stalls or heaps of wares, or milling pedestrians. In other places it simply vanishes. We then are forced to cross the drain and walk in the road. Though we face oncoming traffic, the driving style is bewildering and dangerous. People hoot constantly, trying to force other drivers out of the way. Cars swerve unpredictably, or overtake in the wrong place at the wrong time. Trucks and buses jink about like dodgem cars. In other stretches the drain is covered by concrete slabs, and this becomes the pavement where the real one is too crowded. The problem is that many of the concrete slabs are missing.

At last we clear the town and walk into the rural area. I have no words for the luminous greenery that surrounds us, no knowledge of the mass of fruits and pods and blooms, or the supple trees I've never seen before. I cannot describe the generosity of this forest. Still, we do not reach the vantage point we imagined. We turn back, too hot and thirsty to continue.

When we return, we learn that the water has dried up completely. Patience throws another tantrum.

Dusk in Buea speaks in tongues. Crouching in the plantation across the road is an unfinished church. It is built of naked concrete blocks, with a fine green roof of metal sheeting. The walls are pockmarked in places, as if they have been raked by heavy machine-gun fire, but there has been no war here. It is vast in comparison with the humble dwellings nearby. The arched windows are without glass, but protected by stout steel grids. It seems that theft is a more direct concern than the weather. This is an ark resting on the ground, waiting for the flood, incomplete but serviceable. A tireless choir sings inside it, sweet patience itself. They know their time will come when the Lord shall hear their cries and return. In the background, crickets pulse and release, swelling with song and spawning it. Then, as it grows darker, a new layer of music can be heard. I see only fragments of the players amongst the plantain fronds. They tap hesitantly on percussion instruments, then quickly pick it up: a small marimba, cowhide drum, other tones of hollow wood and bamboo. Each note is liquid, but the combination becomes tedious, as if they have a lovely voice and nothing new to say. And then a steel band starts up, probably from a bar further down the road. It continues for a long time, breaking at last into an aggressive, shapeless drum solo.

We sit on the first-floor balcony drinking warm beer, speculating. What is this choral music? What is this church? We guess that they're Catholic because of their discipline, because the music speaks of hierarchy and promises heaven. But things are harder to explain than that. Twin bonfires burn in the plantation between the road and the hulking church. Smoke pours up, sheaves of fire lick upwards and vanish. Who lit these fires, who tends them? Dim figures are seen momentarily, then they are masked by smoke, flitting in and out of sight. To me they enact a pantomime of hell. I do not understand the relief it brings me.

✳✳✳

Every evening, three of us read from our work in progress. As Patience takes her turn, my discomfort grows. The narrative she unreels might be naive, but it is not exactly original.

"I am woken up in the night by a still and commanding voice," she intones.

The way she reads it aloud, I suspect that she has capitalized "voice".

"I am called upon by this mysterious Voice to leave my sleeping place and go up, and there is no resisting its command. I stumble up in the darkness, fearful and awake. I do not stop to question myself where I am going, or how I know the way. A mysterious hand guides me, though the night is turbulent. At last, with my feet painful and bleeding, I reach the top of the mountain."

I look around the table at the faces of other writers. Some are amused, others are openly astonished. A young writer named Siviwe Mathe looks at her with an incredulity so naked it verges on hostility. Antrobus's face is intent, but without expression, as he gazes down at the table.

"My eyes are opened, and I understand that it is the Lord who has called me here," continues Patience. "I do not see his face for I would die, but an angel appears to me bearing tablets of stone. I am faint, and fall to my knees and weep. I cry out: 'Why do you thrust this burden upon me, O Lord, who am unworthy?' But the angel makes no reply, and inscribes a mighty lettering on the stone tablets with his quill of lightning. And when he has completed his writing, he speaks to me and says, 'The Lord commands you to take this down to your people and to teach them my Law, and to be my spokesperson'."

"This is as far as I've got," she says, and lays down her manuscript. "I haven't been able to do much. Not only because of the power cuts."

Dare I say that a silence moves upon the waters?

Antrobus is the first to break it: "My dear Patience, you have to be very careful if you choose to tread such an immensely well-worn path. If I were to ask you how that differs from the rather obvious original, what would you say?"

"I would say," she replies, "that my character is going to be a female prophet. That is a big difference."

"If you want to write this blatant didactic material," interjects Siviwe, "don't call yourself a writer. Call yourself a teacher, or a preacher, or something like that. But what you are doing is not fiction, it is evangelism."

The lightning on her page now leaps from her eyes, her voice: "Do not impose your patriarchy on me. You are perpetuating what I write against. In the Bible it is only men who are prophets, but women with the same gift are witches. They are stoned and murdered! They are *murdered* as witches! But as you know – as you know, Siviwe! – in our culture there are female prophets who are *revered*. Do you see what I am doing? Open your eyes, young man, and see the space where I work. It is not what you think!"

"Quill of lightning!" retorts Siviwe. "Takes phallocentrism to a new level, for God's sake."

✳✳✳

In the morning, Patience is more than subdued. It seems that her anger has given way to depression. I ask her if she'd like to make a second attempt on the mountain.

"No, I don't think so. I need to work on my story, and it's going to be too hot anyway."

"That shouldn't make any difference. It's going to be too hot whenever we go. And we might actually see the damn thing this time."

"Not likely, I don't believe it."

"Think how you'll be transfigured if we manage it."

She shakes her head, but almost smiles as she does so.

Later in the morning, she knocks on my door. "Do you still want to go up there?" she asks. "I need to get out of this place."

Our conversation is disrupted as we thread our way up the main township road, because it is impossible to walk abreast for any length of time, and the constant hooting is maddening. She says little about the evening before, but I sense from her scraps of conversation how wounded she feels.

Despite the heat and the challenge of surviving this traffic, we do seem to reach the edge of town more quickly. We've taken bottles of water this time, which makes a great difference. Walking itself and the beauty of the forest help Patience to settle down. For a while there is only walking, and a comfortable silence develops. By the time we reach our previous turning point, we have the legs to continue.

As the road climbs, I begin to question why exactly we're on this pilgrimage to see the mountain. We can see it from the balcony after all, though dimly, as the idea or image of a mountain rather than the monstrous thing itself. To add to the absurdity, we'd probably have to walk for three days before it made any difference. Besides, I ponder, can one ever really see the thing itself?

We climb a curving sweep of road shaded by the most elegant trees. As we walk, I begin to construct my own version of the mountain. I lay down its strata and chisel its irregularity, I soften it with forest and populate it with grazing herds of mountain goat, with porcupine and leopard. I work on its lizards and grasses, and grant it a stream or two. There is no particular order or pace in my creation of the world. I am not a laborious god.

Content with my work, I need to see no other mountain. But we walk on anyway, towards the one that calls for Patience.

Ken Barris is a writer, poet and critic. He has won the Ad. Donker-AA Life Prize, the Ingrid Jonker Prize, the M-Net Book Prize and the Thomas Pringle Award in South Africa. He has twice been shortlisted for the Caine Prize for African Writing, and his third novel, *What Kind of Child*, was nominated for the Commonwealth Prize.

Child of a Hyena

Shadreck Chikoti

MATHILDA SITS ON THE CHAIR opposite mine, her long legs stretched in front of her, occasionally lifting them up and suspending them in the air for a while before bringing them down again. Her arms are folded across her torso. She is looking down and her long blond hair flows down on all sides, shielding her oval face. The Metro train hisses forward. I turn to the window and try to peer outside. It is dark. I pull my eyes away from the window and look at Mathilda. She has raised her head and is looking at me. Her arms are stretched downwards now. Her hands rest on the edges of her seat. Mathilda's face! It looks awfully pale, and her hazel eyes have changed colour.

"You said you would tell me when we got home," she says.

I look at her with a blank face. I heard her all right but words fail me.

"Phereni," she calls. I open my eyes wide and lean my head forward to indicate I am listening.

"You said you would tell me at home," she insists.

"Yes," I tell her. Immediately my heart is filled with a lot of sorrow for dragging this woman into this web of confusion.

"Tell me now," she commands me. Her voice carries with it the sound of dried *msekesa* leaves.

"I will tell you when we get home, OK," I snap, and feel hollow inside.

"There's no need for you to get angry with me. I should be the one getting angry with you," Mathilda barks. But I am not angry with her. I am angry with myself and my people back home. In fact, if I pull up my courage to tell her the whole story, she should be angry, because now I have decided that Denmark is my home, not Malawi. I have decided that I will confess to her the actual reason why I did not want to have kids. It wasn't about the family planning I talked about, I had fear; fear that I would be stuck in this strange land, with its skyscrapers, its rivers, its strange life. But now, where else can I go?

"How long did we plan our trip to Africa?" Mathilda asks for the millionth time. I sense the anger in her voice. I do not answer, for I know that any answer to this question will cause her anger to erupt, so I remain quiet, although I know that we had been planning our trip to Africa for a year.

"How long did we say we would stay in Africa?" she asks, without waiting to hear my answer.

"We have been saving money all this time," she begins to say after realizing I will not say a word. "We said we would visit places in Africa: parks, the lake, and spend time with people in your village. Why did we leave in such a manner? I can't believe this is happening." Mathilda loses her temper. Her pale face turns red. She begins to shake.

I move over to sit down beside her, take her hand into mine. But she pulls her hand back with all her energy. I lose my balance and tilt to the other end of the chair. My shoulder rests on a metal bar at the edge of the chair.

"*Du er meget dum!*" she says in Danish.

She attracts a lot of attention and everyone in the carriage looks at me as if I have soiled my pants.

"Amabro!" the metallic voice announces the next stop...

Above, on top of the underground tunnel, the Metro train station, the darkness of night has descended on the region. It's not raining, but the effects of an earlier spat of rain are still visible. The road glistens with the reflection of the street lights. The fragrance of earth when it is mixed with rain water fills the air, and I can hear all manner of night creatures creaking and cooing in the distance. Between us, no other words have been exchanged. She walks briskly ahead of me. Mathilda.

* * *

Our apartment, in Frankrisgade, is on the upper floor. When we get there, Mathilda goes straight to our bedroom. She locks herself in. I go downstairs and wait for her on the living room couch. She does not show up.

"So how many people knew? How many people knew?" I ask myself. I put my head in my hands and begin to sob. I see myself back home, in Katonda…

I am coming from Saidi's hut at the end of the village. I am passing by the baobab tree where the young men of the village have congregated to play *bawo*. As I pass by, they turn to look at me in unison.

"They have known this for a while," I convince myself. I look away and increase my pace.

"Phereni," somebody calls from behind me. I turn around to see who it is. It is Teleza, the chief's daughter, the girl I played hide and seek together with way back. I stop to wait for her.

"So has he told you?" she asks me when she catches up.

"Who and what?"

"Saidi?"

I do not know what to say so I remain quiet.

"There was a fight three days ago, before you came. Your father and Saidi. He went around the whole village preaching, Saidi. Mmmh, that drunkard! That angered your father and they fought. I think he is just jealous of your success, of the fact that your father is the only well-to-do man in this village. Don't listen to him."

I walk on, leaving Teleza rooted to the ground. I do not look back.

"How many people knew, how many people knew?"

I quickly erase the memories from my village. I want to forget everything. I don't even want to be remembered in the minds of those people.

"They knew? All this time?" I am still speaking to myself.

I rise up from the couch and walk to the kitchen where I get three cans out of the food cabinet. I find a plate and empty the contents from the cans. One can has rice, already cooked, while the other two have peas and beef respectively. I warm the food in the microwave and walk back to the living room, back to the couch. My body feels weightless as I walk.

I sit down and begin to nibble at the food. In my mind I am trying to knit some pieces of this puzzle together. I realize now that there have been codes in my life, codes that I would have encoded had I wanted; had I paid attention to the unfolding of my life.

I remember now that I have known Saidi since I was a baby. I knew him as a village drunkard and a polygamist who was always battering his wives. I had no interest in knowing him beyond that, for there was nothing interesting about his life. On several occasions I had spotted him talking to Father, but it had never occurred to me that he was anywhere close to being a relation of mine. I recall that most of the times I saw Saidi talking to Father was during village assemblies; like weddings and funerals.

Saidi never visited Father at home, not at all, except, I think, for a single day. At least that's what I recall.

On that occasion, Saidi was just passing by from wherever he had gone to drink his beer. We had just eaten our supper and I had locked myself up in my room trying to study my Standard Seven notes under the kerosene lamp. Then, I heard Saidi singing in the distance. His singing was so awful and distressing that I had to stop reading and wait for him to pass by. The singing drew nearer. The songs he was singing were obscene and disturbing to anybody's ears. The drunkard was singing about how good it is to make love to somebody's wife. Then he switched to a song about how women despise a man with a small cock, and how a man with money can marry as many wives as he pleases. Then Saidi stopped right in front of father's house.

"Bwande! Bwande!" Saidi called Father.

I heard the unbolting of the door to Father's house. Father was going out of the house to speak with the drunkard.

"Where is my son?" Saidi asked. He was speaking loudly.

At that time, it did not even occur to me that I was the one he was asking about.

"Who is your son?" Father asked.

"I am asking about Phereni. I have bought some pig meat for him," he spoke drunkenly.

Although I heard that, I did not even give myself any liberty to explore his words further.

"Go away Saidi. Is that what you called me for?" Father shouted.

I heard some shuffling of feet and some hissing. The two men were engaged in some sort of silent tug with each other.

"Greet your wife and my son," the village drunkard, Saidi, said while walking away. His voice was fading away now into a song about some houseboy admiring the thighs of his boss's wife.

At the time, it had meant nothing. But now, I realize that what Saidi had done on that day had carried a lot of meaning about my existence....

I put the plate of food on the floor. I drag my body and lean on one side of the couch while I stretch my legs across until they are touching the other end. I close my eyes and I see Saidi in his blue, tattered coveralls. He is sitting on a small chair inside his house. I am sitting on a similar chair opposite him. We are in his hut and it is dark. I can only see his face in part.

"So, Bwande has never told you that I am actually your father. That he just raised you?"

His words cut like a razor blade. I feel a headache coming on. Saidi's picture vanishes from my head. With my eyes still closed, I let my body float. I drift away into nothingness. Sleep comes like a soft wind, blowing me off my conscience, softly.

* * *

"Phereni," I hear my wife calling in the distance.

"Phereni," she gets nearer.

I fumble through the darkness, and struggle to consciousness. I notice that the light of day has crept into the apartment and that the sun has spread its golden beams on everything around the house. My wife is standing in front of me. I reposition myself.

"Why are you treating me like this?" my wife asks me. Something happens inside me and I begin to cry bitterly. Tears run down my face. My wife looks at me with awe registered in her eyes.

Why are you treating me like this? The question reverberates in my mind. I should not be treating her like this. She is the best gift God ever gave me. She could have married some rich boy from Denmark had she wanted. What would have stopped her? She has the beauty and money. What else could have brought her to me except love?

Why are you treating me like this? Something weighs me down and I increase my crying. Back home, women would have easily undressed for me because I was a rich young African working as a doctor abroad. But Mathilda, she truly loves me and why am I treating her like this?

Saidi's face comes to my mind and at once episodes of his life flash through my mind. I see his tattered clothes, his stench, the numerous times he has been summoned to answer charges at the chief's court. I see him walking about the village drunk, obscene songs carried proudly on his back.

Mathilda comes to sit with me on the couch.

"Tell me now, dear, I am so sorry. I love you," she says. She puts her arms around me. She holds me tightly and leans her head against mine.

"Mathilda, you can't understand," I manage to say.

"I will try to understand, dear," she assures me.

"Mr Bwande is not my father, Mathilda." The words come out of my mouth unguarded. I find myself back in the village...

***

I am sitting on an armchair with Father under the Kachere tree in front of his house. Mother and Mathilda are on the *Khonde*. Mother is trying to cook something. She is squatting and trying to fan some fire. Mathilda is watching her closely. Mother tries so hard to keep the fire stable but the wind keeps blowing it off. Finally Mother manages to keep the fire going. Father and I have been looking at her for some time. Then I gather up my courage and ask Father: "Is it true what Saidi was telling me today? That he is my father and not you?"

Father loses his balance and almost falls. He appears transfixed on his chair.

"Who told you?" he is able to ask me that question.

"Saidi."

"It is a long story. We need some time, Phereni."

"But why did you sink so low? So I am a child of a hyena?"

"Phereni, you can't understand... It was long ago. And why was this fool telling you that?"

I do not answer Father. I do not tell him that Saidi had told me that he was angry that Father had stopped assisting him, that Father was the one enjoying his sweat. I rise up from the chair, storm to the Khonde and pull Mathilda by the hand. I am literally dragging her to our house at the end of the village. Mathilda and I built this house so that we could have a place to stay each time we visited the village.

"What's wrong, what's wrong?" Mathilda protests.

"I will explain, Mathilda. It's no longer safe here," I say to her.

"What do you mean, it's no longer safe? What wrong have I done?"

"Please Mathilda, I will explain to you when we get home. When we get to Copenhagen."

"What?"

I am pulling her hand and she is almost running.

"I am confused, Mathilda." I tell her. "We need to pack up now."

***

"Phereni, come with me upstairs. You need to shower. We will discuss this. It's a difficult issue indeed," my wife tells me.

After bathing, I go to our room. There is no change in the bedroom; it looks just as we left it. There is no indication that Mathilda has slept in the bed. All that time my wife was in the bedroom, she was seated on the couch, and maybe she was crying.

I change my clothes. I walk to the window and open it. A chilly breeze forces its way past me. I immediately close the window.

I look down on the street and see some cars that have stopped, waiting for the traffic lights to turn green. I wonder in my heart if my life has halted also. My eyes lose focus on the present and transport me to some world beyond. I do not see the buildings in front of me, or the traffic lights, or the cars, or the tarmac roads, or the women pushing their babies in their prams, or the people that are walking with their dogs. I see a light that is very bright. I can't feel my legs and hands any more. The next thing I know, I am lying in Mathilda's arms.

"Come with me," she is dragging me. She sits beside me on our bed. She begins by apologizing to me, by telling me that she is sorry for behaving in a negative way and that she should have understood that I was going through something big that caused me to behave the way I did.

"I should have realized that there was something big troubling you. I am sorry."

She leans on me.

"Do you think you will be able to tell me all about it now?"

It is difficult to explain to Mathilda about my ordeal but I try. I tell her that the person I had known as father all my life – 32 years – was not my father at all.

"Does this mean you were adopted?" she asks.

"No. My father... fuck!" I put my head in my hands. "That stupid man I have called Father is sterile," I tell Mathilda. I wonder if I am making sense to her and if I should make sense at all.

I explain to Mathilda about the hyena custom. That whenever a man marries, the people from his wife's home provide him with an animal, a chicken, a goat or a piglet. The aim is that the man should be able to conceive before the animal does. The man is also told that he should not wait for more than two years before fathering a child.

"It is an honourable thing to have a child back home," I tell Mathilda, who is listening attentively. I explain to her that any family that does not have children is not respected at all. The man and the woman are not accepted in the circle of the married for they are considered young and ignorant of the ways of life. During functions like funerals, weddings and village gatherings, those that do not have children are the ones who do all the chores, like cooking, splitting firewood, drawing water. Anybody who has a child, whether they are younger than them or not, is at liberty to send the childless on errands. It is a shameful thing for a person, especially a man, to be childless when they are married.

I explain to Mathilda that in our culture, it is acceptable for a man to hire someone to sleep with his wife so that they can conceive. This tradition is called *fisi*. The *fisi* or hyena comes at night and sleeps with your wife. The arrangement is so secret that it is confined to the hyena and the childless couple.

"I am a child of a hyena, Mathilda. Saidi is my father."

I weep bitterly now.

"You mean your father hired Saidi for you to be born?" Mathilda asks. Her question throws me into her lap. She places her hands on me and pulls me to herself.

"Why didn't your father tell you all this time?" Mathilda asks.

"He was not supposed to tell me. I was not supposed to know at all. It is Saidi who told me."

"And your father? Did he confirm it?"

"Yes," I tell her.

I am drunk. I am dizzy. My wife is talking.

"You know, Phereni, I think we need to give ourselves time to think about this. I am sure we will find a way. You have me and I have you, that's what matters."

My wife shuffles and I know she wants to stand up.

"Can we go for a walk around town? I don't want you to think of this now," she asks me.

I nod my head in agreement.

But as we walk around town, I do not see the shops along Amabrogade. I do not see the people that have crowded the town. I do not see the rivers that we cross and the ships on the waters of Copenhagen. I only see the faces of Bwande, my mother and Saidi.

I see myself as a young man going to primary school. I remember how Father was fond of me. He loved me too much, I would say. I was the only child in the whole village that lacked nothing, as far as education was concerned. I had enough pairs of school uniforms. I was given pocket money right from the secondary school. I was the only child from Katonda who put on shoes and who went to school on a bicycle. He loved me so much, Mr Bwande.

"Phereni." My wife startles me out of my daydreams.

"Yes."

"You are thinking too much."

We discuss the weather: how cold it is and how we both dislike winter. We talk about recent movies: *The Book of Eli,*

Tangled, *Avatar*, *Salt* and others. We talk about Christiania and about the people who live there, how they are so free and so confused at the same time.

Shadreck Chikoti is a Malawian writer. He is the author of nine published books. His short story, 'The Trap', won Malawi's 2001 Pygnt Literary Award. Chikoti has just finished writing a futuristic novel about Africa 500 years from now. He lives in Malawi with his wife, Yamikani, his daughter Shamiso and his son Thabo.

No Blood, No Slaves

Dona Forbin

"BINTA! BINTA!" THE YOUNGER Queen Mother calls impatiently. "What is it? I have never had to remind you about your duties before... bring me my clothes."

"My Queen, forgive me." Binta walks to her side, carrying three different outfits, and presents them for royal inspection. This morning, Binta's age sits like a bag of wet clay on her back. There are terrible rumours. The Sultan is dying. Binta has not slept well at all. She waits for the Queen Mother to make up her mind about what she wishes to wear. She tries to be patient and fold away the fear and worry snaking up from her belly to her throat.

"Binta," the Queen Mother turns her superior gaze to her trusted servant. "You have been in the palace for a long time now... what troubles you?"

It is rare for her to pay attention to the servant's health in general but she has known Binta for a little over forty years and they are tied by cords of shared intimacies. Binta was one of the many wedding presents from her late father, a much feared and distinguished hunter from a neighbouring village. She was a thin, tall girl with frightened eyes when she arrived. Today, though Binta struggles for composure, tears fill her brown, gentle eyes and they carry an echo of that almost forgotten haunted look as she attends to her royal charge.

"I know you well enough to know when you are troubled," the Queen Mother continues softly, as she pulls out the dark blue *boubou* and stands from her dressing stool.

Binta is tall but the Queen Mother is a good head taller. She carries herself with the easy grace of a woman well satisfied with life, whose every wish was granted but appreciated that the gods had favoured her. The only misfortune that had ever cast a shadow on her dreamy, deep-set eyes was the death of one of her five infant sons. Her plump dimpled cheeks gave the impression she was always gently smiling as she spoke. Though childbearing and age had matured her figure, it was still easy to see why the Sultan had not hesitated to pick her as his second consort when the first had borne him three daughters. The gods had favoured her. It was custom to prepare the first son of the Sultan to be heir to the throne, though the gods could decide otherwise.

The Queen Mother pulls the heavy *boubou* over her head and ample bosom and wiggles her graceful hips a little as she smooths the dress into shape. She picks up the pieces of gold jewellery that Binta has laid out and fastens them on, one after the other, setting off her dark skin. When she is finished, she studies her reflection.

Carefully Binta paints her mistress's face with black and gold brown. It is a time to be solemn and the Queen Mother has made the appropriate choice in her clothing.

"You know Prince Babali, my heart, arrives soon," she speaks aloud as she adjusts her tiny hand-woven bangles and continues as if she is not aware of the reason for Binta's silence.

"I have to be ready to talk with him before the council whisks him off. Bring me my blue leather slippers."

"Yes, *Mafua*, mother of handsome princes."

The Queen Mother arches her right eyebrow. This type of formal address is one Binta hardly uses in private. She is obviously not in the mood for talk. What is there to talk about? In forty years they have never had any occasion to think of such things. In the last few days, a buzz of speculation has enveloped the slave quarters as they have all pondered who will be chosen to follow the Sultan to the Land of Great

Happiness. There is little the Queen Mother can do but hope this time will be Binta's own time. What slave would not want their name to be remembered and earn the favour of the gods?

✻✻✻

A sonorous call to prayer interrupts the unhurried cool of the morning. In the spacious chamber his own father had once occupied, Sultan Babamou receives a visit from Abu.

The Sultan is old. He shifts his tall, once-handsome body slowly. It is wrung out like freshly tie-dyed cloth and clad in a very soft, white, ample robe. He lies serenely, propped up on a bed befitting his rank. The scents of the 'queen of the night' tree cling to the air. It is cloying and strong but cannot chase the approaching scent of death away.

Several leopard and panther skins cover the floor. Most of his father's personal belongings have been stored away a long time ago but four blank statues stand on either side of the room. They are two heavy, ancient, bronze lions and elephant tusks engraved with small pictograms. They represent the power and wealth of generations of the thousand-year-old Bamouni Dynasty.

Heavy hand-woven blue-and-cream drapes cordon off a part of the room. A small shrine in honour of his forefathers stands behind them. It is neglected. The Sultan is prepared to quarrel with his forefathers about this.

"Abu, I am ready to go... The sun sets for me here, it will rise for the next Sultan. May he live long!" the Sultan says, in a clear, desert whisper of voice as soon as the medicine man announces the reason for his artless arrival.

The strength in the Sultan's diminishing body has moved to his grey pupils and they glitter with the sharp intellect and wisdom of a strong spirit.

"Abu, I refuse to travel like my fathers." He watches the royal medicine man closely. Abu's blotchy pink and grey eyes open wider, slowly. They flash in understanding, then, just as quickly, contempt. The dark skin on his high, wide brow folds, two distinct earth-worms forming. This stretches the rest of the ceremonial chalked symbols on his gaunt face and deep tribal scars. His face is an unusual mask.

"Time has come," the Sultan continues unwearyingly. He ignores this bastion of traditions. "Abu, listen, from now there will be no blood, no slaves."

Abu's thin frame trembles on the traditional stool. He closes his eyes and repeatedly pulls his long grey beard. Of its own will, the divination staff in his left hand rattles twice as he strives for composure.

"Great Sultan." Slowly, Abu's tongue unfurls, his strong lyrical tenor contains his inner agitation. "This time, you ask too much." He rises, leaning heavily on his staff, then paces the room slowly.

"I have delivered my message and I am going." He appears to study the leopard-skin spots intensely before he walks out as he had come. Silently.

∗ ∗ ∗

"Favoured among others, favoured, Binta is favoured," the three younger women sing as they work. "There are many... but she is favoured..." It is a wild medley of high-pitched ululations and excitement.

"Favoured... Favoured," Binta sings softly along with them. She is still and sits on a colourful mat. They are gathered under a big shade tree. It showers orange and yellow blossoms as the late afternoon breeze teases it. The intricate lines of her light brown scalp shine into view as her hair style approaches completion. Her feet and hands are stretched out in front of her. A fertile forest of dark henna patterns has appeared all over them. Slowly their song changes to a mournful farewell chant.

"Abi, love or duty requires sacrifices. Please don't be sad." Binta offers gentle consolation to the youngest girl. She does not want to move since the henna powder is not quite dry. "You too are favoured, Abi, but this time is my own."

"But see how long you waited, Ba," Abi says. "Some of us might never have such honour, such favour, to follow the Sun of Bamouni into the land of Great Happiness." Her sigh is loud. "Our names would just disappear into sand."

"No two people travel the same road, Abi," Binta says slowly and flashes of her most treasured memories surface and occupy her inmost self.

* * *

"Better my unripe mangoes, than your foolish flat chest!" Binta's happy giggle chases after her sister. "When I put this pot of water down," she continues in her singsong voice, wagging her right index finger vigorously, "you will see." They race back home through the tall grass up the hill.

"Mma," she calls out as soon as she arrives, "warn your silly daughter." She lets Mma help her put the pot down on the cool earth. It is a clear crisp day. She wants to hurry with her chores and then head off to play with her mates. Mma looks sad. She sniffs and has been crying.

"Binta, my child." She reaches out and pulls her daughter close to her bosom. "Forgive me. There are some men coming here soon." She sobs, then quickly wipes the tears from her face with her calloused left hand.

"When they come you will go with them. Take this packet." A few almost round red palm fruits peep out of soft, pale green cocoyam leaves. "You will give it to someone waiting for you far away."

"Don't be sad, I will come back soon, Mma," Binta promises solemnly, willing to do anything to stop Mma's tears from falling. It is the last day she ever sees her family.

* * *

"What makes a slave different from another person?" the Sultan asks thoughtfully one night as he lies down next to Binta. His flushed cheek is resting on his wrist and he looks down at her languidly. The moon is full. Its silver light shines through the wide open window onto Binta's firm naked skin. She shivers a little. Her slender frame is covered with their sweat.

"He eats, sleeps and blood too runs through his veins." He tugs gently at her puckered, dark brown nipples with his other hand. It is not customary to invite any slave into his sleeping quarters more than once. The Sultan has lost count of the number of full-moon nights he has insisted she spend in his bed.

"I am thinking, we do not need to send them to early death for our forefathers' pleasure, but Abu would not hear of this." He stretches and takes a few sips from his half-empty bowl of drink.

"Sweetness, speak." He strokes his hand down to her damp thighs softly. "You know you fire my heart. Do I lie? Are not your own kind just unfortunate?"

"My master." She speaks quietly but clearly averting her eyes from his direct gaze. "To win the favour of the gods, is it not our greatest honour?"

"Honour?" The Sultan's laughter rumbles, startling the guards that stand just outside the door.

"Yes. All my life is a preparation." Her eyes flash fiercely. "If I don't follow you to the place of Great Happiness, my life is just meaningless." He is drunk on moonlight and her youth, Binta thinks. Most times when he has talked madness, she has listened carefully with eyes wide open. Tonight, she is not ready to encourage his quarrel with his forefathers.

"Sweetness," his soothing voice cajoles, "I do not mean to upset you." He pulls a cloth over her body. "What will happen if you follow me long after you have seen many more sunrises and the gods call you as they call me?"

"My life will not have been truly favoured."

"To me it is sweetness," he stretches, then smiles indulgently, "and I am the rising sun of the Bamouni Dynasty. I am angry at the thought of anyone bruising and burying your delicate skin in the sand then leaving you parched, starving and exhausted just because you are marked for favour." The Sultan shakes his head.

"No, it must not be for me. I will be patient on the journey to Great Happiness and wait for the gods to send you to me later."

✻✻✻

"Is it true that the thing you carry in your womb bears royal blood?" Abu hisses at the slave girl.

"Yes." Binta nods, her voice trembling. It has already been four moons since she had not declared her uncleanness and she had stopped eating the morning meal. Abu, who checks on the state of the palace slaves' health, had noticed.

"Which of the princes favours you?" Sexual trysts between the princes and slaves were not uncommon at all.

"None of them."

"None?" Abu was surprised. Most of the favoured slave women had nothing to do with other slave men.

"It is the Sultan."

"Do the Queen Mothers know?" he asks, nodding his head in admiration. So the rumours he had heard about her were true.

"No, they do not."

"Good, they must never know." Abu turns and picks up a calabash with a dark viscous potion.

"Drink it," he says as he hands it to her. "Lie down on the mat over there." He points to a corner of his shed.

He mutters to himself, collects sharp instruments and prepares to preserve the blood lines of the illustrious dynasty.

✻✻✻

It is well past midnight. Abu binds one of the father's old knobby hands above the young vigorous son's as custom dictates in twined leaves, earth and animal blood. He murmurs incantations. The father, who had seemed to be asleep, opens his eyes and looks at his son directly, with a faint smile.

"Thank you Abu." Then he turns to his son. "My son, Babali, follow the voice of Spirit, so hard decisions are easy. You are a great ruler." Babali feels a strong current begin to flow from the aging hand bound to his and he trembles in shock. His gaze is frozen on the older Sultan's eyes.

"Take my strength as I took my father's. They are here." His father's voice falters. "Yes, I see them, they approve." His breathing grows more laboured and the lustrous shine in his eyes dims softly. "You know my wishes."

His son nods quietly. Bonds between them stretch and break. Abu looks away. The air is charged with the mysteries of their forefathers as the dark, tall shadow of the spirit of death carries the old great sun of Bamouni, Sultan Babamou, away.

Abu rubs the body with an array of strong, musky, scented potions. He works capably, murmuring more incantations to himself.

"Abu," the Prince says tiredly, "you know my father refuses to have slaves accompany him on the journey to Great Happiness."

"Nonsense." Abu retorts sharply as he traces symbolic figures on the body with a dark dye stick.

"I promised I would respect his wishes."

"Nonsense," Abu repeats calmly. He had expected something like this to happen and is prepared. "You vowed last night in my presence to continue in the customs of our people." He talks slowly. "Is this how? He buried his own father the proper way. Do you think I would let you disrespect him now?"

"But they are his last wishes…"

"Let me help you," Abu knows the young man is disoriented from lack of sleep and emotion. Abu reassures him yet asserts his authority.

"Get some rest. Long before the rest of the Kingdom learns that their Sultan has travelled, they must meet the new Sultan."

***

"Everything is well arranged, favoured Binta," Abu tells her at dawn. Everything is going according to plan. He admires her. Binta's boubou is coarse and stands stiffly from her body. It is loaded with many natural crystal beads and she moves slowly, with effort.

"The others are already in their positions at the sacred grounds waiting for you," he nods his head. "Binta, it is your time. Your name will be remembered by the Bamouni people for always."

"I thank you, Abu, you are kind." Proudly she carries the lavish gold combs in her freshly arranged hair. Nothing can stop her from fulfilling her destiny. She among many is favoured by the gods. She had heard some terrible thoughts from the Sultan's mouth. He wished to forbid her from accompanying him on his journey to Great Happiness. She shudders at the thought. It was a good thing Abu was sound enough to see through the voice of madness that had made such utterances. She would win the ultimate favour of the gods. She rides on a heavily decorated white horse behind the chief palace guard.

In the sacred grounds four of the five young men are buried standing in holes around the Sultan's grave. The cool sandy soil covers them up to their chins. Their eyes are blindfolded. Much later, Abu would uncover their eyes but leave their mouths gagged. All but the last young man and favoured Binta were buried before the Sultan's body.

In the middle, a hole that would receive the Sultan's body is lined with choice fabric and animal skins. He alone will be laid lying down. In yet another, smaller, hole some other things of value he loved are placed.

Binta is lowered to the place allotted for her gently. Abu gives her something bitter to drink.

"It will give you strength for the journey," he promises, then motions to guards to fill up the hole with earth. Once they are done, he smiles into her eyes before he blindfolds her.

"You will be reunited with your sons."

The royal retinue arrives on horseback as their forefathers had before; the Sultan's body is lowered nobly in full view of the adult male members of his household. Abu performs his duties keenly, proudly.

He glances disdainfully at the new Sultan from time to time during the proceedings. Tears are streaming down the young Sultan's face. Thunder rumbles from far away. Clouds gather above the sacred place. The sky darkens and it begins to drizzle. It is unusual; this time of the year is the heart of the dry season.

At the climax of proceedings, Abu flashes his ceremonial knife and spills human blood on the soil of his ancestors. He chants unintelligibly as the last slave is buried with his slit wrists draining his life into the soil. It is all over. Abu heaves a sigh and relaxes as the new Sultan of Bamouni turns to go. No one has stood in his way. He is triumphant as he uncovers the slaves' eyes and then softly chants a farewell song.

***

"Speak Abu. Why do we gather?"

In the palace, the young Sultan, in full traditional garb, taps his left foot repeatedly. He is versed in his court's ancient etiquette. It is three days since the old sun set on the Bamouni Kingdom. The new sun has risen. It is three days since and the drizzle has turned into a torrential rain flooding parts of the kingdom.

The two Queen Mothers sit to the far left on their stools next to the two princes. Seven elders sit in their customary places on either side of the throne. They all have arrived at the medicine man's summons. Everyone but the young Sultan and Abu is calm.

"Why do we gather?" Abu echoes. His gaunt body is still trembling from the effort to contain himself and his speech erupts in short quick bursts.

"You ask me why we gather. See the rain. The gods are angry. You ask me why we gather when the earth has rejected your father and our offerings... why do we gather?"

"Can anyone make sense of Abu's lament?" the Sultan looks around. The silence gives way to a speculative hum. Several of the elders turn to each other, murmuring. The Queen Mothers are heavily veiled and keep silent, befitting their mourning status.

"Summon the chief palace guard into your presence!" Abu shouts. "Since you need a commoner to tell the obvious." He shakes his rattled staff and sits on his mat.

"It is done." The Sultan ignores the breach in protocol and motions to a guard.

"My Master, My Lord, ruler of the Bamouni people, the sun that has risen on the land to never set," the well trained guard begins in his booming voice once he is permitted to speak. He is a thick-set, middle-aged man with bronze bangles on his wrists that announce his position.

"I am honoured to greet you and your council." He looks uneasily in Abu's direction and breathes rapidly before he squares his shoulders again.

"This morning, I was summoned by Abu to the sacred grove beyond the stream. It is there that our great Sultans may begin their journey to the land of Great Happiness. I went there with the royal retinue three days ago. I took charge of the favoured slaves."

"Just get to the point," the Sultan interrupts, tapping his iroko and ivory sceptre on his throne. "Get to the point!"

"My Ruler, your father the great sun of the Bamouni people," he pauses, shifts his weight from the left then to the right foot before he continues. "He is angry and has refused to go."

"What do you mean? How does a dead body that is buried in the ground refuse to go?!" A hush descends as the young Sultan pronounces the forbidden phrase. Nobody dares speak out loud but murmurs make rounds. He dares refer to the great Sultan's mortal cloak as a dead body.

"Foolish guard. You waste our time? Speak!"

"My ruler, forgive me. The earth is rejecting our Sultan's father." The guard shifts his weight uneasily again and folds and unfolds his arms. "His royal remains lie in a pool of foul stagnant water for all common eyes to see. Four of the favoured slaves are lying weak, struck with illness…"

The young Sultan leaps up off his throne. He drops his sceptre. There is a shrill wail from the royal women. Abu jumps up from his mat, laughing madly, and rushes outside unprotected into the pounding rain.

Donna (Dona) Forbin is Cameroonian and works in the Communications service of the Limbe City Council. She is the author of a collection of short stories, *Dancing Heart*, and a collection of poetry, *Primitive Prayer*. She has freelanced for local newspapers and magazines and is currently working on her second collection of short stories.

Twinkle, Twinkle Little Pastor

Lawrence Kadzitche

A GUST OF ICY COLD WIND hit the pastor's face when he opened the bedroom window. Birds and insects chirped and chattered, happy that the rain that had fallen all night long had finally let up. But Pastor John Kalebe knew otherwise. The sky was still overcast with dark clouds. It would just be a matter of time before the rains started again.

"You should be on your way, dear," a voice said behind him.

He turned. It was Paulina, his wife. He hadn't heard her return to the bedroom. A glance at his expensive Rolex showed that it was 7.00am, exactly the time he had planned to leave.

"You're right, honey," he said, and then, taking her hands in his, he added, "Let us pray."

The prayer started on a soft note but, as is usually the case with Pentecostal pastors, his voice rose gradually. Soon, he was shouting, invoking the blood of Jesus to protect him during the journey and bind the devil and all evil powers. To the prayer, Paulina added a chorus of tongue praying spiced with a lot of alleluia and amen.

When he finished his prayers, ten minutes later, he was drenched in sweat. Paulina picked up his suitcase and he followed her out of the bedroom. In the lounge, Sonia, his maid, relieved her of the travel case. Sonia had scarcely gone out of the house when she shrieked with horror.

They ran outside and found the maid frozen with terror on the veranda. She was staring at a small dead bird on the floor. Kalebe recognized it as a nocturnal bird called *nkhwenzule*.

"This is bad luck," Sonia screeched. "When this bird dies, something really bad happens."

The pastor put a fatherly arm on the housemaid's shoulder. He knew where Sonia's fear stemmed from. Because the bird came out only at night, people associated it with witches and evil spirits. It was not uncommon to see people shudder when the bird chirped at night and murmur with fear that a witch was on the loose. But Sonia was a born-again Christian and, as such, she was not expected to believe in such mumbo-jumbo.

"Sonia, this is just a bird like any other bird," he pointed out. "It hit the wall and died. That's all."

But the housemaid was not convinced. "Pastor." She always called him pastor. "Pastor, back home, we found a dead bird like this outside my brother's house and three days later he died in his sleep."

"That was a mere coincidence, Sonia," Kalebe assured her. "We who are born-again Christians should make no concessions to any superstitions."

And to illustrate his point, he picked up the dead bird and threw it carelessly into the shrubs.

"But be careful, anyway," Paulina said, trying to sound as casual as possible. "You never know."

"Paulina, Paulina," Kalebe said in a reproachful manner, "That's blasphemous coming from a pastor's wife. We are Christians, and superstitions have no room in our lives."

He picked up the suitcase Sonia had dropped and walked to the white Mercedes Benz parked outside. The moment he got into the car and started the engine, the heavens opened again. He lowered the window, blew his wife a kiss, quickly rolled it up again and then drove off into the blinding rain.

His destination was Blantyre, where he had been invited

to be the main speaker at a religious revival crusade which was beginning the following day.

The downpour deteriorated into a storm. Gusts of wind-driven rain whipped the car mercilessly so that he could hardly see. The streets, usually full on a Saturday morning, were eerily empty. It was obvious one had to have compelling reasons to venture out. His headlights on, the wipers slashing angrily at the rain streaming down the windscreen, the car crawled along the tarmac road.

He was in no hurry and killed time by rehearsing the sermon he would deliver at the crusade. After the revival meeting, he expected to set up a new branch in Blantyre. An additional branch meant increased membership and consequently enhanced collections.

The thought brought a wry smile to his face. Just five years ago, he had been eking out a living as a teacher at one of the primary schools in the slums of the city. Then he had received the Lord's call, quit the job, and founded the church.

And, as the church's slogan confirmed, the Lord was really good all the time. Starting with just a few people, his congregation had mushroomed to fill the city hall where they met. Thanks to the generosity of his flock, he now lived in the sprawling rented bungalow in the elegant Area 43 suburb. His five children were learning at expensive private boarding schools and his wife was able to go shopping in South Africa. He had overheard the church elders say they planned to buy him a maize mill as his birthday gift this year. God was really working miracles for him.

He recalled a Presbyterian reverend who asked him how he managed to convince his flock to give to him so generously. "They don't give to me," he had replied blandly. "They give to God and they know God will give back abundantly." To himself he added: "I will not be surprised if they buy me a private jet in a few years."

The rain had eased to a drizzle by the time he reached the outskirts of the city. He picked up speed. And that's when he saw her. She stood by the road, a tall figure in a bright yellow raincoat that reached down to her knees. A large bag was slung across her left shoulder.

It was the pastor's habit never to offer a lift to strangers. There were great dangers in doing so. He had heard more than enough stories of unsuspecting drivers being robbed or even killed by thugs they had kindly offered a lift to.

The girl ahead did not wave him down. She brought down her pointing finger imperiously, then indicated with her thumb the direction she was going. The gesture raised the pastor's curiosity. Slowing down, he could clearly see the girl's white teeth bared in an expectant smile. He found himself shifting into a lower gear. Surely there would be no danger from a lone girl shivering in the rain. His mind made up, he pressed his foot on the brake pedal. The car came to a halt beside the girl.

"Get in," he said as he leaned over and opened the passenger door.

"Thanks a lot," she said, scuttling into the car. "I was wondering whether I was not going to melt out there like *Kamdothi*. Honey, you know the story of *Kamdothi*?"

Of course he knew the tale, just as every child who had grown up in the village did. It was a popular tale about a woman who had no children. She liked to mould toys made of clay and pretended they were children. One day, one of the clay toys became a real child. She named her *Kamdothi*, meaning made of clay. However, it was obviously necessary that the child should never be touched by water or she would melt.

Without waiting for his reply, the girl went on, "The tale went with a lovely song. Something like," she paused, closed her eyes and sang, *"Kamdothi run away from the rain."* She opened her eyes and said dreamily: "I grew up with my grandmother. She was very good. But good things do not last, you know."

"What happened?" the pastor asked.

"Well, the usual story, sweet. She died; blah blah blah." She paused and shrugged, "The important thing is I am here, little me."

She threw back the hood of her raincoat to reveal a moon-shaped face framed by pitch-black wavy hair cascading to her shoulders. Her light complexion showed the use of skin-lightening creams.

"Babe, I'm headed for Blantyre for a Revival Crusade which will take place tomorrow," she said, throwing her bag at the back seat. "I was so worried I would miss the great event."

The pastor smiled. "God always has ways of providing our needs, daughter. That's why I came along."

She smiled to reveal again the row of snow-white teeth he had espied earlier and stared coquettishly at him. "Oh? Well, I once heard that there are some days when the Lord determines all our actions. So, honey darling, are you also going to the revival?"

Kalebe nodded without taking his eyes off the road.

"Let the Lord be praised," she said, rolling her eyes. "There is some big pastor that will be preaching there. I've heard his sermons on the radio but never had a chance to meet him. They are very powerful and enlightening. I'm sure you'll enjoy the event."

"Actually, I am that pastor," he said with a smile, allowing himself a moment of pride.

"Holy Mother Mary! This is a blessed day for me," she leaned over and kissed him on the cheek. "Seeing you in jeans and a pullover, you look more like some handsome movie star than a pastor. Cowboy, you're a lady killer."

Kalebe blushed and took a deep breath. "Remember, I am a pastor," he pointed out weakly. "I would be grateful if you could address me as such."

The girl laughed. "Pastor to your flock. To me, your little *moi*, you are sweetie."

The pastor turned to tell her that he was past 40 and fit to be her father. However, as his eyes encountered her provocative smile, the words died in his throat.

The rain had picked up again, pattering on the roof, gushing down the windscreen and forming an almost impenetrable curtain ahead of him.

"Bad weather, I wish the rain would stop," he said to the girl, hoping to change the subject.

The girl dipped her hand into her handbag and fished out several compact discs. "I don't know which music you enjoy, sugar. I'm into the reggae thing. Bob Marley, Burning Spear, The Maytals, you know."

Selecting one of the discs, she slotted it into the car's stereo without waiting for his response. She turned up the volume and Bob Marley's music filled the car. *"I ago tired to see your face,"* she sang along in a corrupted version of the song, while shaking her body, *"Can't get me out of the race."*

A sunny smile spread on Kalebe's face. The music reminded him of the days before he became a pastor. He had loved reggae too. He found himself nodding his head in rhythm with the music.

"You didn't tell me your name," he said, eyeing the girl with some kind of renewed interest.

She looked at him from under her eyelids, biting her fingernails playfully. "Sorry, general. I am Tadala, but you can call me Tada."

Glancing at her, the pastor was aware there was something about the girl he couldn't place. Yes, she was beautiful and exciting, but there was something more than that.

But the girl was speaking again. "Gosh, poor me! I should have taken off the raincoat!"

The vision that emerged out of the raincoat made the pastor's eyes almost pop out of their sockets, his mouth dropping wide open. The girl was in a tight-fitting white blouse that showed her navel. Shapely breasts threatened to burst open her blouse. Flowing out of a miniskirt that barely covered her thighs were shapely legs that tapered into high heels.

He tried to avert his eyes but failed. On that desolate rainy day, she was like the sun breaking out of dark clouds.

"Do you mind if I make up my face?" Tadala's voice broke the spell. "The rain spoiled everything."

"Go ahead," croaked the pastor, his chest heaving. To him, she looked breathtaking the way she was.

He took several deep breaths to calm his pounding heart. He was confused. What was the meaning of all this? When the girl had said she was going to the crusade, he had assumed she was a born-again Christian. But how could someone who had committed her life to Christ dress like that?

He watched her out of the corner of his eyes as she powdered her face, painted her lips and then preened herself in the car's mirror.

"Honey, how do I look?" she asked, looking as pleased as a cat that has caught a mouse.

The pastor had to admit to himself that she looked devastatingly beautiful. But there was no way he could tell her that.

"Hey, loosen up, handsome," she purred. "Let me get you something to put you in the mood."

She retrieved her bag and dug out a bottle, opened it with her teeth and spat out the bottle top.

"Here, have a swig of this, baby. It will make you feel good," she said, handing him a bottle of beer.

He shook his head vehemently. What was she up to? Hadn't he told her she was a pastor?

"Don't give me that pastor stuff," she said, reading his mind.

"I am a Pentecostal pastor," he croaked faintly. "We don't touch alcoholic drinks."

The girl laughed again. "Be honest, beloved. I know of Pentecostal preachers who drink harder than Catholic priests. At any rate, don't worry about your flock finding out. Who will tell them?"

He didn't answer her. There was nothing to tell her. She

wouldn't understand. He watched her take a long pull of the beer. After that she took out a cigarette. When he turned to protest, she blew smoke in his face and that stopped him. He had a feeling that if he tried to let out a word, a kiss on the mouth would be used to silence him.

"So you are still a little boy, sweetie?" she asked gaily. "Then let mother sing you something to cheer you up. *Twinkle, Twinkle little pastor, how I wonder what you are, here in the car, a beautiful girl by your side.*"

The nursery rhyme was infuriating to the pastor but he knew there was little he could do to shut the girl's mouth short of gagging her. He decided to leave it there. He would not look at or speak to her again until they reached Blantyre.

The beer seemed to tranquilize the girl and as the car was cruising along Zalewa Road, she closed her eyes and fell asleep. At the same time, the weather cleared and the sun appeared.

The pastor couldn't understand what was happening. Was this a trap thrown at him by the devil? If this was case, then the prince of darkness had made his call in vain. He was a seasoned pastor and had met temptations of all sorts in his calling. He wasn't going to fall for this one. Not him.

His eyes strayed to Tadala. Fast asleep and breathing softly, she looked so innocent, like an angel. Maybe he had misjudged her. She hadn't done anything really offensive. Her smoking and beer drinking was wrong, but there were a lot of young women who smoked and drank beer. The curse of modernity.

He was now nearing Blantyre. He admitted to himself that the girl had made the journey seem very short. She looked like a nice young girl and with proper guidance she could be returned to the right path. All he needed to do was make sure she really attended the revival meeting the next day.

"Tadala, Tadala," he called softly.

But the girl was fast asleep. Eyes on the road, he put out his hand to wake her up. His fingers touched warm, bare flesh. He retracted his hand as if he had touched a red hot ember. His eyes automatically left the road and fell on the girl. What he saw shook him to the very roots of his soul. It could not be true. He must be dreaming. The girl's skirt had gone up to her waist. Underneath, she didn't have a stitch on!

Kalebe's brain refused to believe this. No, this was too much. What shocked him was not the girl's nakedness but the enormity of his error in offering a lift to a girl who was not wearing any underwear and was obviously trying to seduce him. His mind willed him to take his eyes off the girl but his eyes refused.

Confused, he didn't know that his car was cruising in the middle of the road. As he rounded a corner, that's when he saw the truck. He tried to swerve but it was like dodging a meteorite. His car scraped the side of the truck and rocked violently.

The door on the girl's side was thrown open and she flew out. She crashed on the roadside and rolled into a low ditch. The pastor retained enough presence of mind to wrestle with the car as it danced crazily on the wet tarmac. It came to rest with a crash against an electricity pole.

Kalebe, stunned momentarily, quickly recovered his senses. As he was scrambling out, something caught on his trousers, tearing them. But he paid no heed and limped towards Tadala, who, to his horror, was lying spreadeagled and semi-naked on the grass roadside.

He bent over her. Surprisingly, she was only slightly bruised. He felt her pulse. It was beating. Overjoyed, he cradled her in his arms. The girl's eyes fluttered open.

Relief flooding his body, he jumped up with joy. He was out of the danger zone. Laughter hit his ears and he stopped. Looking down at him from the side of the road was a group of people which was growing bigger as more people arrived. Someone laughed again, pointing at him.

The pastor looked at himself and realized with alarm that his trousers were torn and the waistline was round his thighs. Then his eyes went to the girl who was now sitting up, vainly covering her nakedness with her mini skirt. In the people's eyes and laughter he saw the accusations and in that instant, he knew he was doomed.

"Go away!" he howled.

But they just stood there like vultures, laughing as they watched him and the girl.

Oh God, what a position. He knew it would be out that he had been involved in an accident because he was doing immoral things with a girl while driving his car – and imagine, people would add, on his way to a crusade.

As the laughter reverberated in his ears, he could already hear similar laughter as he moved out of the elegant mansion back to the seedy slum, as his children went back to the government school, as he went from place to place looking for a new job. He was finished as a pastor.

"Go away, fools," he shouted again. "What are you looking at?"

But the only answer he got was more laughter.

He wondered what had happened to his prayers. He was not supposed to be experiencing this. Then he remembered Sonia's warning. Maybe he should have paid some attention to what she had said. Why was he having all this misfortune if the dead bird had not signalled bad luck?

Lawrence Kadzitche is a columnist and prolific short-story writer. His satirical column *Katakwe* has been appearing in one of Malawi's biggest newspapers, *Weekend Nation*, since 2001. He published his first novel in 2010. He currently lives and works in Malawi.

Afritude

Monique Kwachou

CAN YOU A IMAGINE being a pet fish in an aquarium, catered for but never being quite at home? So you fight what you think is a despicable cruelty, then you lose the aquarium, and are tossed on land, forced to breathe like never before. It's sad, right? It's said we never know what we have till we lose it. The aquarium might have lacked the freedom of the sea, but at least it had water! I was that fish, and this is my story.

"Shoplifting, Eli, of all ungodly things, shoplifting!" My mother, Ms Frida Tambe, or Ma Fri as she was commonly called, clapped her hands at her idea of an abomination. "What did you lack? Is it not madness that has come over you?" Her voice was shrill, resounding with confusion. "Am I not talking to you? What did you lack?

"I have told you time and time again! As you see me standing here, I was born in a place that makes this house look like a palace!

"You do practically nothing. I provide you with everything; all you have to do is be a good child! Ah-ah, is that too much to ask? When I was half your age I worked! Do you even know what that means? I would fetch water from a deep well in the mornings, feed my father's swine by noon and then, in the evenings, I'm at the roadside roasting corn! But here you are at twelve years, I tell you to do mere chores – make up your own bed, wash dishes you eat from, clean up your room – and you can't do it without an agreement of $10 a week as allowance!" Ma Fri looked to the ceiling as though seeking God therein.

"Where did I go wrong? Have I spoiled you? How could I? Did I not bring a hoe and a broom from my last trip to Cameroon, just to teach you how to sweep like a child should instead of being lazy and using a vacuum cleaner?" Her voice expressed her distaste.

"Am I not the one who cleared the backyard and taught you how to use the hoe to plant maize?

"No, I did not spoil you! It is this America oh! Eh! Shoplifting! And then you excuse it by saying it was a dare, you want to be accepted in some clique.

"Do you hear yourself when you speak? Don't you sound like a fool? Since when are thieves accepted anywhere in society?

"Cha! I have suffered!

"This child! You will not kill me! Elizabeth, you will not kill me oh!" Ma Fri sat down, taking some time to think so as to make some sense out of the madness in her house.

The subject of her thoughts, I sat, laid back on the loveseat across from her, scowling at the adjacent wall. I was not in the least remorseful, and I did not look it. No, I looked as though I wished that ceiling would cave in and crush my mother. And I did. I thought about what she'd been saying. I smiled as I remembered that, when she had brought that hoe and broom, one of her friends, aunty Bessem, had exclaimed, "Ma Fri, you are the epitome of the idiom that says: 'you can take a man out of the village, but never the village out of the man!'" My mother always had crazy plans like that, claiming she was trying to resurrect the African in me, trying to wipe away American-bred ideas like saying I was from Africa when asked. "Elizabeth! Africa is not a country, you are Cameroonian!" she was wont to say.

I was tired of hearing her complain about my so-called 'attitude', telling me to act like a Cameroonian. I had left Cameroon at the age of five, and I hated it when my mom spoke as though the place was heaven, when I distinctly remember it as a step up from hell. I remember I came to

America with a shaved head and rashes on my skin. And when I began school, everyone wanted to know what kind of cancer I had. I didn't even know what cancer was!

I had explained to her about the dare. The cop had understood. Why couldn't she? Did she know what it meant or how it felt to be an outcast at school? Or how I longed to belong to any group whatsoever at school so I wouldn't have to sit at the table with the geeks whose lives revolved around their computers and the freaks who always wore black as though they were in constant mourning. No, she couldn't understand. All my mom knew was I was not behaving like a Cameroonian, not even like an African. As though anyone cared whether I did or not, apart from her, that is. Being the good African child did not get you accepted in school, or get you friends, or get you much of anything, except your mom's acceptance, and shouldn't she accept me as I am anyways?

"I've come to a decision." My mother's voice interrupted my thoughts. Still scowling, I looked at her; she looked me straight in my face, trying to meet my eyes.

"I'm sending you back home to go to boarding school." My body tensed. I knew what she called home. My first thought was to correct her: home is where the heart is and my heart was definitely not in Cameroon. But I was too proud to show I was hurt by the fact that she would want me to go away. I couldn't let her see the hurt – how could she ship me off like some undesirable element? Pride spoke loudest.

"I want to go, anyways," I heard myself lie. "I can't stand living in the same house with you!"

I was shocked my voice didn't crack. With that I fled to my room. I guess I wasn't surprised; she had always threatened me with boarding school, painting a picture akin to exile in my mind. So all I had actually done was hurt her as she had me. And, as I lay on my bed, I consoled myself, filling my mind with my idea of what boarding school would entail: a room for me and another young girl. No mom, no chores, free to do as I liked. Didn't only rich kids go to boarding school? It ought to be something prestigious, right? It was going to be okay, everything would be great.

My ticket was bought; we had agreed I was going to go for nine months, a single school year after which I'd return. I saw myself as taking a leisurely sabbatical from my mother's authority. My only moment of pause, of suspicion that maybe everything wasn't going to be alright, came on the day of take-off. Before prayers an uncle laughingly asked my mom if she had bought my lance. My mom chided him playfully, saying I'd get one when the time came. When I asked what a lance was, she evaded, answering me by commencing the prayers. When the same uncle asked me one last time if I was sure I wanted to go back, my mom scowled, but I simply reminded him that I was a *pre-teen* and not a child. I therefore knew my mind. I left the aquarium on that false notion.

***

The first thing I wondered as I stepped off the plane onto Cameroonian soil was how the air in the plane, a confined space, could seem more fresh than that of the open space outdoors. The air was thick with heat, car exhaust and the odours of about 300 busy travellers. My mom had said someone would meet me at the airport, but I didn't know who. I began to panic. What had I gotten myself into? I felt queasy in the pit of my stomach. I wanted to get back on the plane, just continue flying, without landing, and definitely not landing here!

I heard my name; well, I heard something like my name. Instead of Elizabeth, it sounded more like *Eliz-a-beth*. As I turned to the direction of the voice, I saw a middle-aged woman approaching me. She called the remix of my name once more and waited hesitantly till I nodded in response. She then proceeded to swallow me in her embrace. She was dressed in full African wear, a patterned wax cloth tailored to suit her, with a matching head-tie elaborately tied. Behind her a swarm of people followed to welcome me. Those I knew and those I didn't. Who could have guessed that my mother's sister-in-law's brother's child could be considered family to the point of welcoming me at the airport?

As we left the airport, the wave of heat that met me made me long for a swim. As we settled in the Jeep an uncle had brought, I asked if there was a swimming pool around the house. After repeating myself about five times so as to be understood my relatives all began laughing. "Did y'all understand what I said? I haven't made a joke, so why are y'all laughing?"

Hannah, one of the far relations, and the closest to my age, spoke up: "You rap too much, but we understood you. The question is funny because it seems you do not know what you're asking. Swimming pools are not common around here."

As I digested her words, my aunt took pity on me. "Don't worry, okay? Maybe during the holiday we could take you to one of the hotels with a swimming pool."

When I heard 'holiday', I thought of Christmas, of snow. It was already September. I laid my head back on my seat, willing tears back as I thought of the strangeness of everything.

When my mom called later that day to check that I had arrived safe and sound, I had to talk to her. I could have complained, could have cried, begged even, but I didn't. "I'm fine, mom." My pride spoke for me and, when looking around, I thought the tears would come anyway. I told her I was tired and passed the phone to my aunt. That night I barely slept. I had been told I was going off to Bamenda, to a Christian boarding school, in three days' time.

✳✳✳

CRHS, Christian Remedial High School, Mbengwi, welcomed me with a barber and a uniform the colour of spirogyra. The barber, a lanky guy wearing a faded polo shirt and sporting a trimmed moustache, had to hold my head still while wielding his evil machinery. I was taken to the dormitory, where all the nice clothes, the only perks of my journey to Cameroon, were seized. I was told to wear the uniform, a shapeless sterile garb so fashion-less it would be cruel to give it to a nun. Upon reaching the dorm, I received another blow as I looked around what was to be my home for the next nine months. I cringed. My image of boarding school – having a room of my own, privacy, freedom independence – burst like the bubble of fantasy it was. When a swift breeze came through the window, sending a chill through my newly shaved scalp, I stood unmovable in the midst of the dorm with its iron beds, rough cement floors, and greyish stained walls with little sign of life. I felt tears threatening. I willed the tears away at least until I had somewhere I could shed them and still keep my pride intact. As I skirted around other kids, most of whom looked at me with open curiosity, I tried to ignore their murmured comments.

"Cha! Na form one that? how e fats so?"

"Na America wanda! Na so dem dey whether dey di chop na fertilizer oh?"

Once outside, I tried to get to the back of the dorm, with feet not used to coping with what seemed like the rubble left behind by a volcanic eruption. Trying to avoid the rocks, I attempted to walk on the sides of the cemented gutter. I promptly found myself on the ground, with half my body in the air, the other half in the gutter. The tears which had been building up since I had proudly left my mother's care, tears I had restrained for days, fell unbridled, uncontrolled. I couldn't take it any more. As I sobbed, I felt the stares of those around me, and instead of clinging to that pride I had held on to for so long, I sobbed all the more.

A young girl came up to me while the others who were laughing and pointing looked on.

"Hi," she said, "I'm Yaah."

I was down to sniffling now and she helped me up off the ground. Looking down at the ugly uniform, made all the more ugly by my fall, and at the dribble of blood from where the cement had scraped my legs, I resumed my sobbing again but muted this time, restrained, as tears of self-pity streamed down my face.

"So what is your name?" Yaah asked, trying to get me to stop crying.

"Eli- Elizabeth," I stammered. She smiled and, still holding my hand, led me to a nearby bucket to rinse my wound.

Clang! Clang! The unmistakable sound of a gong made me raise my head to see what had happened. Yaah's eyes, however, did not mirror my surprise.

"It's time for supper," she said simply. "That's the warning bell; you don't want to be late." With that she left me to my own devices and fled.

I looked around. The gong had caused an uproar, with everyone moving hurriedly, busy with one thing or the other. I stood lost in the centre of a whirlwind. I saw Yaah with another group of girls far ahead. I rushed into the dorm and rummaged through the things in my trunk. I found my plate. A minute later, Yaah was nowhere to be seen. I attached myself to a group of older girls, following them to the refectory. At the doors a tall boy stood, looking imposing. My heartbeat quickened as I saw he barred the doorway.

"Refecto, abeg sorry oh, we bi di follow form one dem for cam Ref." The statement was made by one of the tallest girls in the bunch.

"Elise, don't you know you shouldn't be speaking in pidgin beside these new students?" The boy nodded at me. The girls, noticing me just then, turned their astonished gazes on me.

"Where are you from?" asked one, wondering when I had joined their group.

"Are you not the *bush-faller* who fell in the gutter today?" asked another.

"When you heard the gong, why didn't you run to the refectory?" It was the boy's turn to speak, "You did not want to eat, not so?"

I did not move. I had been in this situation before. If I answered him, I would be speaking back to an elder. If I didn't, I would be ignoring an older person. Either way, I would be considered rude. I decided not to risk it.

"Since you have nothing to say for yourself, you will sit outside here." With that he let the other girls pass, entering and shutting the door behind him, leaving me outside. I stood there like a fool, praying it was a nightmare. A chilling breeze blew in my face, a cold blast of reality that mocked my wishes.

Twenty minutes later the population of the refectory spilled out, everyone busy talking, hurrying forward. I was scarcely noticed. I spotted Yaah and rushed to her.

"I didn't get to eat," I blurted out, as though expecting her to solve the problem. The girls around her giggled. I ignored them, only to have my snub destroyed by the hungry growl of my stomach.

"I told you to hurry when you heard the gong *na*?" Yaah couldn't help but pity me.

She gave me her plate with what looked like her leftovers. "Take, finish it," she said.

"What is it?" I asked.

Her friends snickered, and she rolled her eyes. "Garri and okra."

One taste of the meal had me offering it back to her. The food had lost its warmth and was now a cold tasteless mass. I knew I had food in my trunk back in the dorm. I would eat later. Yaah shrugged at my refusal of her food and we hurried on to class.

Two hours later I was sure I had never been so hungry in my life. Upon arrival at the dorm, I found the store room where our trunks were kept was locked. Yaah found me on my bunk bed weeping in my hunger. After attempting in vain to console me, she asked, "Haven't you ever slept hungry?"

I looked at her, baffled at the absurdity of the question. "No, why should I?"

She turned surprisingly solemn eyes on mine. "Why should anybody?" She returned to her own bunk, leaving me with unexplainable feelings of immaturity and guilt.

Somehow, by some inborn will I didn't know existed, I survived the weeks that followed; the horror of the pit toilets, the labour of scrubbing the rough cement floors of the dormitory or, worse, the spirogyra of the gutters. I braved the insults of elder students and the lashings of teachers for late-coming or some other inconsequential crime. I endured the assaults on my way of talking, walking and, yes, even eating. Above all, I lived day by agonizing day through the rigorous schedule, the lack of privacy, freedom, independence – of all the things I had sought. Yes, I lived, not only survived but lived through broken dreams.

*** *** ***

"Elizabeth! Eli!" The voice sounded like something familiar yet so strange. I turned to see Jubsia calling from the entrance of the girls' dorm. The discipline mistress had told me that my childhood friend was coming to school at CRHS but I couldn't believe it. Now I was seeing it.

I walked up the pathway to meet her, slowly taking in her appearance. She's much larger than I am now, larger than I was when I had just arrived. That was going to be a problem for her, recalling the insults I had endured. Her face held a mixture of resignation and hope. I knew exactly how she felt. Hadn't I felt the same way that first day?

"Juby!" I yelled, forcing exuberance into my voice to cheer her up. We hugged and I noticed she held a plastic bag fast in her hands so that it made a rustling sound when we hugged. As I withdrew, I gave the plastic bag a pointed look, and then looked quizzically at Jubsia.

"It's my hair," she said by way of explanation.

"What?" I blurted out, not believing my ears.

"They shaved it," she said, stating the obvious. "I couldn't let them throw it away." I felt her loss. The need to hold on to something you had cherished. I just shook my head.

Together we carried her things into her dormitory. It was reopening day, the first day of Form Three for me. Nine months had somehow turned to three years. But I was resigned, even content with it.

"So, girl, tell me, what are *you* doing here?" I asked, as though I couldn't guess. We were sitting on her bed, after I had helped her make it up. I checked my watch to make sure we had time to chat before the gong would sound.

"It's your mom's fault, you know?" That surprised me, but not too much.

"She caught me smoking pot with some friends last month and immediately tattled to my mom, advising her to ship me here for some time."

I wondered if my shock at hearing marijuana – not even cigarettes, but marijuana – was apparent on my face.

"Juby! Pot! Marijuana? What for?" If the shock hadn't shown before, I had passed on the message now.

She shrugged casually. "It's supposed to help you lose appetite and weight and stuff. So I said what the heck, I'll try it, and then here comes your mom just crossing the street and she sees me and my friends at the kerb puffing away." She smiled at the memory. My mouth was slack.

"But that wasn't the real issue. I think my mom was going to send me here anyways – you know my dad is here, right? He's got a wife here and kids older than me. Well, I've practically been living with my boyfriend for this past year and it's been making my mom worried. It serves her right; she's too stiff, for Christ's sake."

I sat dumbfounded through this speech. A million thoughts raced through my head.

"Can you believe I'm fifteen and my curfew is still 10pm?"

She shook her head as though it was too illogical. I wondered whether to remind her that we were age mates and I didn't have a curfew, I wasn't even allowed out. I decided not to.

"And can you believe, my boyfriend wanted to take me to Florida for spring break? He's in college, by the way," she said, looking proud.

"And my mom like totally refused! That's what really blew things up! I moved in with my boyfriend after that!" It was stupid of me, but I wanted to ask her if she was still a virgin. I restrained myself.

"So here I am for a year, just one year," she said. "After that I'm leaving, even if it means going to the American Embassy here and reporting my mom for child abuse. I mean, I know my rights."

"My mom won't dare, she knows what I can do. Her only flaw is she's too old-fashioned, she just can't understand, you know?" She posed the question looking at me as though expecting an answer.

And it all came back to me then. Yes, I did know. That was me spouting such rubbish three years ago. And here I was looking in the mirror yet not recognizing the image therein. How did it happen? When did I change? When did I learn to be time conscious, to see something wrong in staying out late, or losing one's virginity so carelessly? When did I become the girl who would prefer reading a good book to watching TV? And when did my taste change so much that I had Makossa CDs next to my Beyoncé? And would rather dress maturely than look like a stripper?

Should I tell Jubsia? Should I warn her of what was to come? The rigour and moralization that was life changing, the hell she had to pass through to fit in?

No, I probably shouldn't bother. Some lessons cannot be merely taught, they must be experienced. Thinking of the fact that my nine months' contract had extended to three years, I smiled. She had time.

I thought of my mother, of that American attitude she had

complained about so much. Who would have guessed she was right? What would she call my attitude now, I wondered?

I laughed; Jubsia looked up from the school timetable she was perusing.

"What is it?" she asked.

I smiled. "You've got to get the *Afritude*, Girl!"

She looked at me as though I had lost some screws. "Explain," she said simply.

Clang! Clang! Clang! It was the gong. All of a sudden I was alert. "Never mind," I told her. "You'll find out eventually. But right now we've got to hurry. You really don't want to be late!"

***

Did I liken myself to a fish? I was wrong. I was a tadpole, still to mature into a full-grown frog. I can breathe, live both on land and in sea.

Monique Kwachou, born Cameroonian, is a mixture of Cameroonian and Western upbringing. She is currently enrolled in double-major programmes of Gender Studies and Sociology at the University of Buea, Cameroon. She has freelanced for local newsletters and magazines and published her first book – *Writing Therapy*, a collection of poems – with Langaa RCIPG in 2010. She is currently working on her first novel.

Bottled Memory

Beatrice Lamwaka

AYAT DREAMT ABOUT BIDONG AGAIN. This time, she held him close to her chest and swung him around until she felt as if she was drunk on *arege*, the local brew. She pinched his ears like she did when he was three months old. Her heart thumped loud and it could be heard two kilometres away. People stopped selling *malakwang*, *boo*, sweet potatoes and mangoes. They watched her with envy. She didn't mind. It was one of those occasions where nothing mattered but her son. Bidong's dimples deepened with every smile. His small arms clung to her body like he was afraid to let go. He kept calling her: "Mummy! Mummy!" His voice was the sweetest she had heard in her whole life. People clapped as they watched her and her son. Then, suddenly, his fingers began to slip away from her. He was falling into a deep hole. She screamed for help but people went back to selling their *malakwang*, *boo*, sweet potatoes and mangoes. She screamed again but her voice could not be heard. People looked past her and her son.

She suddenly wakes up as a dog barks in the compound. For a moment she is confused. She does not know where she is or where Bidong is. She grapples frantically in her bed to look for clues. Then she remembers. She is in school. The sheets are damp. Fresh sweat from her neck drips on her pillow. She lets the sweat drip for a while. She uses the tip of her nightdress to dry her face. She does not like the smell of her bed. With her left hand she throws the pillow to the floor. I will pick it up in the morning, she thinks. She looks around in the dark dormitory which she shares with about twenty girls. She does not see any movement or hear anybody talk; only Eva snoring in the corner of the dormitory. She does not know what time it is. She hopes it is not three o'clock because she believes that is the time that Satan moves around the world. And that is the time when most people die.

She tries to force her mind to create a picture of Bidong's face but her mind only brings pictures of her nieces and nephews. Why can't I remember my own son? she asks herself. His memory is all I have. I cannot forget my son, she says, as she gets out of bed. She walks in the narrow corridor between the beds. She paces for a while and still she does not get a picture of Bidong. Only dimples come to her mind. She wishes she had talked to her friends about Bidong, then maybe it would be easier for her. She knows that the school environment is not good for mothers or even talking about children. Most of the girls do not even talk about sex. If the students saw her talking to herself and walking about that would confirm she was totally mad, as they had often said of her. They don't know what she is coping with.

Students of Namugongo are always displayed in the *Monitor* and *New Vision* newspapers for getting triple As in exams. Ayat knows she will never appear in the newspapers. Her best marks are Bs, which she gets in office practice and religious studies. She would be happy just to pass her O-level exams. Her dream of university seems distant but she hopes to get there. She hopes to get into Makerere University, which she used to sing about when she was in primary school. Her final exams will start in about a month's time and she does not want anything to clutter up her brain. Trying to cram what is in her notebook is becoming harder than she thought it would be. Every time she closes her books, whatever she has read goes with the page.

She is happy that the students have not yet discovered that she has had a baby. They would have told her she should have known human biology better. Students can be mean, she thinks. Sometimes, when she walks around the school, she hears students whispering about her. 'Joseph Kony,' they have called her a number of times, in reference to the rebel leader who has created anarchy in northern Uganda. She has decided she won't be bothered by any of the things they say though sometimes it does get on her nerves. But school isn't supposed to be easy, her mother has always told her. She remembers when Nakato, one of her classmates, was found to be pregnant. The nurse pushed her fingers to every student's womb to feel if they had babies. Ayat felt nauseated after the experience. Nakato was called out during assembly, with the whole school standing in lines on a hot Monday afternoon. Nakato cried as the headmaster said she was such a bad girl. Later the school pick-up took her home.

Ayat didn't realize she was pregnant, even after her stomach started to swell. She drank warm water to cleanse her stomach but it swelled more. It was only later, when her friend told her that a baby was in her womb, that she realized she didn't know how it would come out. But her friend encouraged her to wait till the time was right because she would know what to do. And, when it was time, Ayat wailed until a piece of cloth had to be stuffed in her mouth to avoid soldiers from finding out their whereabouts. She was excited to see what had come out of her. He was a little thing. Later, Ayat noticed that he had dimples on both his cheeks. She noticed that he would grow to have a gap between his teeth. She liked men with gaps between their teeth. She thought they were handsome. Bidong would grow into a handsome boy.

Thinking about Bidong has brought tears to Ayat's eyes. She cannot dwell on that part of her life. Focus on your school, she forces herself to think. But her mind takes her right back to Bidong. He must be well. I can feel him calling for me, she thinks. He must be wondering why his mother never returned.

Yes, it was almost four years since she had last seen Bidong. She hadn't meant to leave him behind. Everything had happened so fast. She hadn't had time to think. She had left the rebel camp to fetch water. Bidong had remained with one of her friends. She hadn't wanted to carry her gun, Bidong and a jerry-can of water, which would have made it impossible for her to walk the hills of Agoro. When she had heard the gunshots, she hadn't stopped to think. She had just run and run until she had found help and been put on a bus back home to Katikati.

On the day that she returned home from the rebel camp, Ayat's dress was torn and her nipples peeped through. She would never be able to wear that dress any more. But it was the only dress she owned. Her feet were cracked and swollen from the long walk home. She was thirsty for water. The water that she had drunk at the swamp had made her want to drink more. She hadn't eaten food in a long time but she was used to that. She wanted to sleep. Her mind was blank on the trip home. She didn't know what to expect and she wasn't sure she would find her family alive. She had heard of rebels talking of how they had looted villages and killed people. She was angry that they talked about it with such ease. They seemed to have enjoyed every moment.

As she stood by the roadside she didn't know if she would find her mother. She could see the path leading home but her father's land was now filled with hundreds of huts. She had seen some of the camps on her way from Kitgum but had never imagined that her home would house so many people. This was the new way people lived – in camps, driven from their half-burnt houses that now stood amidst overgrown grass. Before she had been abducted by rebels on her way to school, only her aunt and a few other people had asked her father for plots of land where they could build new houses and grow some vegetables. In the beginning her father had been glad to help out. It was only later when the number of people became overwhelming that he had urged the people to ask other neighbours. But, from the look of the houses, the number had increased.

Trucks of the World Food Programme loaded with sacks of grain drove past her. She knew that they had brought food for the people living in the camp. She saw people run after them. It was hard for her to watch women with empty sacks and saucepans run after the trucks instead of running from the rebels. Adults only learned to run during the war to get away from the rebels or the government soldiers.

The children remained behind, not bothered by what the adults were doing. She herself had enjoyed playing *dulu* while she was young. She peered at the children to see if she could recognize any of them. They continued to play, unaware of her presence. She could not recognize any of them. She assumed that they were children of the people that had moved to her father's land. The men also had remained behind, drinking *marwa* with straws sticking from pots. They spoke loudly about how they could never get out of the camp to go and farm. How they were treated as children by the government soldiers. *Kaa chini*, the soldiers would say. One of the men told the group how he had been forced to sit by the roadside. The soldiers had bullied him but after a while had let him go when he promised he would not leave the camp without permission. "I am not a child. Why should I be treated that way?" he asked his peers, who remained silent.

Ayat continued to look for her mother's house. The mango tree on the compound guided her to it. She wondered what her mother would say and do when she saw her. For a moment, she felt as if she had been caught stealing sugar. It wasn't her fault, she thought.

The day she was abducted, Ayat had set off for school just like every child in Katikati. Little did she know that the rebels were hiding in the bushes waiting for schoolchildren. Sometimes she thought she saw a man wearing dark clothes hiding in the tall *obia* grass. At first she wasn't bothered, but suddenly a rude voice asked her to stop and she was forcefully led to a group of whimpering children.

Ayat never thought that she would be haunted by her actions. She pinched herself for not having completed the rituals she should have observed. She should have done better. Maybe if she had done *mato oput* then she wouldn't dream about Bidong any more.

When she returned from her captivity, her mother said *"lam dogi latina wek rubanga okonyi"* and sprinkled water mixed with millet over Ayat before she entered the house. Ayat closed her eyes and said *"apwoyo dwogo gang"*, "I am happy to be home". Her mother quickly sprinkled water on her forehead with *oboko lwedo* leaves. She kept whispering, "My daughter, I never thought I would see you again." She was shaking. She called the neighbours, who gathered in a short time. "My daughter, who everybody said was dead, has returned. What can I do to receive her?" she asked again. "You are doing alright. The gods are happy," one man shouted from the crowd.

Maybe she should have said something more, thinks Ayat. She should have said something good to appease the ancestors. Or she should have asked her mother what to say. Maybe the dreams would have dried with the water that clung to her forehead. She was sad that, four years after she had returned home, Bidong was still crowding her mind. Maybe she wasn't meant to forget about him; after all, he was her only child. She should have kept his memory in a bottle, like *arege* was kept to enhance its potency. He would be her bottled son.

She had expected her mother to ask her where she had been or what had happened to her, but instead her mother had provided her with water to bathe, clothes she could wear and food to eat. Ayat had decided she would never tell anyone she had had a baby that she had left behind. Days became years and nobody asked what had happened to her. Her mother developed high blood pressure and it seemed like that occupied her mind. Maybe she was happy that Ayat was home and that was all that mattered. And then they began to find a way for her to return to school.

Every moment she wanted to tell her mother about her son, but it was never the right time. She wanted her mother to know how she missed her son, how she dreamed about him and how she wanted to see him. She was only fifteen then. Before the war, her mother had always told her that should keep away from boys. The existence of Bidong would mean she had been close to another boy. She didn't want to disappoint her. She wanted to be a girl her mother would be proud of.

There are days when she wishes she had returned for her son. He must be around five years by now. She does not remember the date he was born. All she remembers is the pain she underwent and her friend encouraging her to push. When he came out she was happy to hold him. She hated to carry Bidong along with her gun. He was a small baby. He never cried. He smiled at whoever carried him. He started eating *boo* at about three months. And he drank chicken soup. He would play with chicken bones. She hardly had any breast milk so she gave him whatever she could find. He ate without complaining. Just smiled and showed his dimples.

While in the bush, Commander M told her that her life depended on her gun. He beat her up when he called him Otim. She was looking for some form of connection with him and had recognized him. He was from her village, Katikati. She had gone to the same school as him before the war – he had been in senior four while she had just joined senior one. He had probably never noticed her.

How could she have borne it when she was handed over to Commander M like she was some piece of cloth? She watched him with disgust as he panted over her. She didn't care what he did so long as he didn't hurt her. He would quickly leave the room as if feeling guilty about what he had just done. She hardly saw Commander M but she learnt from him how to shoot her gun. He showed her how to aim at targets. He told her to keep her gun close, just in case she had to use it. Commander M barely noticed Bidong but, when he did, the little boy would smile with excitement. He would try to jump and would make noises only he could understand.

In the two years that she spent with the rebels she only had to use her gun twice, when the government soldiers shot at them. She was excited to use her gun. She shot randomly until she finished all the bullets that had been given to her. When it was silent again and the rebels buried the dead, she received more bullets that became hard to carry along with Bidong. It didn't seem easy then but now that she thinks about it, she feels she could do it over and over again without complaint. She would have carried Bidong and five guns and walked many hills just to see him again. She aches for him. She wants to replay every memory of him.

Ayat switches on the lights. She knows it isn't allowed to switch on lights at this time of the night. She waits to hear if the senior lady or guards will rebuke her, but nothing stirs. She opens her religious education book. She finds the story about Jesus turning water into wine appealing. Ever since she had returned from the rebel camp she had been confused about religion. The rebels talked about creating a holy group of Acholi according to the Ten Commandments and yet they killed, stole, raped and distributed girls among themselves. She didn't want to join them but that was the only way she could survive. She carried her gun around and then Bidong became part of it too.

She tries to recall Bidong again. This time nothing comes to her mind. Not even her nieces or nephews. Her brain is dumped completely. She freaks out. She jumps in circles. Beds bump against her hips. She is not bothered by the pain.

The more she tries to get a picture of Bidong the less comes to mind. I have to find my son and then everything will make sense, she thinks. She closes her book as Eva stops snoring. "You mad girl – switch off the light. You read as if everyone in your home walks around naked and you are the only one who can save them." Eva's words do not make sense to her. She keeps repeating to herself, "I need to open that bottle where the memory of Bidong lies."

She wants Bidong to hug her the way he did in her dreams. She will not read about Jesus or Bismarck tonight. Not until she finds her son. It is the best thing I can do, she thinks. It is the only thing she wants. She tries to think of what she will tell her mother when she hears that she has walked out of the school – her mother had sold the only land she owned to pay the school fees. She wants to know where Bidong is. What he is doing. If he is in school. Does he have dreams about her? Does he like to eat *malakwang* the way she did? Does he look like Otim?

She picks up her *lesu* and wraps it around herself. She is still wearing her nightdress. She finds her slippers by her side. She puts them on without looking at them. She walks towards the door and finds the key in the keyhole. She turns the key and the door opens. She walks out of the dormitory. She does not hear when Eva shouts: "Mad girl, where are you going? Come back and close the door." The only words she hears are: "I need to open that bottle where Bidong's memories lie. I must find my son." She walks away from the blue and white dormitory. She walks past the sleeping guards into the night. She does not feel the cold wind. All she hears is, "I must find my son". The morning dew wets her feet as she passes through the grass to find her son.

Beatrice Lamwaka is the General Secretary of the Uganda Women Writers Association (FEMRITE) and lives in Kampala. [For full biography see page 59.]

The Menagerie of the Accused

Ayodele Morocco-Clarke

THE EVENING WAS SULLEN: leaves drooped from the branches of the mango trees in the compound; listless. Flies, engorged, were perched on ripened fruit and Udo, crouched behind the tree, was playing hide and seek with his sister and the neighbours' children.

Kufre dragged Udo out from his hiding place. "I've found him, I've caught Udo," she shouted, pulling her squirming brother away from the tree. When no one came out from their hiding place, she shouted, "I am not lying o. You people should come out, it is Udo's turn now." The other children came out to join them.

"Why didn't you come out when I said I had found Udo?"

"We thought you were trying to trick us, so you could catch us," Edem replied. "Oya Udo, it's your turn to count to one hundred while we go and hide. Turn your back. Don't cheat o."

Udo was still counting when Ekanem called him and Kufre inside to tidy up before their father got home.

***

Okon's day was an oxymoron. He woke up to Ekanem's warm buttocks rubbing against his groin and the gentle breeze of the old fan whirring overhead. For weeks, she had been trying to convince him to have another child and any protest he had was stifled under the intensity of her amatory ministrations.

Ekanem was in a good mood and prepared boiled yam with eggs for his breakfast; humming a hymn and gyrating her backside, she moved back and forth between the communal kitchen and the parlour. Okon felt his loins respond and hurried past her to put on his work clothes.

He started for work on his Vespa motorcycle, with Udo firmly clamped between his thighs and Kufre's little arms clutched tight around his waist. He dropped them at the end of the road to their school before continuing to his Oga's house. Parking his motorcycle near the sentry post, he walked up to the kitchen door to tell the house help to get the car keys and inform Oga that he had arrived. He took a bucket, added some Omo detergent, filled it with water and washed the Infinity Jeep that Oga preferred to ride in. Then he drove the vehicle up to the front of the house, carefully positioning the back door of the 'owner's corner' of the Jeep directly in front of the main door.

"Oga, good morning sir," he greeted and immediately opened the car door when the Chairman emerged from the house.

"Good morning Okon. Madam's driver is sick, so she needs you today. When you drop me at the office, make sure you come straight back to the house."

"Yes sir."

At the local government secretariat, Okon rushed round to open Oga's door. The Chairman reached into his pocket, pulled out a wad of notes and gave Okon 5,000 naira, saying "I know you must be broke by this time of the month." Okon prostrated himself on the floor, "Oga, thank you sir. God bless you sir." The Chairman waved him away and went inside the building.

The grin on Okon's face had not diminished when he returned to the house. Madam sent him on errands all morning; first to drive the house help to the market, then to take her car to the petrol station for servicing, and later to pick up some clothes from the tailor.

By the time he got back from the tailor, she was dressed and waiting impatiently. He pushed the garments he had collected from the tailor into the house help's outstretched hands and rushed round to open the back door of the car for Madam. He did not see the stone half buried in the sand. Pain shot up from the big toe of his left foot and he stifled the yelp that rose to his lips; the nail on the toe was stained scarlet. Hoping this was not a foreboding of some sort, he shut the door after Madam got into the car, then hurriedly limped back to his driver's seat.

"Madam, where are we going to?" he asked.

"Take me to the bank."

"Yes ma." He swung the car in a U-turn and exited the compound.

The sun played peek-a-boo all afternoon; darting behind clouds, then re-appearing when it got tired of its silly game; progressing steadily each time from east to west. Every time the sun disappeared, Madam peered heavenwards, trying to determine if she needed an umbrella. Suddenly, the skies shuddered; bloated clouds parted their jaws and spat out cold rain: fat drops which raped the parched earth, penetrating and churning it into potters' clay.

With the first rat-a-tats on the roof and windscreen, Okon turned on the car wipers, hunched forward in his seat and peered through the foggy glass. All of a sudden, he saw a chicken dash into the path of his car and tried to veer left to the opposite lane when he saw an oncoming lorry, forcing him to swerve back. Madam was screeching, "The blood of Jesus, the blood of Jesus," in the back of the car; there was a massive thud as the car made impact; a spider web criss-crossed the windscreen; then the car bounced up and down as its tyres climbed over something uneven before careening off the road into a ditch.

Okon came to as fingers clawed at him from behind. Madam was hysterical. The rain had petered out and the first thing Okon saw was a rainbow, marred by a trickle of blood flowing from a gash which had opened up beneath his left eyebrow. An irate crowd of people had gathered around the car; rocking it from side to side as they tried to open the doors. Okon could not make out what they were saying and just stared at them. This annoyed the crowd further.

"See as he dey look us like mumu. Make una no let am escape o," one man from the back of the crowd shouted.

"Don't worry," another said. "He will not go anywhere."

"And look at the useless Madam wey him carry. See as she siddon for back of car like say na party she dey go," a new voice added.

"Na so all these yeye rich people dey do," someone else said.

"Make una comot from road, I get jack here," someone shouted, elbowing his way to the front of the crowd. He hit the cracked windscreen with the jack and it caved in whole. Some men pulled Okon out and started beating him.

"Na God go punish you. You don kill person and instead make you come down from car come look the bad thing wey you do, you just lock the car door like say na thief surround your moto."

"I did not kill anyone o. It was a chicken that ran in front of the car."

Okon's ears rang with the force of the slap that followed his statement.

"Look at this bastard," said his assailant. "Is it a human being you are calling a fowl?"

"I swear to God. It was a chicken that crossed my path."

"Does this look like a chicken to you?" someone asked when a group of men dragged Okon to the bloody mass on the road; a greyish substance oozed from the top of the victim's head and his eyes were wide open: frozen in shock. One of his shoes had flown off his foot and lay face down several metres away; shards of glass from the car's headlamp were strewn on the road; bright red blood inched away from the body until it formed a pool in a dip in the road.

Okon collapsed and began weeping. "It was a chicken. I swear it was a chicken that flew in front of my car."

"First the chicken ran, now the chicken flew. You will speak the truth when you get to the police station."

"Please! Please. I did not see him. All I saw was a chicken."

"You can tell that to the police when we get there. Oya, let us get the body inside the car."

That night, when Okon finally left the police station on bail, he was no longer employed. Instead of going straight home, he stopped at Mama Akpan's beer parlour and tried to forget how a day which started so well had become a nightmare.

That evening, Ekanem and the children sat waiting for Okon. Supper had turned cold and Okon's mobile kept going to voicemail. He did not come home that night.

***

Ekanem was sitting under the guava tree peeling cassava when a motorcycle glided to a stop before her. "Oh my God," she exclaimed, jumping up from her stool. "What is wrong? What happened?"

The motorcycle rider helped the teacher carrying Udo off the back of the motorcycle. "Madam, we don't know what happened, but some of the pupils ran in to report that Udo had fallen in the playground and was foaming in the mouth.

"Eeeeeee," Ekanem wailed, jumping up and down and stamping her foot. She snatched Udo out of the teacher's arms. "Why would he just fall down and his mouth start foaming? I am sure those thugs you people call children did something to my son."

"Madam, nobody did anything to him. We took him to the clinic and the doctor said he has epilepsy."

"EPI-Wetin? It is you and the doctor's family who have epilepsy. My son does not have epilepsy. It does not exist in our family."

"I am just telling you what the doctor said, Madam."

"And I am just telling you that your doctor is a quack."

Ekanem was convinced the teacher and doctor did not know what they were saying. Since he had been brought home, Udo had been his usual self. He did not leave a morsel of the *garri* she served him on his plate. In the evening, he nagged until she let him go out in the yard to join Kufre and the other children. They were playing police and thief, chasing one another across the yard, when Udo fell to the ground for a second time. Some of the other children thought he was messing about and started laughing and mimicking him, until they saw his pupils disappear into this head and his tongue loll outside his mouth. When he began to thrash about violently, Kufre screamed for her mother.

Udo suffered two more fits over the next two days. When he woke up on the third day, Udo had lost the ability to speak. All the neighbours heard Ekanem's dirge right up to the main road. Okon buried himself deeper in the bottle; often coming back in the wee hours of the morning and sometimes not bothering to return home, leaving Ekanem to bear the increasingly heavy burden alone.

Three days after Udo had become dumb, Mama Edem came to visit. She made all the sympathetic noises other well-wishers before her had made but, unlike her predecessors, Mama Edem did not get up to leave after a few minutes. Her mouth was heavy and she had no intention of leaving until she made it lighter.

"Hmmmmm, there is more to this your problem than meets the eye, Mama Kufre," she said to Ekanem. "Only one person cannot have so much bad luck." Then, casting a suspicious glance at Kufre in the corner of the room, she lowered her voice, "I overheard Kufre telling Edem that she always eats in her dreams." Ekanem stared at her without comprehension.

"Must someone use all their mouth to talk before you understand?" she snapped.

"I don't know what you are talking about."

"I just came to warn you as a friend. People who eat in their sleep are witches. I am sure Kufre has a hand in all these misfortunes that keep befalling your family. You have to find a way to counter her before she finishes you off," she whispered from the side of her mouth, keeping her eyes on Kufre.

"Look, Mama Edem, I do not want any trouble o. Why would you come into my house and start calling my child a witch?"

"Why are you shouting? You want your daughter to cast her evil eye on me? I am only telling you what everyone knows. There is a pastor who specializes in witches. He has helped many people."

"Mama Edem, leave my house," Ekanem said, getting to her feet and walking to the door.

"Is it me you are throwing out of your house? Me? Mama Kufre?" Mama Edem asked, beating her chest.

"Please, I don't want any trouble, just go."

"Okay, when that witch of a thing you call a daughter finishes with all of you, do not say I did not warn you."

"I said GO!" Ekanem shouted, pushing her out and slamming the door.

Mama Edem stood outside the door shouting, "We do not want a witch in our midst. I don't want your child to come and transfer her witchcraft to my children."

"What is the matter, Mama Edem?" another neighbour asked.

"Is it not Mama Kufre and her witch child? Edem told me that Kufre eats in her dreams and I just came to advise Mama Kufre and she pushed me out of her house."

A few people had gathered round to listen to Mama Edem and they crossed themselves, hurrying away from the front of the building which housed the witch.

"Edem! Edem!!" Mama Edem shouted as she stormed off to her quarters. "Edem! Where is this stupid boy?"

"Mama, I am here," answered Edem as he ran up to her.

She latched her fingers around his ear, "Don't you ever let me see you playing with that Kufre girl again. Do you hear me?"

"Yeeeee.... Yes Mama," he cried.

"If I catch you even talking to her, I will kill you myself. I will not let anyone bring witchcraft into my house."

From that day, Ekanem made sure both Kufre and Udo slept in her room. For a long time that night, she could not sleep; her eyes alternated between Kufre and Udo. Silver streaks of dawn were tentatively laying claim to the sky by the time Ekanem fell into troubled slumber.

Udo did not suffer a fit the next day; nor the day after that, but, in the night, Ekanem heard Kufre laughing in her sleep.

Udo did not wake up the following morning.

✷✷✷

The day after the police came to the house to pick up Okon for arraignment, Ekanem went with Mama Edem to Freedom Bible Church. It was three days after Udo's burial. The women took Kufre with them to the church. The head of the church, Pastor Inyang, glanced up as the three of them walked into his office and said, "This child is a witch."

Mama Edem gave Ekanem an 'I told you so' look.

"Kneel down there," he said to Kufre. She looked around confusedly and made to hold her mother's hand. Ekanem shoved her forward.

The pastor walked around from his desk, grabbed the top of Kufre's head and forced her to the ground.

"When darkness comes before the light, it must bow down," he said. Then he prayed. "In the name of Jesus, I come against every evil spirit in this child."

Say Amen, Amen," he shouted at Ekanem and Mama Edem.

"AMEN."

"Father in heaven, I bind the spirit of witchcraft in this child. Holy Ghost fire! Holy Ghost fire, burn all the witches. Burn, Burn, BURN!" He screamed, then began to speak in tongues, bouncing on the balls of his feet. To Ekanem's surprise, he thrust his right fist forward; then the left: he was fighting spiritual enemies. Exhibiting the foot shuffle made popular by Muhammad Ali, he ducked his head, threw three swift jabs: left-right-left and continued ducking and weaving in the confined space. He never stopped praying. "I command all my enemies to be consumed by fire. Die, die, die, die, die," he chanted. "I bind all demons and witches and cast them into the fiery pits of hell."

Kufre began to cry. She got to her feet; Mama Edem rushed forward to push her back down; Pastor Inyang, caught up in his spiritual combat, was momentarily distracted. He hurried behind his desk, grabbed a broom made of palm fronds and whipped Kufre with it. Her screams were magnified in the enclosed space. Ekanem was shocked.

The pastor did not stop with a few strokes. The movement of his arm was frenetic. The louder Kufre screamed, the harder Pastor Inyang whipped.

"Confess, you witch. I say, confess your evil deeds," he shouted.

"I am not a witch, I am not a witch," howled Kufre.

"I said confess. Confess!"

Ekanem moved forward to come to Kufre's aid, but Mama Edem grabbed her arm. "Leave her," she said.

Wrenching her arm away, Ekanem threw her body over Kufre's prone frame. She had just lost a child, she was not going to let anybody kill the only one she had left.

Pastor Inyang turned on her angrily. "You are the reason this child is a witch. If you had not pampered her, she would not have been able to have powers. Now, her powers have multiplied and unless we remove the witchcraft from her, you and your family will not be safe."

Mama Edem nodded her head at the words of the pastor.

"Let me tell you," he continued. "The Holy Spirit revealed to me that this child has tied your womb. It is her plan to destroy you. As long as she remains a witch, you will never be able to conceive, talk less of having another child. Where is her father?"

"Pastor, the police came to take him away yesterday," Mama Edem said and proceeded to tell him about Okon's accident and about Udo's sickness and death.

"I knew it. I knew it," Pator Inyang was getting excited. "Everything bad that has been happening in your household is the fault of this child. While I was praying, I saw a vision in which you were crying. You looked like you had lost something, but this child sat on top of your chest laughing. The harder you cried, the more she laughed and she was not alone. She was with a group of children who joined her in laughing at your sorrow."

Ekanem sat sobbing on the floor.

"Your husband was not lying when he said he saw a chicken. Witches know how to manipulate shapes and forms. They can turn themselves into any animal and influence people's minds so that they believe they are seeing an animal instead of a human being. But it is not too late, the time to take your destiny in your own hands is now," Pastor Inyang insisted. "I pray that every plan the devil has concerning you fails in Jesus' name."

"Amen," shouted Mama Edem.

"Follow me," Pastor Inyang said.

Mama Edem helped Ekanem up and she reached down to give Kufre a hand.

"Leave her alone," snapped the pastor. "We need to give her time to realize that no child leaves Freedom Bible church as a witch. We know how to deal with them. Come with me, I want you to see something."

He walked out of the office, carefully locking the door behind them, and led Ekanem and Mama Edem round the back of the office block and towards the far end of the church compound, all the while talking about how his ministry had been founded to deliver the world from the evil clutches of witches.

A pungent smell assailed their noses and the wind carried a humming noise towards them. As they progressed further, it was clear that their destination was in the unkempt part of the compound which most of the church's congregation seldom visited.

They came up to the back of a small building. As they rounded the building, the smell became almost unbearable; Ekanem drew up the edge of her wrapper to cover her nose. The humming had progressed to a din.

The building, when seen from the front, was a bizarre menagerie. It contained a single room which had bars instead of a front wall. The room was filthy: the concrete floor was stained yellow with urine and there were fingerprints of brown excrement trailing along the walls. A veranda on which people could walk and observe the room ran the entire length of the building. Inside the menagerie were 23 grimy children, crouched or lying down, whose ages ranged between six and fourteen years.

Pastor Inyang climbed on to the veranda and everyone became silent; dozens of eyes watched his every move. Mama Edem followed him, but Ekanem shrunk back.

"Come, woman," he beckoned. "All the children you see here are witches. We have taken it upon ourselves to reform them." He walked to the end of the veranda. "Do you see that child there?" he asked, pointing at a girl of about nine years huddled in the far right end of the room. "You! Mercy, come here." Mercy stared at them with doleful eyes and did not move.

"Are you deaf? I said come here."

She got up slowly and hobbled to the front of the room. Ekanem saw that her ankles and wrists were shackled and she turned to the pastor in shock.

"Tell these women what you are," Pastor Inyang said to Mercy.

She looked at her grubby feet.

"I said tell them what you are," he shouted, banging on the iron bars that separated them from Mercy and the others.

"I am a witch." The voice was feeble; resigned.

Pastor Inyang turned to his audience of two. "She is a witch," he repeated. "Do you know what this witch did?" He did not wait for an answer before continuing. "She wiped out the whole of her family single-handed. Her father, mother and two brothers."

"How did she do that?" Ekanem asked.

"She caused their death by making a trailer run over their car. The trailer crushed the part of the car she was sitting in, but she was the only one who survived."

"But that could have just been an accident," Ekanem said. Mama Edem elbowed Ekanem in the side.

Pastor Inyang said: "If that was just an accident, how do you explain the fact that after her father's brother took her in, he lost his job less than three months later? A job he had worked at for more than twelve years, and then his son suddenly became sick and died."

Ekanem saw many of the children trying to hide behind others.

"You see those two boys over there? They are twin wizards and killed their mother during childbirth. They did not want her to have any more children. Look at that girl on the left. She made her sister lame and killed two of her father's wives."

"But why do they have to live like this?"

"They are witches, and witches are worse than animals. They know the difference between good and evil, but still choose to practise evil. They have to confess their sins, repent and renounce their witchcraft. Only then can we finally cleanse them of the evil spirit of witchcraft. Until this happens, they are not fit to live among human beings. They will remain here on display, so that they know that only repentance will save them."

"But pastor...," Ekanem said.

"Let me tell you," Pastor Inyang interrupted. "All of these witches have been rejected by their families and even their villages. Our church does not believe in turning anyone away. Jesus Christ loves everyone, even the sinners. This is why we bring them under our wing when no one else wants them."

He beckoned at a lanky girl, "Uduak, come here. Turn to your other side."

Both Ekanem and Mama Edem gasped. The left side of her face was shiny molten ebony wax. Her ear was unrecognizable; sealed into the side of her face and extending to the back of her head.

"Her father poured petrol on her and set her on fire," Pastor Inyang said. "See the boy near the front with the sore on his head? His uncle drove a nail into his skull. Here at Freedom Bible church, we do not treat them the way many out there do, but we will not pamper them either." He stared at Ekanem; eyes burning with intensity. She looked away.

They made their way back to Pastor Inyang's office. He unlocked the door: Kufre sat cross-legged in the middle of the floor, snot and tears running down her face and the front of her dress. Ekanem saw Kufre steal a quick glance at her, then cower when Pastor Inyang looked her way.

Ekanem crouched in front of Kufre, gathered her in her arms and to the incredulity of both Mama Edem and Pastor Inyang, said to her daughter, "Don't worry, we are going home."

Ayodele Morocco-Clarke was born in Lagos, Nigeria – a descendant of kin from the West Indies, Sierra Leone and the Republic of Benin – and is currently living in the United Kingdom. Often describing herself as 'Stubbornly Unconventional', her prose and poetry have appeared in numerous print and online journals and anthologies. Her short story 'When the Chips are Down' was shortlisted for the International Students' Short Story Competition in 2010.

The Lost Friend

Elizabeth Ngozi Okpalaenwe

I AM A GENIUS WRITER. I was brought up in a family where education was paramount. At the age of four, my father began to teach me how to read and write. He believed that I was the cleverest of his five children though I was the youngest. His desire to take me to the ladder of learning spurred me on. When I was ten years old, my father would compare my writing with that of my elder brothers and sisters and abuse them for being so slow to learn. By the age of eighteen, I had written five short stories that were waiting for publication.

My school friends exclaimed at me, clapped their hands. They surrounded me; tall, beautiful, impossibly glamorous, and I shrank away from them as they turned me into an object of caricature.

"A genius writer, what a stupid title for an insipid person," Jane blurted out. "You claim to be a genius and you carve yourself out of our circle." My cheeks blazed, as I pulled my hands under my cloak. "I hope your little brain will not cajole you to think that just because your dad adores you, we all must bow down to your arrogant and unattainable utterances," she sneered. My whole body was getting warmer as I wondered how far I could stretch and swallow these abusive utterances. The danger was that I exposed my temper, but it could be risky to face them alone. I became Jane's shadow, and was usually ignored by her friends.

It took me a little while to sort out who was who. Of her inner circle, Jane was the only one from Bamenda. Henrietta was a brisk, cheerful girl from Kumba – I think she would have been happier sailing or playing tennis than practising music and studying poetry, but she had a crystal-clear soprano voice which made me tremble when I heard it. Newly arrived at the college, her roommate, Jessie, made a big show of her superior knowledge of the world, although Beatrice said that she could not see how spending two months abroad qualified her to patronize us. She had inherited her dancer's body from her Barossa mother, and I always felt uncomfortable when she was around. Tina, the plump girl, made me uneasy. She had started her studies in Beta, but transferred to St Agnes's College a couple of years ago, although I was not sure why. She had calculating grey eyes, and whenever they came to rest on me – which wasn't often – they seemed to look beneath the surface and be unimpressed by what they saw. I felt unsafe when Jane and her group of glamorous friends were around me. I was part of that group until jealousy came in.

Jane herself never missed an opportunity to make an annoying comment about my writing or criticism over my use of a new word. Although Jane closed her eyes to many things, her expression changed constantly with her thoughts, like sunshine chasing clouds across the mountainside. Instead of the tight little pout affected by most Bamenda girls, her lips were large and mobile, and never seemed to quite close, and her creamy skin was freckled, as if she had been lightly dusted in brown sugar.

I turned pages at her recitals, carried her music, ran errands to the post office or the pharmacist to make peace. I hated myself for serving her to no avail. Her cronies split their sides, of course, but the names they called me – "Slave! Bitch!" – hurt me. They also teased me about Rita, my best friend. Rita was a vulnerable person who was hated by her family, especially her stepmother. They threw her out in the street when she became pregnant.

I was lonely and withdrew from them, but the more I sought the seclusion of my inner self, the more Jane became a pain in the neck.

We all hired a three-bedroom flat together close to the school. The building was a bit hidden in the corner of the city. It was a popular place where students would gather to gossip after school. When the front of the house was in shadow, silhouetted against the diffused light of the moon, the two small windows of the cold room glowed like golden eyes, which made the house look like a black cat, its haunches up, head down, ready to pounce.

One night, I walked down the drive and the stones crunched under my laboured steps, sounding unnaturally loud. I was finding it difficult to concentrate on my writing. The thought of Rita distracted me and I felt sad. This was where we used to come to be together. I needed a quiet place to work and I went to the orchard with my notes. I stepped into the dense shadow at the side of the house, where the branches of the trees arched over my head. Even in the light breeze, I could hear them scraping against the brickwork, like teeth gnawing on a bone. I felt like I had walked into a feral creature's mouth. There was rustling in the wood. I jumped at the sound of twigs breaking. When I turned to look into the blackness, I saw nothing.

Even though I was glad to get back indoors, the air in the room was too warm and stuffy. I walked through to the kitchen and sat down but, in a moment of uncertainty, I turned, half expecting to see other girls, but instead the house was empty. I picked up the manuscript I planned to publish. As I was about to move out of the house, Jane appeared and said:

"Oh, do stop showing off, Nelly, we all know you are a circus act. The little secret you have concerning your friend Rita seems to be turning your head round like a circle. That is not enough reason to avoid our glamorous group." I kept quiet but she continued. "Are you deaf and dumb? Where is your so-called best friend?"

"Jane, two people cannot be mad at the same time."

Her countenance changed instantly. She screamed.

Her screams attracted the attention of her friends who instead cheered and clapped their hands. Delighted at their behaviour, I could not help myself. I lifted her up and threw her to the ground.

"You claim to be religious but you are evil. You want to kill me," Jane stammered beneath her breath, as she struggled to disengage herself from the ground. I picked up my books and went away. The others looked at me as if they were scared.

Having been helped by her friends, Jane and the rest of them entered the house. I could hear them talking at the top of their voices. It was like a noisy train singing 'Ho o o o', not making sense. It was not surprising that none of the girls spoke to me that day.

The rain was threatening. I had no umbrella but I went on all the same. The wind snatched the red cap on my head and ran off as if someone had sent for it. I followed, not knowing how far it would go before I caught up with it. There was a drizzle for a while, quenching the hot air that had possessed the day.

Eventually, I took my work to the manager of the Sunshine Publishing Company, Mr Putty. He was short, stout and had a rounded stomach like a pot which made him actually look more like a chimpanzee than a human being. His eyebrows were really bushy, exposing the two eyes that stuck out like rats from a hole. In no sense did he have a handsome bearing that women would love to hang around with. I restrained my giggling when I looked down and saw his small legs. I wondered if he could find his size of shoes in the market. Everything about him was below average.

"I will give you a call," Mr Putty said.

I decided to check on him after two weeks of patiently waiting to receive word by mail, letter or phone. He took me into his office. The office was not the epitome of superior quality as I had imagined. It was disorganized to the highest degree, cluttered with papers and manuscripts scattered all over the floor. There was hardly a space on the table. The floor was dirty. The long glass windows were decked in light brown curtains that added to the dirtiness of the office. One could hear the birds chirp as they moved from tree to tree. A rainbow bird perched on the window, made a piercing noise and flew away. When he sat on the chair, I could see his legs dangling in the air under the desk. He invited me to a seat. For the next ten minutes, he kept looking at my manuscript.

"Had he not read my work for two weeks now?" I wondered. After what seemed like ages, he looked up and sighed.

"Young lady, you are an earnest writer. I like your choice of words because it helps to bring your message across. You clearly expose the ills in our society and the moral decadence that has devoured society like a cancer. But the general public will not be interested in such things as morals and good etiquette. If you want the general public to read your work you must avoid such things."

I opened my mouth wide and closed it again. What nonsense! Sweat settled on my palms and my forehead. I saw my pride crippled beneath my feet. I found it impossible to comprehend how anyone in his right senses could condemn a good moral story. My fingers cracked momentarily on my lap. I was angry, afraid and resentful of Mr Putty. I was barely listening when he continued.

"You have the gift of writing all the same, but you have to take this manuscript back and rewrite your story. You must add things that interest the readers. We cannot take this for publication because there is no market for it."

"With all due respect, sir," I began, "I did a lot of research."

He frowned, nodded several times. "I see. Would you want us to edit your work before publication or would you do it yourself?"

"I would like to publish it the way it is, sir," I answered emphatically.

"Then you have to take your work back. Your work is good, but you need to spice it up more to meet the public interest."

"How do you mean, sir?" I inquired.

"Well, if you want to publish your work the way it is, you have to pay for the production and publication. I do not think the publishing company would like to embark on this project. Will you be ready to pay 500,000 francs for the printing and 500,000 francs for publication? Can you afford that?"

I looked at the floor and tears slid down my cheeks.

"I do not have time for your tears. As you can see, there are many people waiting out there." He became more emphatic. "Young lady, people these days prefer to enjoy life while it lasts. If you want this establishment to publish your work, you must talk about things like erotic love, jealousy, suicide, politics and things like that or else you take your work to someone else." He got up from his seat, handed me my manuscript and pretended to be busy.

"Excuse me sir," I said, getting up as well. I wanted to explain further my idea of writing but he walked away from the table and turned his back to me. Screaming could not bring out the turbulence that formed in my chest. It was difficult to go back to the house and face those irresponsible girls. That was not my main preoccupation anyway. Then I recalled my father's words: *never despair or give up in the face of adversity.* I picked up my manuscript again, read through it. I did not see the point of either changing my writing or my thoughts. "Buck up a bit," I told myself.

I sat outside the office feeling a bit annoyed at his ideas, which were totally different from mine. Well, it was only one man's opinion. I was relieved that, after all, there were other publishers, and I also felt resolved as I went out again.

As I walked, I felt dejected. My legs were heavy and felt like they could not carry me any more. The weather suddenly became cold and chilly though the sun had risen. The trees were as still as death. I was nervous and walked slowly back to my room, not caring about who would know or see my tears. Reflecting over my meeting with Mr Putty, it was clear that he required me to revisit my writing style and his suggestion that I pay money to have my book published was done only to make me accept his conditions. I was not happy with the reasons he gave me for rejecting my work. He felt it was a moral story and did not have the social aspect that would interest the public. I needed a break and time to think again. Before I could do anything, Jane appeared.

"Oh, there you are," she said. "The police came to our flat to seek information about Rita. You were not around; I did not have much information to give them."

"Why are they looking for me?"

"The police discovered the body of a young girl on the bank of the river. And the examination of her body indicated that she must have committed suicide. She was your friend, Nelly. They wanted to know more about her life."

"Oh my God, but what makes you think I know what happened to her?" I exclaimed.

"You were there at John's party. They were discussing her, over dinner."

"I wasn't there for dinner."

"You came late with your so-called boyfriend, Leng, but you sat at the table while they talked about her. I remember I was standing opposite you."

"You are very observant." There was a long pause, but I remained silent, and eventually she spoke again.

"Rita was a highly talented but disturbed young woman. She had asked me for help a number of times, but, but…"

"But, what! You refused to help her, so why are you so interested in knowing about her now?"

"No, it is the police who wish to know whether she threw herself off a bridge and drowned, or if someone pushed her." Jane was looking at me in a strange way, as if I might have been the one who pushed her. "You *saw* her! You were there."

I didn't move a muscle, but the tension in the room increased perceptibly.

"Nelly, no matter what the situation, we are still friends. I just want to know what happened to her, that is all," Jane said.

"No, Jane, we are not friends. I am sick of you interfering with my life."

"This is not about your life anyway. I want to know if Rita died because she was neglected. She was our friend too."

My mouth went dry.

"Jane, who sent you to find out about Rita?" I asked impatiently.

"Nobody, but all the girls living in the flat are concerned after seeing the police."

I burst into tears. "None of you cared about her when she was alive. She died depressed and starved of love and care. So what *do* you want her story for?"

"I just want to get the information from you. The police need to know what happened and how she died."

"You are not the police." I said quickly.

"I understand that. But you may be the only living witness to what happened to Rita. She was with you most of the time," Jane responded.

I nodded in spite of myself. "I don't have to give evidence to you," I challenged.

"If you don't tell me what happened I will go straight to the police."

How could I explain? I took a deep breath. "I knew Rita very well – better than most people. I knew about her depression and unhappy situation. What I mean is... I can see that, after what happened at home with the issue of her pregnancy, the state of mind she was in... what she did was inevitable. It made sense emotionally, at least. But I didn't know that her body was discovered about twenty kilometres away by the police."

"Please now tell me the whole story," said Jane insistently.

"Jane, it is a long and sad story," I began. "Rita was depressed and unhappy. I had tried on various occasions to advise her in my own little way but she was really in a difficult situation," I paused and continued, almost in tears. "She is the only child of her mother. Her mother was the third wife. She died when

Rita was five years old. She was brought up by her stepmother who treated her like a slave. Rita never knew what love was like in her home. When she gained admission to the school, it was her cousin who brought her to our flat with practically nothing: no fees, books, provision, even the basic things a girl of her age required. I felt sorry for her and gave her some of my clothes and food as well. She was a lovely girl."

"Poor girl, but how did she die?" Jane's voice had grown softer.

"Her situation went from bad to worse when she went home during the holidays and was raped by her stepbrother and she became pregnant. I advised her against opting for an abortion. She was so depressed and the issue of what would happen to her and the child tormented her. When she informed her father, he did not believe her. Instead it earned her another beating and of course the family did not want to hear that her stepbrother was responsible. It was an abomination. Poor girl, she had nowhere to turn and she chose to end it."

"Did you report this to the police?"

"No, I did not tell anyone. I did not know that her body would be discovered and moreover no one cared about her, not even her family. The knowledge of her death had weighed me down too," I paused. Light could be seen through the cracks in the walls. The lamp shone pale, and the shadows in the room were less well defined.

"Two days before she died, which was the day she had the abortion, she disclosed to me how depressed she was. She suffered intensely. She made me promise that I would keep it secret but offer prayers for her. Ignorantly, I agreed to keep her secret as my last respect to her."

"She was really emotionally vulnerable. A victim of denied love," Jane observed. "Nelly, you look far away from me. What is going on?"

"I am thinking, instead of telling the police how she died, which may not yield much empathy, I am going to write a story about Rita and how she committed suicide. There I will be able to speak about the circumstances that lead unfortunate people to death. I am going to elevate her as a hero."

I shivered as the cold evening air seeped through my worn jacket. Though the moon was still bright, cloud had started to drift in from the west and the stars were hard to make out. I pulled my hands up into my sleeves and Jane came closer to me.

"I think that will make for compelling reading."

The more I thought of it now, the clearer it became to me that such a moving story would satisfy both my publisher and me. Yes, I am going to write a story about suicide. By the time the police finish their investigation, Rita's story will be displayed in all the bookshops.

Sister Elizabeth Ngozi Okpalaenwe is a Holy Rosary Sister and the author of two novels, *The Power to Succeed* (2005) and *The Power to Make a Choice* (2011). She is also a playwright: *Two Plays*. She draws on natural myths, daily experiences and uses flashback symbolism to enrich her dramatic style. She did her master's degree in counselling at the University of East Anglia, England. She loves praying, travelling, reading and writing. She is a Nigerian currently on her way to Sierra Leone.

The Man with the Hole in his Face

Namwali Serpell

"I CAN'T BELIEVE YOU'VE never partied in the bush," Scholie said with his mongrel accent, a voice like flipping through satellite TV stations. He touched the small of Tandi's back as he helped her onto the Landrover. He sat her on the bench behind the driver's seat and tucked a blanket around her. She thought he might kiss her on the forehead. When he started the engine, it thrumped like a dying animal, then the rhythm accelerated to a screechy hum. They jerked forward violently. He glanced back. "Oops," he said in his own voice; she shivered and off they went.

When he turned the Landrover onto a dirt road, the rumble of the tyres gave way to an uneven crunching, with the occasional splash as they went through a puddle. The breeze of their momentum became satiny. Soon the vehicle was submerged in sound: spiralling calls and burps and gurgles. There was a buzz that sometimes whined louder and then insect wings would flick Tandi's cheeks. She held the blanket over her mouth and stared into the darkness. There would be animals out there. But she saw no sign of life and if the headlamps now and again caught beady flashes on the horizon, she could not distinguish them from the stars.

Her eyes were growing tired when the Landrover suddenly stopped. Scholie held his hand up and said, "Shhh". She reached for his shoulder and, just then, the vehicle leapt ahead at top speed, its roof scraped by low tree limbs. Tandi instinctively lifted her bum and the blanket slipped off. Insects catapulted off her body. Her hair weave, carefully pressed that morning, tangled in the wind. There was a sting in her right eye and then another. She rubbed at it but the stinging grew worse, coming in progressive stabs. Her blinking became like a seizure. Tears looped down her cheek, buffeted into odd paths by the wind. She screamed with frustration and Scholie looked back. Only when she heard her voice did she realize she was shaking. He slowed the Landrover and turned off the engine. He stepped over the division between them and switched on the torch on his key ring.

"Stop blinking."

"I can't."

"I can't see what's wrong unless you stop blinking."

Torch in one hand, he used the fingers of the other hand to stretch her eye open, exposing the pinpricks of pain.

"There's an insect in your eye."

"Oh God," she stuttered, "it's biting me from the inside."

"Keep it cool, it's the one's gonna die," he smiled. He pulled her eye open again, wider this time. He pursed his lips and blew with quick force. She blinked. Again. His breath rushed against the tender skin and the moment grew still and wide, so wide she could almost feel the spray of his saliva. She shuddered, tears welling from the socket. Her eye still felt sore but the stinging was gone.

"Why were you driving so fast?" she snapped.

"I heard something," he said, grinning. "You can't be too careful."

When they got to the bushcamp, Scholie helped her step off the Landrover but it was in a practised way that annoyed her. He glanced down at her heels and she stumbled, cursing as he left her easily, striding toward the fire to slap palms in greeting. He grinned, his teeth glinting in the light of the bonfire. By the time Tandi had made her way around the puddles, Scholie was seated with a beer between his legs, shaking the pale hand of a white girl.

Among the tourists, nobody knew anybody but everybody knew everybody: recognizable knots in the informal net of backpackers draped over southern Africa. There was a group of Nordic creatures gleaming under the crisp of their sunburn; a gaggle of British girls who soon took over the drinking, dictating its pace and quantity; a South African couple who spent much of the night entwined; and finally, the American girl, wobbly and giggly and all on her own.

There were three other safari guides apart from Scholie, all Zambians. Tandi waved hellos to them over the fire. They all knew her from JollyBoys: she would ring them to arrange drives or hikes for the hostel guests. Two local girls sat with the guides, whinnying and tossing their plaits. Tandi was thankful for them; her outfit was tame in comparison. She went to sit by Scholie nevertheless. She didn't want anyone to get the wrong impression.

As she approached, she noticed the American girl's grandfather laugh and that Scholie didn't look up. Tandi levered herself down, negotiating her heels and her tight jeans. She looked around, taking in the canvas tents that circled the circle of people, and the darkness that circled them all. She leaned forward to catch Scholie's eye. He smiled and winked, except the wink fluttered as he mimicked her from earlier. She shook her head sheepishly but her pulse raced with the memory of his breath on her. She wished that she'd checked her hair in the Landrover mirror. Scholie leaned away from the white girl, who was sitting on the other side of him.

"Little TandyCandy," he said. "You were so cute. You shook like a chicken in the rain, you."

He sounded Zambian, his accent shorn of the twangs and twirls he'd accumulated over years of making himself clear to tourists. Tandi smiled. He *would* like it that she had been so helpless. Their ongoing joke was that she was a dam and he was the water and if he persevered, she would one day open her floodgates.

The American girl leaned forward to look at Tandi. Or through her: the girl's gaze was thick with drink and she scratched absently at her arm, the bracelets strung there like remnants on a clothesline. Tandi reached across Scholie's legs and introduced herself. The girl clasped Tandi's hand loosely and replied with her forgettable name. Tandi caught a whiff of her. She smelled like tea biscuits on a tin plate in the midday sun. Her hair was ragged as the flames and almost the same colour. At that point, Tandi was naïve enough to pity her.

The wind lifted. The bonfire hollered and the tents sounded like clapping hands. Scholie and the girl resumed their chat. There was nothing for Tandi to do but eavesdrop and stare at the fire's unruly death. The girl was explaining that she had started drinking early, that she had snuck into the Royal Livingstone for afternoon cocktails on the patio. She called it the Loyo, an inside joke among locals, and Scholie asked where she'd heard it.

"My bungee instructor."

"Really? Who was that?" he asked, testing her.

"His name was Chongo."

"I love that guy, he's mad," Scholie laughed. "His name means shut up. When d'you jump?"

"I bungee... jamp? I mean jumped," she giggled, "yesterday."

"What did you think?"

"Oh-my-God. Spiritual experience. Like I was truly alive for the first time in my life."

Tandi stood up and moved to the other side of the fire. Scholie didn't notice. One of the Nordic tourists sitting nearby caught her eye and lifted a hand. Tandi smiled and smoothed her hair, subtly slapping the seam of her weave. She wished she had moved up her plaiting appointment; she would have to withstand the needling itch for two more days. The tourist moved closer and handed her a beer and she thanked him. They sipped in unison and conducted a *pro forma* interview: where they were from, what they had studied at Uni, their names. She was about to ask the tourist whether his job suited his degree any better than hers when she heard Scholie's voice – "It's biting me from the inside!" – and then his baritone laugh.

She turned to look at him. He was lying on his side with his head tipped back as he laughed. There were already three empty Mosi bottles leaning against his thigh. The tourist called out to him.

"Vhat is so funny over dare?"

Scholie had to look past Tandi to reply and his eyes flinched as if burnt by the anger in hers.

"It's her story," he gestured to her with his beer. "You tell it," he said.

Her anger was engulfed by nerves. Everyone was looking at her. Tandi took a sip of beer and told the story quickly, mocking herself to temper it.

"It happened just now," Scholie confirmed with a grin. "I'm the one who saved her."

"Ach, sat. Shuttup, *iwe*." She sucked her teeth under a smile.

Scholie goaded another guide, Muli, into telling a story. Muli's voice was booming, his tone mellow with Mosi. His story unfolded at its own pace and grew more and more amusing and soon everyone was fitting their laughter into his pauses. The stories that followed were the same as always, each teller trumping the last until the insect in Tandi's eye had led to Muli's hyena, an elephant trampling in Zimbabwe, a mauled baby in Kasama, and a drowning in Lake Malawi. The two local girls made their exit. Clinging to Muli's arms, they teetered over to his Landrover, trailing excuses.

"Wow, wow. That's deep," Scholie was saying about the drowning. He faced away from Tandi but she could see from the ripple in his shoulder that his hand was on the girl and it was moving. The conversation seemed destined to fragment. The South African couple was snogging again and Tandi was reaching for a beer when the American girl sat up and spoke.

"I had this really intense thing happen to me last week, close to Impala," she began. Mbala, Tandi thought irritably, it's a town, not an animal.

"We had stopped earlier in the day to see that crazy British guy's house? It was super fascinating, you know, so we stayed longer than we'd planned. The couple I was with was fighting so I was like, look: I'll drive. But then it gets dark and it's clear we're like nowhere near Impala. I'm totally fine, I'm sober, driving straight, lights on full blast, not going super fast. So me and the guy in the passenger seat, Matt, *we* start fighting. He's saying we should gun it and I'm like, no, let's pull over and sleep in the car. We can't convince each other so we decide to ask his girlfriend, who's sleeping in the back. We're looking back at her, going Jess, Jess, wake up. Then: bam!"

Scholie sat up.

"Bam, what?" he asked.

"We hit this guy."

Tandi's head tipped back slightly, like she'd been knocked on the chin. Maybe it was just the beery drowse but it felt like they had all stumbled into a private room.

"Did he die?"

"No, no," the girl said hastily, spinning her hands. "I hit him but then we swerved off the road into a ditch. It was wild. We literally felt the tyre blow, like" – she trapped her curled fingers behind her thumb and flicked them forward in a spraying motion – "poof! The car slams into a bank and the only light in this whole place is coming from us. It's pitch black. All we can hear is the seatbelt alarm and the crickets. Jess wakes up but she doesn't know we hit someone so she starts talking about how we're already using our only spare. I'm shaking like I've just done a skydive or something. Matt starts explaining and then we see these eyes glowing in the dark. Jess thinks it's an animal and starts freaking out but it's a kid, a little African boy. He comes up to the car and knocks on my window and I open it. He's got no shoes. He has that little potbelly from starving and his face has this rash. He doesn't speak English and he's super young and he's crying so hard, I can't hear what he's saying. Then he reaches in and grabs my arm to come come, he knows that word: come.

"I get out and my legs feel like jelly and I almost fall but I keep going with the kid. I see a man lying on the road. There's a bicycle a few feet away. The guy was riding with his son and I hit his back wheel and sent them both flying. The boy landed in the grass so he's not so beat up. I just give him some Kleenex to hold against a scrape on his arm. I take a closer look at his dad. The guy's bleeding some, mostly from his leg and his face, and he's moaning and stuff. I know some first aid so I tie my t-shirt above his knee. The kid is whimpering and staring at me because I'm in my bra and he's in shock and I'm in shock and his dad's bleeding on the ground and it's just a clusterfuck.

"I yell back to the car and they come over with a flashlight and, first thing, Matt gives me his t-shirt. Up close, the guy's a mess. So intense. Lots of blood and there's a hole above his lip where you can see the gum. Matt says the guy's drunk on the local drink. It smells like rotting fruit..."

"*Chibuku*," Scholie said.

"Yeah," the girl continued, "he's wasted on that stuff. So we decide that I should stay with him because Jess is too scared to stay there alone and Matt doesn't want to go for help alone. We find this concrete building without a roof, you know, it's unfinished? We use our tent to make a gurney and we carry him to the building: his leg doesn't look broken but he's definitely too drunk to stand up. Matt and Jess take off with the flashlight so they can find their way back to a town we passed a few miles back. I wait with the guy and the kid and some Castle to keep me company."

The girl described how the night had passed. How the boy fell asleep but the man kept moaning. How the man became delirious and she got a bit drunk on the beer. How dawn arrived and they were still waiting. Tandi could see the scene: the boy curled like a scared *chongololo*, the waxy rainy-season light coming through the holes in the cheap concrete. She thought she knew how the story would end: a patched tyre, a race to the hospital, a resuscitation. Perhaps there would even be a quasi-adoption of the boy: sponsored schooling, rashes fading, potbelly diminished. But then the girl just stopped. Her words trailed off and she looked down. After a pause, she spoke.

"It was super intense. The guy had this hole in his face. Not quite skydiving but, you know."

She laughed and after a beat, the rest of them laughed too. Except for Tandi, who wasn't laughing, who was somehow certain that she wasn't telling the whole truth. But the girl was already on her feet, raising her beer with a whoop. She wanted to dance, she said. Someone pulled out a radio and rumba was soon twittering out of it. Tandi watched Scholie rock his hips in front of the white girl. Sex had arrived, with all of its tender collusion. The wind picked up, raising copper in the embers. The canvas tents applauded.

Two days later, she saw the white girl again. Tandi was sitting on the kerb, waiting for the coach back to Lusaka. Most locals couldn't afford it but Tandi knew the manager from making bookings for JollyBoys. She had called in the favour that morning, knowing she wouldn't be able to withstand a minibus. Drinking had been an inevitable part of her job at the hostel but Tandi had never quite gotten used to it. The party the JollyBoys staff had insisted on throwing for her the night before had left her utterly wrecked.

Two packs of tourists showed up around the same time to catch the coach. One was a group of guys from JollyBoys: she remembered their unplaceable accents. Tandi smiled weakly and waved but she didn't have to avoid eye contact. Now that they had checked out, they wouldn't bother with her. They didn't find her interesting. Tandi had just been the woman who spoke uncluttered English to them as she handed them keys and printed their bill.

The others were Americans. Squatting on her bag, knees tenting her skirt, the girl joined their lazy morning revelry: beer and *chitumbuas*. It's that girl, Tandi thought, and felt an itch in her mind. What was her name again? The girl's raspy laugh dredged up that night at the bonfire: seeing them together, those fingers gleaming on Scholie's arm. She could have been any girl from any time during the months that Tandi had worked in Livingstone, but she wasn't. She was that girl from that night and Tandi swiftly hated her.

She was incredulous when the girl pitched up in the aisle next to Tandi's seat and asked if she could sit. Tandi looked around. The coach was nearly full.

"Yes, no, I guess it's available," Tandi said sullenly and moved into the window seat.

The girl smiled and slung her bag into the gap in front of the aisle seat. The bag looked heavy and where its strap had hung on her shoulder, the skin was wrung red. The girl sat, one foot on her bag, the other leg bent as if she were a half-collapsed chair. Tandi looked at the girl's shoe resting on her bag. They both wore their layer of grime patiently, in the way of martyred objects. The girl – Tandi still couldn't remember her name – took out her ponytail, filling the air with a candysweat smell. Tandi reached for her bottle of ice water. The girl's hair, the colour of unripe maize, made her thirsty just looking at it. The girl was combing her fingers through it, pulling it into a new ponytail possessed of its own gravity: heavy in its lightness.

The girl didn't seem to recognize Tandi. They had met before Tandi had gotten her hair plaited. Still. The girl pulled out a paperback. She tried to fan herself with it but the pages released only a weak sugary must. She puffed her lips out at Tandi to signal her discomfort. Tandi mimed commiseration and opened her bottle of water, the plastic crackling unhappily as the vacuum released. The chill crept down her throat – a feeling both delicate and sharp – but when the water hit her stomach, she felt the hangover descend like a demon. She shut her eyes to fight the nausea but it was slippery and coiling, she couldn't wrangle it down. She needed to eat. She pulled the food warmer out of her *kiyondo*. The shortbread biscuits the JollyBoys cook had baked for her this morning were still steaming. The girl looked over.

"Would you like one?" Tandi held out the container reluctantly. The girl peered inside.

"Oh, a cookie? Sure," she said, taking one with her closebitten fingers. What was her name? Tandi seemed to recall that it had the snap and purr of a fickle cat but that was about it. Scholie would know, of course, but Tandi would never see Scholie again. And she wouldn't ask him about this girl even if she did see him. Which she wouldn't. The girl crunched into her biscuit.

"It's just like those ones on safari!" she said. The biscuit's dust cast a loose galaxy on her lips.

"What did you see on your safari?" Tandi asked with the exact rhythm and tone that she used at JollyBoys. The girl responded at length, chewing through Tandi's biscuits along the way. This was the way all the tourists spoke after they returned from a game drive, naming the animals one by one. Her forearms on the front desk, Tandi would nod and smile at them, watching their wind-brightened eyes dim with each animal they listed. The things of the world are better left unsaid.

The bus gave a hitch and its bowels began to grumble. Tandi's bowels responded in kind. The air conditioning gushed down with the smell of scrubbed dust. Biscuits or no, Tandi was going to be sick on this bus. Something was crawling up her throat and saliva brimmed in her gullet.

"Who was your guide?" She knew she was only hurting herself by asking.

"This guy, um—" Tandi didn't wait for his name.

"Was he any good?

"Oh, he was amazing. I met him at a bonfire a couple nights ago. We went for a drive the next morning."

"What did he teach you?" Tandi flexed the tone so the girl might catch her meaning.

"He told me about the musting, you know how the bulls – the boy elephants – go in heat. It kind of made me think of my period, you know the way it runs down their leg." She paused with a grin. "That's probably because my guide told me this joke: what's an elephant's tampon?"

Tandi raised an eyebrow.

"A sheep."

The girl rocked into her grandfather laugh but Tandi sneered to show her distaste. The girl noticed and when she had properly sorted through her laughter, thoroughly explored every nook of it to her satisfaction, she put her hand on Tandi's shoulder and complained.

"But it's hilarious. Come on, you're not so innocent."

The bus descended into a gorge in the road and Tandi turned to the window as it rose, her plaits strumming the seat in front of her. There was nothing she could do; she caught it in the warmer. Barely anything came up: a grainy mush, water, and something with a putrid yellow colour with no purpose but to warn people away. Tandi closed the lid on the mess. She wiped her mouth.

"Sorry."

"You okay?" the girl stroked her back. "I used to get car sick all the time growing up."

"No, I'm just hungover," Tandi whispered but the girl had already begun to recount her childhood. As the bus heaved along, Tandi fixed her eyes on the girl's face to stave off the nausea. She stared at the thin beige nose, its smattering of dark freckles like make-up she hadn't rubbed in.

Tandi wondered what would happen if those spots grew in number, merged, crowded the girl's face with darkness.

How different her life would be, the life she was still stitching into a threadbare story with her patchy memories of a small town in California.

When the bus turned onto the tarmac road, it was like an exhalation and it gave Tandi an excuse to look away. She stared out the window as if lulled by the blur. There was a pause, then the girl opened her paperback. Tandi closed her eyes and rested her head against the glass, her fresh plaits squeaking. She hated that this girl felt free to talk to her this way, to touch her. But wasn't that why Tandi had come to Livingstone? To meet new people. To befriend them in the name of that mantra: opportunity. She had mostly just wanted to get away from Lusaka but when she had moved to Livingstone, she had met Scholie, and now she was going back to Lusaka to get away from him so that when he pitched up at JollyBoys and said, Hey man, where's TandyCandy? they'd say, Sorry man, she's bounced.

Tandi woke from her nap. The clouds had darkened and rain was tapping the window. The bus climbed a winding road, spots of death on the banks marked with plastic flowers and white crosses. Down in the shadowy valleys, she could see the carcasses of unclaimed wrecks. The rain made diagonal slashes over the million scratches on the window. Through the crosshatch, Tandi saw her face reflected: big eyes, small nose; big lips, small chin. She kissed her lips inward to spread the lipstick and then she saw the girl's face behind hers, looking not at the world outside the window but at Tandi. Their glances touched in the compounded reflection. Tandi felt obliged to turn.

"Are you feeling any better, you poor thing?"

Tandi nodded.

"I've never taken this bus from Livingstone to Lusaka. It was my first time at the Falls."

"What did you think?"

"Oh my god. So. Fucking. Beautiful. I've seen a lot of waterfalls, like in Cambodia and this amazing one in

Thailand. But this was something else. The perfect circle rainbow? So amazing."

She reached for her bag and her head bounced against the seat in front of her.

"Oops," she said like a child who had made a mistake. "Good thing it's so soft," she laughed, stroking the fuzz on the seat back. Tandi noticed then that the whole bus was furry: the ceiling, the aisle, even the walls, every surface coated with a coarse grey flecked with primary colours. An inside-out animal. Her scanning eye hit a mirror at the front, a large disc above the driver. Rows of heads danced in its reflection and she felt another surge of nausea. Even the eyes were inside.

The girl had pulled out a camera that looked expensive despite its nicks. She scrunched closer to Tandi, bringing the smell of her hair with her, and she turned the flat side of the camera toward them. She thumbed a button and the camera flashed a montage: monkeys stole nuts; arms and oars spoked from rapids; another bloody sunset tracked across the sky; and a girl jumped from a bridge, arms extended like Christ, the cords tied to her feet twisting like the water below her.

"Is that you?"

Still thumbing, the girl turned to Tandi with a solemn look in her green-grey eyes.

"It was like a spiritual experience. I saw death coming straight toward me. Then the bungee caught and I felt truly alive for the first time in my life."

The girl had reached the pics of Vic Falls. They looked like a cluster of errors, all spurting white chaos and none of the torque that the rocks give them in the dry season. The girl's thumb slowed and every time it pressed the button, Tandi could see the nail whiten and then blush again as she released. There were pictures of the Falls and the Falls and Livingstone's bulky, cartoonish statue, some masks and a boy with no shoes, then the Falls again, and finally, a perfectly circular rainbow.

"There it is," the girl said with wonder, as if seeing it had reminded her of what she was looking for. Tandi peered. The girl looked pretty, standing with her knee cocked and the prismatic halo around her. Tandi remembered being foolish and unseeing inside one of those rainbows, about to walk right through it until Scholie had made her look again. Tandi felt for the first time and with a certain clarity that there was something just about the choice that Scholie had made that night. Tandi opened the warmer but nothing came up this time.

"Are you sure you're not sick?" the girl asked as she stroked Tandi's back.

"Ya, I'm fine," Tandi said impatiently, spitting into the warmer. "I just drank a lot. Going away party."

"Oh! I thought you had malaria! Why didn't you just say you had a hangover?" The girl tapped the tip of Tandi's nose. Her finger smelled of dead cigarettes. "I know the feeling. I had a rough night a couple days ago."

"I know. I was there," Tandi said shortly, surprising herself. She had somehow assumed she would play out this farce until they got to Lusaka.

"What, you *were*?" The girl burst out laughing. "Yeah, wait, of course, I thought—"

For a moment, relief bubbled through Tandi but then the girl's laughter caught.

"Wait. I'm just trying to place… did we actually meet? At the bonfire?"

"Yes."

"You know what? I think I do recognize you. I just remembered, from your braids! I've been wanting to get my hair done like that. Do you know where—"

"No, I came with Scholie." They exchanged a glance. Tandi had a flash of memory: two backs hunching to enter a tent as dawn poured out of a hole in the clouds.

"So. Wait. Are you *with* Scholie?" The way the girl said his name was jarring, the O too long.

"No." Tandi smiled and shook her head. "He tried, but."

"Oh. Okay." The girl looked relieved. Then she cocked her head with a knowing smile. "He must have been hard to resist. I mean, I was drunk but he was definitely persuasive."

Tandi looked away. She didn't want to have a little chat with her new mate about Scholie and his moves. She was not inclined to tell the story of their failed courtship, to explain that a rush of air to the eye is the closest they ever got. There had been other girls around, of course, from the very beginning; they were the reason for Tandi's reticence. But that night had been the first time Scholie had actually left her to find her own ride home. She supposed it was his way of saying he would no longer besiege her dam wall. Before he had gone into the tent with the white girl, he had looked at Tandi and shrugged and wiped his blinking eye. Tandi had spent the last two days weighing what he had meant by that. She still didn't know exactly which inside joke had curled his lip and lowered his eyelid into one last wink.

The rain had stopped and light was splitting the clouds. The weather was so short-tempered these days. The sky raged but was quick to forgive, cool and placid afterwards, lacking only a certain warmth. Concrete buildings slid by, iconic pictures advertising their purposes. The people on the side of the road thickened: women selling tomatoes in pyramids, men on bicycles warping under firewood. In the distance you could see the buildings drifting in the exhaust haze of Lusaka.

"So. Did you hear the stories?"

"Yes, I was there. I heard yours as well, about the accident. The injured man."

The girl nodded. There was a pause.

"You know, I really thought he was dying."

The girl's voice was soft, her eyes forward.

"It was so sad. His boy was sleeping. He was going to die and all he wanted was to be touched. You know, in that way. I could tell from the way he was pulling on me and looking at me."

Tandi held her breath. The girl's eyes still faced forward and it felt like a mercy.

"He didn't ask. Even if he had, I wouldn't have understood his language. I could just tell, you know? From his hands and his eyes. I tried to talk to him. I whispered so I wouldn't wake his boy. But he didn't seem to get it. He was pulling on the neck of my shirt and reaching for my hair and he even put my hand on him. I thought he was dying and this was something I could do for him. I was drunk and I thought if I touched him there, he would understand. About how sorry I was."

The girl turned to Tandi. She looked thin and tired.

"And I was right. He did."

They were so close that Tandi could see the raw whites of her eyes, a fallen eyelash curving in one. It looked like a cut but she knew it would be as light as air.

"I can plait your hair for you if you want," Tandi said finally. She touched the hair wisping at the girl's temple. "Your hair is too soft, it will fall. But I can try."

The girl smiled and said nothing and then they were like children. Tandi sat sideways with one knee bent and her back to the window. The girl sat with her feet in the aisle and her back to Tandi. When she pulled out the ponytail, the hair swept down and static lifted a blonde mist. They were quiet while Tandi smoothed the girl's hair and parted it, threaded her fingers in it and began to rotate her wrists. The focus stilled her stomach and cleared her head. She wondered if the girl would try to pay her. Her hands did the work automatically, twisting the rising mayhem into order.

The sky blushed as they approached town and even though the windows could not be opened, the smell of woodsmoke seeped into the bus. By the time they had arrived at the bus depot downtown, it was night. The girl was asleep with white pods in her ears that reminded Tandi of the electrodes you use to monitor a patient. The plaits in her hair had already loosened.

Namwali Serpell was born in Lusaka, Zambia in 1980. She is an assistant professor in the English department at the University of California, Berkeley. She has published nonfiction in *Bidoun* and *The Believer*. Her first story, 'Muzungu', was published in *Callaloo*, selected for *The Best American Short Stories 2009* (edited by Alice Sebold), and nominated for the 2010 Caine Prize for African Writing.

Wolf Blue

Alex Smith

1. Cormorant Head

Formidable eyes, upper lids lost beneath wiry brows, a singular nose, irregular as a sweet-potato, and those lips... Lilita Tshinavhe paused from contemplating the monochromatic features of a portrait in an auction catalogue. The car was travelling at high speed, but she heard footsteps. *Outside? How is it possible?* She peered into the darkness beyond the back seat window and shrieked when a flaming chain struck the glass. There was the sound of a heartbeat, loud and fast, then silence, and everything was black again.

"Something the matter, Ma'am?" the driver asked, unfazed.

Lilita took three slow breaths, the way her psychologist had advised for these situations, but again – *crack* – the fiery shackle, the fearful heartbeat, and those footfalls, pounding the night grass. She opened her window. Air gushed against her face and in the billowing of southeaster she felt adrenaline fear, that of a creature chased, and she knew a woman was in danger.

"Stop the car!"

The driver slowed. "It's not safe, the highway, at this late hour, Ma'am."

"Stop the car, I said!"

He slowed the BMW more, almost, but not quite, stopping.

"Did you hear?" she asked. "Did you see something out there?"

"Definitely nothing there, Ma'am," said the driver, after checking. He accelerated and turned up the music.

Her own judgement was no longer to be trusted. Lilita closed out the burly wind. A flute concerto played, serene and so aloof from life beyond that leather interior. *Why care about a stranger? Ignore it!* She tried, but still, she could feel the woman's fear. Lilita's dread mounted too. *I should have taken my medication.* She touched a cormorant-head pendant hanging at her neck; began whispering a prayer to whichever god would hear, but winced where amen should have been because the white gold bird at her neck had become hot as an element in an oven. She pulled her burning finger tips away and sucked them, aware of an unpleasant phosphate smell, as when a match is struck. She scrabbled for her mobile and phoned her psychologist. "Ella, Ella, answer please..."

2. Wolf Yellow

In the vineyard beyond the triple-volume window, vines shook in the wind, but inside Villa Libertas all was calm, and whales were calling. At his granddaughter's insistence, the study was fitted out with energy-saving bulbs, but the light they offered was regrettably cold. Jans Boshoff chose darkness over coldness and found his way by instinct to the wall of books behind the velvet sofa. After returning *Frankenstein* to its position in the S shelves, Jans switched on a table lamp – his little secret – and its regular bulb gave warmth and revealed Clerval, the Mastiff, curled up among the cushions of a floral armchair. Jans poured himself a hearty glass of whisky and settled down to watch whales on the Discovery Channel. The whales in their great deep sea were a temporary comfort; Jans was anxious for that night to end, and along with it two unfortunate 'situations'. For a man in his position, he had, in his opinion, solved the problem of murder surprisingly easily. Gleaning a few tips from recent newspaper articles, he'd taken a drive down to Wynberg station and made the sort of queries which led him via a dealer of stolen mobile phones and pirated DVDs to a family of willing killers in Albert Road in Woodstock.

"I'm looking for professionals," he'd said to Yusuf Cupido, who wore a Red Nike T-shirt and sat across from him at a kitchen table full of mobile phones and who looked more like a football player than a gangster. But options for Jans were few, and urgent action was required. The Cupido brothers would have to do.

"Quality and good service guaranteed," Yusuf Cupido had replied. One of the contraband phones had rung, but he had ignored it at first. "Isn't that right, hey, Yaseen?... he's my youngest brother," Yusuf had said to Jans and then said to Yaseen again, "You're a pro aren't you, Yaseen?"

The kid, Yaseen, had nodded and looked up from the puppy sleeping in the blue tog bag on his lap.

"Handsome dog, you've got, Yaseen," Jans had said. "What is he, or is it she?"

"They think Pitbull crossed with Dalmatian."

Yusuf had answered the ringing phone with silence, listened and then turned it off.

"I got her at the SPCA this morning," Yaseen had said.

Then began negotiations, in the midst of which, another pair of youths had arrived, one wearing a green tracksuit and the other, fit to be a sumo wrestler, wearing a pink tracksuit branded loudly with roses and skulls and *Ed Harvey*. After they'd emptied a couple more bags of phones onto the kitchen table, Jans had argued down Yusuf's non-negotiable price for the job.

Satisfied, Jans declared it was necessary to be more discreet about this project in future, so at his request, they'd settled on code names for the job. Due to the maizey hue of his silk tie, Jans was christened Wolf Yellow.

3. Babel Towers

On the top floor of Babel Towers, as she liked to call it because the twin blocks housed refugees from all over Africa, Ella was trying to decide what to wear for her first date with an Internet match. On the lower slopes of Table Mountain, the southeaster raged and the towers, the tallest in the Cape, swayed back and forth; each slow journey and return enough to make the non-habituated giddy. There were clothes in her closet of course, but that evening none of them spoke to her libertine mood. She wanted a dress that said 'Aphrodite'; she wanted to dance under palm trees, smoke Cuban cigars and drink margaritas.

She had settled for a green silk wrap dress and was brushing mascara onto her lashes when the phone rang.

Moving a pen and a vibrating magazine, she uncovered her mobile; a client's name was flashing.

"Lilita, what is it?"

"I had another vision."

Ella wedged the phone between her ear and her shoulder and continued a languid act of stroking layers of kohl liquid onto her lashes as Lilita described what she had seen and heard.

"Why are you on the highway?" Ella asked, "I thought you were flying to Joburg this evening?"

"Driving. They sent a driver for me. This time, I'm certain the chain, the footsteps, the heartbeat are a presentiment," Lilita said, "I'm frightened, I'm wor...."

"Take a breath." Ella breathed with her client and at the same time, put down the mascara wand and dipped her finger into a small silver tin of duskflower lipstain. "Let's consider this calmly." Smiling so that her cheeks made apples, she applied a dot of pink onto the apple of her left cheek and did likewise with her right cheek. "Tell me what makes this vision different from the delusional manifestations we have discussed so often?" Ella began to smooth and spread both bronzey-pink dots into her skin, giving the apples a subtle rosy glow.

"It's impossible to explain, but something awful is happening or going to happen, somebody is hunting a woman. I feel her fear, like I'm inside her head. I could hear her heart beating. She's running..."

"Take three slow breaths and remember how we talked about acknowledging these flashes of 'presentiments' as you call them, but realizing they are no more than a mind trick. Don't be sucked in by them. You know how anxious they make you, how unhappy. Breathe in and let it go."

4. Wolf Blue

Yaseen Cupido had chosen the code names and his was definitely Wolf Blue, because it was his blue tog bag of a brand represented in logo by a wolf that had given them the wolf idea in the first place.

As he pounded through the grass, his long legs were arguing with each other like a Djinn and Allah, praise be to Allah. On the left, the Djinn was saying "do the job". On the right, Allah the Exulted was saying "reconsider, murder is a far cry from stealing mobile phones". Not that Allah the Most Merciful and Compassionate would condone theft, but still, this was several degrees more serious. The holy squabble in his legs crept up into his lungs, seizing them like he had asthma. He asked Allah for forgiveness, and thought of the money this hit would earn him, and remembered a game his mother taught him before she chose seventh heaven over Woodstock and left him an orphan.

"When you have to face bad things, like this," his Ma had said about getting stitches, "play the alphabet game." She had distracted him from the needle sewing his flesh by telling him a cautionary tale for each letter. 'A' was for Aubrey who ate himself to death. 'B' was for Bismilla who stuffed samoosas with naughty boys... Ha! She was a mischievous storyteller, his Ma, but stories were for children, and the escaped woman's Nokia Communicator was bleating in his pocket, reminding him of the dirty task ahead.

Hoping it would work this time too, make it possible to block out the bad things he was about to do, Yaseen resorted again to the alphabet game.

A is for Astronomy: Science of stars, like Mr Fischer at school said, I could study that at UCT, specially now, with the money we're getting for this job.

B is for Bloedskiet: spilling blood, the only way into the Kingdom of Numbers, doesn't my Pa know it.

C is for C-block: in Pollsmoor, where Pa is, ag, fok dit, fok Pollsmoor, C is for Cherries: nickname of the English Football League's Second Division team AFC Bournemouth, them that wears the cherry red jerseys.

D is for...

"Faster, man, Yaseen, she's getting away," said his cousin, Brandon Festus, who, for this job, was supposed to be known as Wolf, was it Pink? No, Green.

"You're supposed to call me Wolf Blue." Even though he could never remember if his cousin Brandon was Wolf Green or Wolf Pink, Yaseen knew he was definitely Wolf Blue.

5. Bather

A beautiful sight, a comforting sound: hot water gushing from the taps, filling a bath to an inch of its brim. Water from taps, particularly hot water for bathing, never failed to delight Inspector Jonny Mthethwa, who grew up in a township where the only running water was in the river. He added a drop of Green Tea foam bath to the water. From his jeans pocket he removed a little black book and set it on the side of the bath with a pen before undressing, briefly admiring his six-pack in the mirror, and climbing into the bath.

Beyond the green tea's scented steam was a window ledge of potted succulents.

"Good evening, Sharpeville," he said to a yellowish-green plant with sprays of prickles. He'd broken a stem off a wild succulent near the Sharpeville memorial and so, like the other plants in his 320-strong collection, it was named for its auspicious home turf. "Hello, Che's Grave," he said to a trailing orange one. "You are an absolute wonder! Look how you've grown." A friend who'd travelled to South America had returned with a tiny cutting of that succulent and, from a single fat leaf, after some struggle, it had flourished and matured into a glorious plant. As a hobby, a distraction from the bodies in his day job, Jonny sold plants grown from cuttings.

Jonny dried his hands on the towel hanging near the bath. He picked up the pen, the black book and added an idea: *building a monster? Dr Frankenstein* to a series of notes – *access through open window, strangulation, hand sawed off, any link to the CM murder/mutilation? Revenge?* – all of them about a politician found dead in Claremont Park.

6. Reclaimed

Things might have been different if Lien hadn't tripped and twisted her ankle back when that BMW seemed to slow down, almost stop. That was the last real chance she'd had to get away; the men behind were closing in, she couldn't go any faster, she was feverish, her head, where they'd whacked her with a crowbar, was bleeding. Though she'd recovered from concussion enough to escape, she had to fight focus, to keep reality straight. Confusion was increasingly taking over from terror, and over and over with every step she forced in spite of the agony of a fractured skull, she heard a medley from *The Sound of Music*. One song with a line about dogs biting and thinking of favourite things kept returning to her; as she pushed on blindly, stumbling on rocky ground beneath tall grass and between thorny shrubs, she could see Julie Andrews in that white apron, smiling, singing. Maybe it was because her teenage son, Judah, played what she, as a proud mother, considered an inspired saxophone version of that song. *Judah, my baby.* It was the need to get back to him alive that was pulling her through the absolute darkness. Between seconds of blank delirium, she was lucid, and knew the men were sent by Jans Boshoff to kill her because she, together with an Advocate, the Deputy Director of Environmental

Affairs, had refused a bribe after finding proof of extreme corruption. There was Julie again, with her strawberry-blond page-boy haircut, doing a polka in a meadow, and Lien was running towards her.

Until, "Fok!" Her foot had landed deep in a hole, twisted, stuck, and she went face first into grass and sand. She sobbed. It was dark, but Julie turned on a light and was promising hills alive with... Lien screamed... A boot had tramped and pinned her hand to the ground.

"Daarsy," said a man's voice. "Thought you could get away, huh?"

For months, she'd been investigating the hydraulic fracking scheme planned for the area where her family farm was and, as a result, in the last two days, her life had turned into some kind of sordid rip-off of an Elmore Leonard novel. There was Julie again willing Lien to think of happy things. She thought of Judah, she thought of reading him bedtime stories –above all others he'd loved Dickens and Enid Blyton. Happy things, Julie in her apron insisted. Lien could think of nothing happier than Judah relishing the Famous Five having a picnic with 'lashings of ginger beer'.

7. The Saxman Cometh
With wrinkles both ways, it's a vertical and horizontal frown; even his eyes are participating in directing concern to the crags between his brows. Lilita could feel the shaven-headed driver's eyes on her in the mirror. He was the emissary of her employer and was listening to the conversation with her psychologist. No doubt he would report it all back.

"No, my fingers aren't burnt anymore." She looked at them. She touched the cormorant pendant. "There's no mark, but there was. Something terrible is about to happen. Maybe this time, I can stop it. Remember the vision about the old man, strangled, remember I saw, I dreamed..."

"Are you taking your meds?" Ella asked.

She never listens, even though I pay fortunes for her to listen. Why won't she believe me? Lilita stared at a painting entitled 'The Saxman Cometh'.

"Why aren't you flying to Joburg?"

"I can't fly." How could Lilita explain it, without Ella using the new phobia as further evidence for medication? "It's too dangerous." She was due to guest star in a TV show there, but had developed a fear of flying, so the producer had sent a driver.

"I'm late for a dinner meeting, Lilita, please, please take your meds. It's the only way to stop the hallucinations."

"It wasn't an hallucination."

Or maybe it was, these visions were getting more frequent, maybe Ella was right. What to believe? She was reluctant to take the medication, it gave her tremors, it caused her to put on weight, but worse, it made her feel disconnected from herself. "Once on the Discovery Channel, I saw a programme about a woman who had visions, premonitions..."

"We've spoken about this, Lilita. Did you read that Derren Brown book I lent you about how all those so-called miracles and psychic powers are unsubstantiated and invariably some form of mind trick?"

"That's a very jaded, Western interpretation, Ella."

"And that's a red herring, Lilita. Take the meds. Forget the woman. She does not exist beyond your mind."

"Maybe there are two kinds of minds in the human world: those who accept mystery beyond our limited logic, and those who can't. What's more improbable, Ella, a universe limited to bounds of human reason and our sciences, or a universe more intricate than our minds can possibly conceive?"

There it is again, the horizontal-vertical frown.

8. Wolf Blue Green

"Wolf... What colour are you again, Yaseen?"

"Blue. I'm Wolf Blue. You're Wolf Red."

Yusuf cuffed Yaseen. "Don't be stupid, I'm know I'm Red. It's you and Brandon I get mixed up. Okay, Wolf Blue, Wolf Pink, get the fuel and the tyres. It's quiet enough to do it here."

"No," Brandon said, "I'm Green. Fadhl is Pink."

"Fok off! I don't care. Just get the stuff."

Wolf Blue made the mistake of looking into the tied-up woman's eyes, and Allah knows by some magic she snared him with those eyes, they were begging him and they wouldn't let him go. He found it impossible to turn away from her, but he didn't want to think about her. He stood locked in a stare, thinking of letters in the alphabet game.

K is for KFC Streetwise Feast: Two drumsticks, two wings, two breasts, two mash with gravy and three bread rolls. Finger Licking Good.

L and M are both for El Diablo: Marco Etcheverry, the best player in the history of MLS. They surprisingly great soccer players those Americans. L and M, L-Diablo,Marco, famous for his wicked sexy free-kick goals.

"Hey!" Wolf Red pushed him, he stumbled and followed Brandon to the car that Fadhl, Wolf Pink, had parked on the side of the highway.

"These Communicators are heavy as bricks," Yaseen said, tossing the woman's Nokia into a bag of other phones in the car.

Nobody commented; they were unloading tyres.

"Hey, Wolf Pink," said Yaseen, chuckling. "Did you ever hear the true story of Nasrin Orrie, the dead bricklayer's daughter?"

Fadhl shook his head. "Why are you laughing? It's the Pink isn't it? Pink is for moffies. I don't want to be Wolf Pink any more. From now on I'm Wolf Orange."

"You can't do that. Do you want to hear the story or not?"

"Ja, whatever, but I don't see why I have to be Wolf Pink."

"Agh, shut up and listen. Skinny Nasrin Orrie had a secret and it made her the most powerful person in Woodstock."

"Why? What's her secret?" asked Fadhl, leaning against the tyres to catch his breath.

"Nasrin Orrie had a kind of power..."

"True story se gat," said Brandon, "that's a bleddy urban legend."

"It's not," Yaseen said. "It's from a book. They don't lie."

9. Wolf Yellow Pink

Jans Boshoff had grown tired of the whales on the Discovery Channel. His transparent Breguet wristwatch, with all its wheels and pivots turning in full view beneath the glass face, told him the deed should be done. He opened a box of chocolates and popped a hazelnut Lindt ball into his mouth. When it was almost gone, he telephoned his Woodstock associates. Thinking of their table of stolen phones made him smile; they'd have to sell an awful lot before they'd ever be wealthy enough to move in next door to Villa Libertas.

One of the Woodstock kids answered.

"Wolf Red?" he asked.

"No, no, sir, it's Fadhl, ah, Wolf Pink, um, Wolf Yellow, no that's you, I mean Red, Wolf Red is not here, but you can speak to Wolf Blue or even Wolf Green if you like, sir, ah Wolf Yellow."

"Don't be absurd." Jans regretted the code names. In the background, he could hear voices arguing. "Just tell me, is it done?"

The argument sounded like typical male rivalry, a battle of one-upmanship.

"In about ten minutes," Fadhl said, "she'll be dead."

10. Interior (the studio at night)

All the lights were out when Judah and his Dad pulled into the driveway scented with Cape jasmine.

"No lights even, typical," his Dad said. "Your mother's irresponsible. She knew I was dropping you back tonight, didn't she?"

Judah nodded.

Before kissing him goodbye, Judah's dad ranted about his mom, Lien's lack of care, her selfish stupidity, her loose ways. Upon seeing weeds growing through the brickwork of the driveway, he quoted the bible. "I went by the field of the slothful, And lo, it was all grown over with thorns and nettles," his Dad said.

Judah's mom, Lien, had told Judah his Dad was an abusive zealot, and a misanthropist, like Scrooge in Charles Dickens' *A Christmas Carol*, a book Lien used to read to Judah when he was still a child. His favourite part of the day had always been after bathtime, when he was tucked up in bed and Lien would read to him.

His Dad waited irritably, watching Judah make his way to the door. Judah waved, "It's fine, Dad, you can go." The door was open. His Dad backed out of the driveway, but waited for Judah to press a button, and for the gate to close out the dangers of the street.

"Lien?" Judah called, pushing the door. "Lien, ma? Are you home?" Their town home was a tiny place filled with art and musical instruments – Lien's art, Judah's music. Judah took the stairs to the upper floor two at a time. "Lien?"

Her bed was empty.

He turned on the globe of the world that served as Lien's bedside lamp, and checked around for a note, but there was nothing. He tried phoning her.

It rang; it was answered with silence.

"Lien, Ma, can you hear me?"

Nobody spoke. The phone went dead.

He rang again. This time it went to voice mail. "Ma, I'm a bit worried. I didn't know you were going out tonight. Are you at the cinema? Please give me a call."

Through the bedroom window he was relieved to see a light on in her studio. He ran down the stairs and through the garden to his mother's studio, a garden shed painted yellow.

"I've been looking for you!" Judah said, flinging open the

studio door. His joy vanished. She wasn't there. The only trace of his mother was a charcoal self-portrait of soft contrasts. She was wearing a checked shirt, and her hair was like she always wore it: soft, loose and tucked behind her ears.

11. *Speitata Leggerezza* (Ruthless Levity)

After the violent winds of earlier that day, Kalk Bay was calm again and the restaurant strip was merry. At Cape To Cuba, a Portuguese woman was singing of excruciating anticipation, and steel drums glittered with bonfires.

Four margaritas and a kiss into the date, Ella was laughing at Paul Tabata's story about how, on his way to Kalk Bay, some crazy woman had first run him and his bike over and then punched him. Ella's phone rang.

"Not again," Paul said.

"I'm so sorry," she said, answering.

"I'll get us more drinks." Paul seemed irritated.

"What if you're wrong, Ella? What if I'm not mad and there is somebody out there in trouble tonight? It's like I'm inside her head, and she's terrified."

"Lilita, you're still fixated on the man who was strangled on the same night you had a dream a man was strangled." Ella tugged at the label on a bottle of Sol that served as a candlestick holder. "You have to acknowledge this is a world of coincidences. Tonight, yes, there are people in trouble, but they're all over the world." Ella watched her date with his torn jacket, ordering them a pair of Margaritas at the bar. What a surprise he was. She'd met up with a few Internet matches before and mostly they'd been a disappointment, but Paul was different. Turned out they were both book lovers and both addicted to Terry Pratchett. They'd both read and owned all his novels, they'd both been disappointed with his most recent one, *Unseen Academicals*, they'd both concluded that due to his Alzheimer's Pratchett probably didn't write the whole novel, and they'd both lamented the inevitable end of a beloved author's career. The last thing Ella wanted was for an obsessive patient to screw up what could be a monumental night.

"Take your meds, Lilita."

"Somebody is going to die. Do you believe me, Ella?"

Ella looked at the blackness of sea beyond the bar; patients had no concept of her having a life apart from their problems.

"What I believe," Ella said, "is irrelevant; it's not about belief. It's about peace of mind, it's about living a normal life, enjoying yourself instead of being plagued with these visions..." There was Paul, carrying drinks, already on his way back to their table. "You need to live a little, Lilita, to laugh, when did you last laugh? To fall in and out of love. For goodness' sake, just take your meds."

Paul sat.

"Somebody out there needs help," Lilita said.

Paul folded his hands, stared at the floor.

"It's a statistical certainty, Lilita, a devastating fact, that there are women in peril in the Cape Province tonight, many women, women who will be raped and women who will be assaulted and some even killed, but you cannot be responsible for them. It's your depression taking over. That responsibility belongs with the police. I'm sorry, take the meds, or at least take a sleeping tablet, that'll help. I have to go now, Lilita. I'll phone you in the morning."

"To meds," said Paul, recovering his smile. "This may be cheesy, but I have to say you're even more beautiful in real life. Usually, Internet dates look better in their profile pictures, but you look so feminine in that silky dress. Such a startling shade, what is it? Emerald?"

He leaned forward to kiss her. The phone rang.

"Jesus," he looked away.

"I'm sorry."

"Can't you turn it off?"

"Lilita, this has to be the last call." Ella looked roofwards where bunches of tobacco leaves hung from the beams.

12. The Aviator

Lien was on her knees, shivering; her head throbbed. *I don't deserve to die like this.* The voices of her captors blurred. The fuel they were dowsing her in caused her skin to itch, the fumes made her dizzy. Two men with jerrycans were arguing about colours: Pink, Green and Orange. *Seven hundred million rand from Boshoff's company... split between the Petroleum Agency of South Africa and the Minister of Environmental Affairs to approve a series of applications for a list of schemes all gas, oil, energy related.* Lien began rambling, occasionally lapsing into a pidgin language, Afrikaans, French, English, mixed as a result of fever; mostly, though, she was fully aware, yanking at the chains that bound her to brutal fate. *First the Advocate disappeared and now me. Oh God, Judah knows too much.* "No!" she shouted, "No!" *Judah, my boy, I won't leave you.* Noxious liquid streamed down her forehead, over her nose and cheeks. *Judah knows, my parents know.* She saw her parents and the family farm in the Karoo. Such good memories there, in that tumbling-down Cape Dutch homestead, a disaster with squirrels nesting in the rafters, an overgrown rose garden tangled with crops gone to seed. Lien's wrists were bleeding from the tight chains around her right and left arms. Both chains were wrapped around stacks of tyres, but as she struggled, she felt the tyres give, and instinct told her there may be hope yet. She threw back her head and allowed her mouth to fill up with the accelerant fluid the men were pouring on and around her.

"You're tatie man, what difference does it make now if you're Wolf Orange or Wolf Green?" said one of the men to the other. "The job is pretty much over."

The other replied. "Pink! I'm Wolf Pink and that's the problem, and it matters to me. I'm not a bleddie moffie."

"Green, Pink, Orange, fok off both you, back to car," said another man.

Through stinging eyes Lien saw that man toss a box of matches to another with a jerrycan at his feet, and she heard him call the one who caught the matches "Wolf Blue".

"Do it," said a voice. "I'm going to sort out those two idiots; cousins or not, I'm never working with them again." The man walked off into the night.

That left the one called Wolf Blue. He struck a match.

With all the fury of a protective mother, Lien spat fuel in the direction of the match in Wolf Blue's hand, the air around the match exploded with flames, Wolf Blue yelled, gravity drew the fire into a column leading to the jerrycan at his feet. Lien threw herself backwards, pulling at the chains, collapsing the pile of tyres. One chain came away completely, but the other was fixed to its tyre. Still shackled, but possessed with a kind monster force, she roared, and she ran as a swell of flames swept over and swallowed Wolf Blue. Behind her, she heard him screaming and the night filled with the smell of his shoes, his jeans, his skin burning, and his hair burning.

But Lien, dragging her fetters, ran on, wildly, sprinting, hard and fast, faster than she had ever been able to run before, towards Frank Sinatra who was singing *Come Fly With Me*.

13. Psyche #2

In shorthand form it all went into Inspector Jonny Mthethwa's little black book – *no identity, body next to N1, charred, legs destroyed (no toeprints), face destroyed (no dental rec.), footprints, tyres, fingers severely damaged (no fingerprints?), cause of death?, evidence of accelerant fluid, male/female?, homeless person? Missing person?*

Back at the office, he emailed a memo to a colleague to request names of missing persons. He wasn't optimistic. It was a hopeless case; the body was too far gone. Whatever life it had once contained, whoever the person had been, his or her struggle was over.

Jonny tested the soil around Harare and Maputo, a pair of potted succulents on his desk. "Parched," he said and from a deep bottom drawer he took out a yellow plastic watering can with a long, elegant spout. In the men's room he filled the watering can and encountered a colleague who regularly told him tales of the latest most crazy calls to the Crime Stop, a toll-free number.

"How about this for nuts: that model who won the Face of Africa, Lilita Tshinavhe," said the colleague, mid-pee, "she phones this morning, she says she had a vision last night and wants to know if we've found the body of a woman." The colleague zipped up his fly. "So I say to her, Ma'am, is this woman a friend of yours? No, she says, she never met her. How is it you know the woman is dead, I ask, and she says she'd had a vision. So I say did your vision mention the dead woman's name and surname by any chance? No, she says, no name but she thinks the woman was somehow burnt or set alight, somewhere on the highway, N1, and she says she had a recurring dream too."

The watering can was nearly full, but Jonny had lost focus on it. "Set alight along the N1?"

"Yes, and in the dream, following the vision, if you don't mind, she hears the burning woman singing *lean on me, lean, lean, lean* and she insists it must be significant."

"Give me the Tshinavhe woman's number." Water was spilling over the edges of the yellow can, splashing onto the white enamel of the basin.

Alex Smith's novel *Four Drunk Beauties* was published in South Africa by Random House's African Imprint, Umuzi, in 2010. In the same year, she won the Sanlam Youth Literature award and her story 'Soulmates' was shortlisted for the Caine Prize for African Writing. She was born in South Africa, has lived for short spells in London, Wuhan, Taipei and Chiang Mai, but is happy to be resident again in Cape Town.

Dark Triad

Olufemi Terry

FROM THE BEDROOM WINDOW, an arc of the city is in view: squat towers serried in uneven, slanting rows. Far below are streets like ribbons of light, filled with slow-going cars; the air is icy clear. In his journal, Ebanks writes, *An old, settled city, the facades plain and difficult to read: Europe.* It had not been apparent when he alighted from the taxi that they've fetched up near the brow of a hill. The city forms a bowl rimmed by four or five such peaks. He sees unimpeded all the way down into the basin, the city's heart, where street lanterns blend and blur into an amber haze. He hunts for a phrase that will cap his sense of the new city. He knows this already: it's not right for his next project, which will be an installation. Somewhere in the world is an inchoate city, a new Berlin or Buenos Aires. All is stale in London, in Paris; nothing untried.

"Yann, do you want some of this?"

Samia's in the living room. Chopped out on the coffee table in front of her are four lines of cocaine.

"Where did you get that?" Ebanks says.

"Tewodros left it for me." The flat has been loaned them by Tewodros, for as long as Samia needs it. "You thought I brought it with me on the flight?" Samia's not a frequent user but a social one; in the six- or seven-month span of their relationship, she's invited him to join her in snorting a line perhaps eight times. He doesn't much care for cocaine. In an unfamiliar city, on a shivering cold night, it's the last thing he wants. He turns away. The view from Tewodros' living room is obscured by a residential building 500 yards or so downslope. Samia snorts two lines. "What are you doing?"

"Looking at the city." He opens his leather-back journal and skims what he's written about Aleppo, about Oran. Tomorrow or the day after perhaps, he'll begin an exploration, tracing the streets on foot with his notebook and cameras.

"The taxi driver's probably downstairs." Samia tips the rest of the powder back into her wrap. "You ready?"

Ebanks goes to find a t-shirt that fits his mood. He inspects one he printed up himself, a green cotton one with yellow lettering that reads: *Baal shoots...* On the back of it are the words: *Jesus saves.* Serifs on the B and the S connote Hebraic script. Ebanks possesses another version, one which invokes Mammon rather than Baal, but in either case the joke seems less clever than it did a year ago. He chooses at last a different shirt, one given him by Samia, an ironic gift; *Dark Triad* is blazoned on this one in a plain font. The irony is a fine one. "Let's go, Yann." Samia's wearing a short coat, balloon pants and boots. Ebanks slides his journal into the pocket of his jacket.

There will be six other guests; this is all Samia knows, or discloses, about the dinner party to which they're invited. She gives the taxi driver a slip of paper with an address on it, written in an unfamiliar hand. The roads are straitened and deserted; seen from a taxi, the town is provincial, with low walls and iron gates.

A man opens the front door to admit them. "Good to see you again." In the warm foyer of a grand house, he kisses Samia's cheeks. "Call me sir," he tells Ebanks, who has no answer to this advice. *Sir?* He's tall, the stranger, very tall with fine, dark skin. And something about him is familiar. The man seems to know Ebanks, to recognize him. He looms close, Ebanks' hand clasped in his, as if trying to see beneath the skin. Ebanks pulls free; he's reluctant to be known without first knowing.

The townhouse – a loft – is vast. Towering ceilings, tiny and discreet light fixtures. On the white walls are empty picture frames, man-high squares and rectangles that will never be filled. A postmodernist's house: mocking and self-referential.

Samia is already in the salon, where other guests are milling. Ebanks has an idea what to expect: voyeurs with one foot each in the worlds of art and hedonism, their greed couched in expressions of ennui; or else, long-serving academics, purveyors of critical theories of kizomba or dubstep. It's Samia's crowd; he doesn't have one.

A Nigerian woman, a television journalist with short bleached brown dreadlocks, gives him a vicious handshake. A blond man with a reddened Adam's apple is wearing a white t-shirt with two words on it: K(no)w Africa. Beneath the black letters is a stylized map of Africa with national borders delineated. Ebanks stares at the shirt, wanting to decipher the paradox. He will, first chance he gets, jot the formulation in his journal. "Howzit, man?" the t-shirt's wearer says, taking no notice of Ebanks' curiosity. The accent is unplaceable.

Another man there, a black, may be famous but it's hard to be sure; his eyes are hidden by silver-studded sunglasses. On his cheeks and forehead are smears like jaundice. In Guadeloupe, Basse Terre, there are many faces marred, like this one, by hydroquinone. Skin bleach. The man's shoes are dagger-like and upcurling; his feet appear inordinately long. Dubai shoes, Samia calls the style. Grand Vizier shoes. Hovering at his shoulder is a reedy woman who seems continually on the point of saying something to him and then deciding against it. Ebanks introduces himself, giving his last name. The woman inclines her head in greeting, a gesture that strikes Ebanks as old-fashioned. She's French, he guesses, or perhaps Spanish – Galician. A semiotician or a deconstructionist. The letters KO are stamped in yellow on her brown t-shirt and Ebanks feels a faint irritation that his is not the only t-shirt bearing a legend.

He recalls no one's name. It's unnecessary. He fixes people by what they've said, by observation. He's met so far a mildly hysterical journalist: the man, K(no)w Africa. The semiotician, whom he's already named Ms KO; and there's her companion, yellow fever. Ebanks comes up behind Samia – she is, for the moment, alone – and says, "Why did that guy tell me to call him Sir?" He means the one that opened the door, who seems now to have vanished.

Samia regards him with pinprick eyes. "It's a shortening of his first name, Tamsir." Her nostrils flare. "That's Tamsir daSouza-Jones." She's gone before Ebanks has a chance to admit he doesn't recognize the name or to ask, *how do you know him?* Parties, in Samia's view, are for meeting new people, not for sticking close to one's partner.

There's a fourth woman, wearing a laced peasant blouse, whom Ebanks has not yet met. She's tall, with a domineering, determined face and a complexion a few shades lighter than his own. He takes her for a lecturer in a conventional discipline: English or History. He does not introduce himself, instead ducking into the bathroom so he can take notes undisturbed. *Artificially eclectic dinner party*, he writes on a new page. *Academics and wealthy pseudo-artists. Samia's milieu.* And yet these people – yellow fever comes to mind – do not correspond precisely to his expectations of Samia's milieu, the members of which he finds tiresome. *Who is Ms KO? Dasouza-Jones (sp?) resembles a cultivated pimp. His poison? Ayahuasca or datura.* He does not write that he perceives something of the shaman in daSouza-Jones' long dark face, an occult tendency concealed beneath an anglophile facade.

He resurfaces and finds the others have taken seats at the high, round table in a dining room adjacent to the salon. Having absented himself a while, daSouza-Jones has reappeared and is seated between Samia and the English professor. Like rowdy schoolchildren, several guests talk at once and, under cover of the pretence of disinhibition, of being at ease, each scrutinizes the others. Couples, it seems, are discouraged from sitting together. Ebanks slips into the sole available place, between the Nigerian journalist and Ms KO. On her right is the blond man, K(no)w Africa. Yellow fever sits at Samia's right hand, sunglasses in place. He's so unresponsive to the shouts, to the faint tension, that he might as well be deaf and blind.

A server circles the table, pouring wine. Samia, eyes downcast, accepts only water. In a minute, Ebanks predicts, she will get up, go to the bathroom and ingest another line of cocaine. "What the hell," wonders the woman from Nigeria, looking at no one, "is a Dark Triad?" She has a voice that will penetrate any chatter.

"It's a cluster of personality traits, typically but not exclusively found in men." Ms KO is the one who answers. "The main elements are narcissism, psychopathy and Machiavellianism. Women find the combination irresistible, apparently." Samia opens her mouth and then closes it. Like Ebanks, she prefers to remain inconspicuous, although narcissism is a subject on which she's able to speak at length.

"Interesting." The journalist eyes Ebanks with a hint of reassessment. He ignores her. He wants to ask Ms KO, *Are you an analyst?* but he hesitates and the opportunity is lost.

"Tell me," Ms KO turns to the man at her right, "what exactly is K(no)w Africa?"

K(no)w Africa sits up straight. "It's an NGO I founded to encourage people to think differently about the continent."

"The *African* continent?" wonders the TV journalist. A server enters the room, steps over daSouza-Jones' outstretched legs and begins ladling soup into bowls.

"*Our* continent, yes," K(no)w Africa's nodding. "I'm South African." It sounds like *Sairth Effrican*. "We all have broad and fuzzy ideas but no one seems to know or care much about the individual countries, hey? Hence the parenthesis." He glances at the shirt with a furtive satisfaction. "The name invites the world to know the continent and at the same time to refuse to perceive it as an undifferentiated mass of suffering and disease."

"Intriguing," says Ms KO, not at all intrigued. She watches Yellow fever in much the same way daSouza-Jones peered at Ebanks as he shook his hand.

Samia smiles, mouths 'Excuse me' to daSouza-Jones and stands up. Ebanks tries to catch her eye. Into the silence, K(no)w Africa asks, "Do you know who the Wodaabe are?"

"Who?" asks the journalist.

"Wodaabe. Nomads in Niger and Chad. They hold narcissistic mating ceremonies that last for days. The men use kohl and powder..."

"Fulanis," the journalist kisses her teeth. "Bororo. Of course now. I covered one of their marriage festivals in my show. What's this Wodaabe nonsense?"

"I'm Foula," announces daSouza-Jones. Ebanks has a feeling he's missing something, that it's no accident talk of narcissism has resurfaced.

"You sound British," someone else – Ebanks cannot be sure which woman it is – tells daSouza-Jones, as if laying a charge.

"You're Foula?" asks the English lecturer. "With a name like daSouza-Jones?" K(no)w Africa is assessing her, Ms KO also, as if her knowledge of the Fulani is suspicious.

"We have such names in Gambia," daSouza-Jones says. "Downs-Thomas, Beckley-Lines. My mother's Foula." The topic bores him. He's slouched in his chair, the whiskey in his tumbler brilliant beneath the lights. The shifts in the conversation are jarring and Ebanks experiences a momentary disembodiment, a sensation like freefall within a dream. Although it might be attributable to fatigue from the long flight. After the meal, if not before, he'll return directly to Tewodros' place and sleep.

The guests are eating soup now, each one talking to his neighbour instead of to the table at large. Ebanks remains curious about Ms KO but the Nigerian journalist snares him in a conversation. There are, she confides, too many projects on her plate. She cannot find time for friendships, let alone a romantic relationship. "The last two months, I've been in Mauritius, Ukraine, São Tomé, South Africa... the conditions in rural Ukraine... not much better than the North." She goes on without concern for whether Ebanks is listening. Swallowing careful mouthfuls of asparagus soup, he supposes she means northern Nigeria. Fragments of other conversations filter through her chatter:

"It's interesting, with the Wodaabe..."

"What are narcissists," says daSouza-Jones, "but black holes, sucking everything into themselves, swallowing all light, energy, all creativity and spitting back nothing."

"Wodaabe, Wodaabe," the journalist complains and it startles Ebanks that she is also eavesdropping. He strains to overhear Samia's answer to the Gambian's remark. "As if Wodaabe are the only people worth knowing about in Africa."

"I was sure," the English professor says, finishing her soup, "I'd be the lone South African here, but there's actually three of us."

"Who's the third?" asks K(no)w Africa.

"I think that gentleman there's from the Western Cape." She stares at Ebanks' face. "Jy is van die Kaap, nê?" she says in a loud voice and the unaccustomed language cuts through all talk.

"Excuse me?"

The English professor makes a face of disbelief. *Don't pretend*, her expression seems to say. *Don't deny.* "You look like a Capetonian."

Ebanks has heard he could be Persian, or Moroccan, even Israeli. But never this. "I'm not South African," he says.

"What are you?" asks the English professor, causing daSouza-Jones to hike his eyebrow.

Ebanks has decided to omit mention of Trinidad and Guadeloupe. "I'm a doogla," he tells her.

"What?" The journalist says. "Whetin be doogla?"

"An Antillean of mixed Asian and African parentage." It is, once again, Ms KO answering a question intended for Ebanks. All the while, she's looking at Samia and Samia gazes back. Whatever passes between the two women goes almost unnoticed.

K(no)w Africa says to Ebanks, "What did you say your name was again?"

The English professor tells Ebanks, "Ah, like whatshisname? Suresh." She turns to K(no)w Africa for confirmation. *Suresh?* Ebanks shakes his head at her, signalling ignorance.

"What about you?" the English professor is addressing Samia now. "What's your story?" And without transition, the weight of the room's attention has swept over Ebanks and on to a new subject. His replies have been immaterial. Whether or not he answered seems also unimportant.

Samia tilts back her head. "I'm doing research for an anthropological book." "What field of anthropology?" Ms KO wants to know.

"I'm making a study of whiteness."

"Whiteness?" says the English professor. K(no)w Africa repeats the word like an echo.

Ebanks makes for the bathroom. The server, a woman in an apron and tight black trousers, is gathering up soup bowls. DaSouza-Jones is appraising her figure and he draws in his long legs and comes in an instant to his feet. He's noticed Ebanks departing the room. "Excuse me," he says.

The Nigerian journalist chooses this moment to ask, "What are you working on now, Tamsir?"

"Are *you* white?" K(no)w Africa is asking Samia.

Ebanks, at the door, hears Samia answer, "Parsi," which is not strictly accurate.

There's no opportunity to enter the bathroom; at the threshold, daSouza-Jones catches up with Ebanks, who tenses for violence. "Come with me," the Gambian says and he moves off in the opposite direction to the dining room.

Ebanks trails him, curious. The house has been designed so that access to upper and lower storeys is concealed. The two men traverse a storage room full of plinths and sculptures. On one wall is a string of surrealist paintings, sunsets, variations on a theme Ebanks cannot interpret. "I thought Down and Out was genius, Yannick," daSouza-Jones tells him without looking round, a reference to Ebanks' most recent project. His walk is a lope. "I want to show you something."

The room daSouza-Jones steps into is dim, if not entirely dark. He holds the door ajar for Ebanks, who, entering, sees a projected image on the wall facing the entryway. A minotaur, a 3D animation; the deep chest heaves with each inhalation and it turns its horned head from left to right as if hunting for a scent. At his back, Ebanks hears the door shut. For a moment, he cannot comprehend what he's seeing. "Where did you get this?" he asks.

"Try it out," daSouza-Jones says. There's an undertone – amusement – in his voice. "It still works." Ebanks gapes at the screen. DaSouza-Jones holds in his hand a visor, and he proffers it to Ebanks. A large LED has been affixed to it so that the beam will shine upward. Ebanks thumbs the switch and, without pulling the visor over his head, he takes two darting strides forward. The LED emits a hard white gleam. The projection changes all at once and Ebanks is facing an image he's very nearly forgotten: a labyrinth of his own design, viewed from above. Within it stand two humanoid figures; one of them is recognizable as the minotaur. The second avatar shifts its position in mimicry of Ebanks' quick steps and now the minotaur hastens toward it. Ebanks sidles to his left, and his avatar does the same. The minotaur appears to lose interest in its pursuit and once more falls motionless. *It works still. Perhaps even better now.*

"Where did you get this?" Ebanks says a second time. There's no need to inform daSouza-Jones that this is his master's thesis; the Gambian already knows it. An intricate project, assembled from multiple elements: a powerful LED; a video camera mounted on the ceiling and aiming downward is linked by fire wire cable to a desktop computer, which runs software capable of tracking the movement of any bright light and replicating it on the screen; a video projector; and of course, hours and hours of coding went into the project. Curiously, Ebanks has done no programming since.

"Samia, of course." daSouza-Jones turns on the light and the labyrinth pales into near-invisibility. "She keeps it here. I cleaned things up a bit, of course. A costume designer built the visor, it's more durable than the original." He says it without reproof.

Samia? Ebanks is looking at daSouza-Jones and a Trinidadian expression of his father's occurs to him: the Gambian is trying to mamaguy him.

"You're not at all what I expected." DaSouza-Jones stoops again over Yannick, his eyes piercing. "You know, I lived in Berlin around the same time you were making *Down and Out*. Funny that our paths never crossed." He turns pensive. "What will you do? Here, I mean. The city's nothing like Berlin, let me tell you."

Ebanks is trying to concentrate. "I'll think about my next project. Something very different from *Down and Out*." It's true. He'll leave Samia to her writing, her theory of embodied whiteness, of the sublimation paradox, none of which he ever understood. "I don't expect to be here long. And I'll be travelling quite often." He knows already the city does not fit into his plans.

"Not long?" The Gambian laughs. "You're mistaken, my friend." The next moment, he says, "Where would you move? Buenos Aires is going the way of Paris or New York. You've done Berlin. And Syria and Vietnam aren't ready for you yet. Ebanks shakes his head in confusion. "Tell me," daSouza-Jones is asking, "was *Down and Out* your idea or Samia's?"

The question confounds Yannick. "I got it from Orwell," he says. "You know, *Down and Out in Paris and London*."

"Of course, but didn't Samia give you that book? I'm sure she made suggestions?"

"I can't recall. A remark from a few moments earlier snags his attention. *She keeps it here.* Ebanks asks, "Isn't this your house?"

"It's Samia's." DaSouza-Jones turns off the installation and retrieves the visor from Ebanks, who concentrates on the blank wall where the minotaur had been visible. *Why did he never give the project a title?* At the time, *Theseus* seemed too obvious. "She's the one who knows these people. Although, between you and me, I'm not convinced anyone out there is who they claim to be." He ushers Ebanks from the room with a wave of his arm. "You'll get used to it here. You may even decide it *is* right for an installation."

Samia's house? They are walking back to the front of the house, to rejoin, presumably, the others. Ebanks' head is swimming. DaSouza-Jones seems to know a great deal. Plans for an installation. The trip to Aleppo. He tries to dredge up memories of the sequence of events leading up to Down and Out. He knew Samia only slightly when he hit on the idea for the project. Still, without consulting his old journals he cannot be sure.

"By the way, this dark triad thing," the Gambian seems determined to confound Ebanks, "is it ironic or real?" And he turns around to get a look at the t-shirt.

Olufemi Terry has published poetry, nonfiction and fiction in numerous publications, including *New Contrast* and the online magazine *Guernica*. His short story 'Stickfighting Days' won the Caine Prize for African Writing in 2010. Originally from Sierra Leone, he now lives in Germany and is at work on a novel.

Rules

The prize is awarded annually to a short story by an African writer published in English, whether in Africa or elsewhere. (The indicative length is between 3,000 and 10,000 words.)

'An African writer' is normally taken to mean someone who was born in Africa, or who is a national of an African country, or whose parents are African, and whose work has reflected African sensibilities.

There is a cash prize of £10,000 for the winning author and a travel award for each of the shortlisted candidates (up to five in all).

For practical reasons, unpublished work and work in other languages is not eligible. Works translated into English from other languages are not excluded, provided they have been published in translation and, should such a work win, a proportion of the prize would be awarded to the translator.

The award is made in July each year, the deadline for submissions being 31 January. The shortlist is selected from work published in the five years preceding the submissions deadline and not previously considered for a Caine Prize. Submissions, including those from online journals, should be made by publishers and will need to be accompanied by six original published copies of the work for consideration, sent to the address below. There is no application form.

Every effort is made to publicize the work of the shortlisted authors through the broadcast as well as the printed media.

Winning and shortlisted authors will be invited to participate in writers' workshops in Africa and elsewhere as resources permit.

The above rules were designed essentially to launch the Caine Prize and may be modified in the light of experience. Their objective is to establish the Caine Prize as a benchmark for excellence in African writing.

The Caine Prize
The Menier Gallery
Menier Chocolate Factory
51 Southwark Street
London, SE1 1RU, UK
Telephone: +44 (0)20 7378 6234
Fax: +44 (0)20 7378 6235
Email: info@caineprize.com
Website: www.caineprize.com